LIBRARY
WITHDRAWN

The Little Gift Shop
on the Loch

MAGGIE CONWAY

ONE PLACE. MANY STORIES

D0188992

This book is dedicated to Margaret Couttie

This novel is entirely a work of fiction. The names, characters
and incidents portrayed in it are the work of the author's
imagination. Any resemblance to actual persons, living or
dead, events or localities is entirely coincidental.

HQ
An imprint of HarperCollins*Publishers* Ltd
1 London Bridge Street
London SE1 9GF

This edition 2019

First published in Great Britain by
HQ, an imprint of HarperCollins*Publishers* Ltd 2019

Copyright © Maggie Conway 2019

Maggie Conway asserts the moral right to be
identified as the author of this work.
A catalogue record for this book is
available from the British Library.

ISBN PB: 978-0-00-833087-3
ISBN EB: 978-0-00-829658-2

MIX
Paper from
responsible sources
FSC
FSC™ C007454

This book is produced from independently certified FSC™ paper
to ensure responsible forest management.

For more information visit: www.harpercollins.co.uk/green

Printed and bound by CPI Group (UK) Ltd,
Croydon, CR0 4YY

All rights reserved. No part of this publication may be reproduced,
stored in a retrieval system, or transmitted, in any form or by any means,
electronic, mechanical, photocopying, recording or otherwise,
without the prior permission of the publishers.

This book is sold subject to the condition that it shall not, by way of trade
or otherwise, be lent, re-sold, hired out or otherwise circulated without
the publisher's prior consent in any form of binding or cover other than
that in which it is published and without a similar condition including this
condition being imposed on the subsequent purchaser.

This book is dedicated to Margaret Ogilvie

Chapter 1

No matter how tired she was, Lily Ballantine prided herself on keeping to her strict morning routine. Her battle with sleep – or rather lack of it – had crept into her life over recent months, insidiously stealing precious hours of blissful oblivion.

She tried to regard her sleep deprivation as a measure of success; her inability to switch off from deadlines and to-do list was a good thing, a sign her career was on the up. So she endured her tiredness, wearing it like a slightly warped badge of honour, although some mornings were harder than others.

Earlier she'd stumbled through to the bathroom, her bleary-eyed, pale reflection confirming the few glasses of wine last night had done their worst. The alcohol sometimes helped, just enough to tip her over to sleep. But never for long enough. Somehow, frustratingly, she always managed to wake up at that deathly hour of 3 a.m., when the world was at its darkest and she just knew she was the only person on the entire planet who was awake.

The scalding shower and transformative contents of her make-up bag had worked wonders and now she was preened and polished, ready to face the day. Her unruly hair had been straightened into submission and she was dressed in her customary dark trouser suit and crisp shirt – pink today because it was Friday.

Lily automatically checked her watch as she closed her front door at precisely seven o'clock, pleased she was on schedule. Situated in a quiet cul-de-sac, the flat's location meant she could make the walk to Edinburgh's city centre in under thirty minutes. She walked at her usual brisk pace, weaving her way through the cobbled streets, past the elegant Georgian tenements and narrow alleyways.

The spring morning showcased Edinburgh's unique charm to perfection, its turreted buildings silhouetted against a pale blue sky. Lily loved this time of day, while the city remained largely untouched by the throng of workers and shoppers and the air still held a clarity in its gentle breeze.

She took a deep breath thinking back to the previous evening when she'd joined a few colleagues for drinks. She rarely went out these days, but it was best to show face now and again and it had made a change to drink in company. She'd found the bar rather noisy, and had trouble hearing Harry from menswear recount his latest hysterical story. Something to do with slim-fitting trousers and inside leg measurements.

She wondered at what age it was acceptable to admit you hated noisy pubs, certain that 28 was too young. She simply wasn't used to it anymore. Not like the evenings she'd frequented the best of Edinburgh's bars, immune to the clamorous voices and pulsating music vying to be heard. Erin and Clare had been her willing accomplices but since they'd both left, Lily was less inclined to go out and making excuses had become a habit. It was amazing how quickly invitations stopped and people fell away if you constantly turned them down.

Lily slowed her pace as she approached her usual coffee shop, anticipating the extra hot skinny cappuccino which provided a pleasant kick start to the ten – possibly more – hours that lay happily ahead of her.

With her coffee in hand, Lily turned into Princes Street. After six years of working there, she still felt a little thrill as she approached Bremners department store. For over a hundred years it had dominated Edinburgh's skyline, sitting on the corner of Princes Street like a grand old lady; graceful and enchanting and just a little bit formidable. To most people, Bremners department store was the iconic building which stood opposite the castle, its beautifully ornate facade a testament to Victorian architecture. To Lily, the building was like an old friend, one she was always happy to see.

As usual Lily was the first to arrive, slipping in through the staff entrance and nodding to the security guard as she entered. Soon the shop would be fully awake, the lights on and doors open, and shoppers would start to filter in. The staff would be ready to spend time with their valued customers, providing the antidote to the quick and cheap retail fix offered by so many other shops. Lily had always thought there was something magical about the old-fashioned store. Bremners oozed an old-world charm and elegance from another era. A place where you could still buy tweeds and reliable underwear, a place where dreams were lived out. The perfect wedding dress, a special gift for a lover or simply a treat for yourself. Shoppers could drift from shoes to cosmetics, stop for lunch or visit the bookshop. Lily thought there was something comforting that people still wanted to buy darning needles from the haberdashery department or silk handkerchiefs from menswear.

Lily skirted around the perfume department on the ground floor where notes of jasmine, amber and magnolia lingered in the air, and headed to the lifts. She knew the layout of the shop, knew how every department operated. Her new boss thought it was important that all staff, no matter their role, should be familiar with the stock and ambience of the shop. It was just one of the things that made James Sinclair such a wonderful boss. Lily sighed, thinking of him, and wondered if she'd see him today.

The lift pinged its arrival and Lily stepped in and pressed the button for the seventh floor. Although she was familiar with the

3

shop floor, it wasn't where she belonged. Instead, she was happy to retreat behind the scenes, to be part of the invisible workforce on the top floor dealing with HR, legal and – in her case – financial matters.

As she entered her office, a sense of calm and purpose took hold of Lily. This was her world, her cocoon of order where she felt comfortable and in control. Swapping her well-worn trainers for three-inch Carvelas, her eyes scanned the room, checking everything was in its correct place.

She sat down with a small contented sigh, with a sense that all was as it should be. Only then did she allow herself the first sip of coffee, now at the perfect temperature. She booted up the computer, her mind running over the day ahead.

An hour later Lily was engrossed in a spreadsheet and when her phone rang, she answered it without thinking. Her pulse quickened as she heard the icy tones of James's secretary. 'Can you come along to Mr Sinclair's office, please?'

And although her day had started like any other, Lily didn't know the phone call was about to change everything.

***

As Lily walked into James Sinclair's office she thought back to the first day she'd met him. After months of rumours, speculation and negotiations, a multimillion-pound deal had finally been agreed and Bremners department store was now part owned by Dunn Equity. Although it had always been hugely successful, Bremners wasn't immune to the economic pressures brought by spiralling costs and internet shopping and the deal had given a huge injection of much-needed capital. Bremners was no longer an independent store and – amidst reassurances its unique identity would be preserved – had been thrust into the corporate world.

James Sinclair belonged to that world and had swept into the

4

boardroom one bleak Monday morning. The mood was sombre and speculation rife amongst the administrative staff gathered for the much-anticipated meeting. Lily had felt the hairs on the back of her neck prickle when James had entered. For the next hour she'd sat transfixed as he'd explained he was part of the management team whose job was to put procedures in place to standardise systems and provide the necessary in-house training to ensure a smooth transition.

It wasn't just the way his blonde hair flopped over his forehead or his penetrating blue gaze that Lily hadn't been able to tear her eyes from, it was his sheer energy. The very air around him seem to crackle.

'What do you think of him?' she'd whispered to Erin, perched on the seat beside her.

'Looks like a ruthless bastard to me. Wouldn't trust him an inch,' she'd muttered darkly while Lily had remained silent.

There followed an uneasy period of redundancies and jostling amongst management and Lily was bereft when Erin and Clare both decided to take the package on offer. They had all started at the same time and had quickly become confidants. Clare, already struggling to balance work with 1-year-old twins, saw it as the perfect opportunity to embrace full-time motherhood. Erin, recovering from a messy break-up, had declared she was taking herself off around the world to eat, pray and love.

'Come with me,' she'd implored Lily, her voice filled with excitement. Lily had considered it for all of five seconds – she'd never really been one for spontaneity. And so she had stayed put, feeling even more isolated when the other two senior accountants both nearing retiring age, had left. James's team included accountants and Lily worried her position was precarious.

Shortly after that, James introduced himself personally to Lily and up close he was even more impressive, his disarming eye contact and firm handshake staying with Lily long after he told her he was looking forward to working with her.

5

As it turned out, she needn't have worried. With her knowledge of staffing, costs and systems Lily soon became James's go-to person. Lily accepted most people might not find preparing balance sheets particularly sexy and she'd be the first to admit the prospect of filing tax returns didn't always leave her fizzing with excitement. But when she started working with James, her job rocketed to a whole new level. She'd never considered herself overly ambitious but now, under his watchful gaze, she'd stepped out of her comfort zone.

Reporting directly to him, Lily found herself compiling reports, analysing data and presenting business plans. Work became a different place. Exciting. She attended meetings and sat on committees set up to oversee the integration process. On several occasions she'd travelled with James in his sleek company car to meet new and existing suppliers. Over meetings, coffee breaks, and sometimes dinner, they discussed business, the conversation occasionally veering onto something more personal as they shared snippets of their lives – the line between professional and personal blurring pleasantly over a glass or two of wine.

The work had been consuming, exhausting and Lily thrived on it. 'I don't know what I'd do without you,' James said to her one day with a look that sent a thrill through her.

With furtive glances she watched James operate, marvelling at how he commanded a meeting, winning people round to his way of thinking. A room changed when he walked into it, people noticed him. Charismatic, dynamic and tough when he needed to be, she breathed him in, hanging on his every word, his every movement.

She'd never met anyone like him before and as she watched him, Lily knew this was what she wanted. Because somewhere along the line, between the meetings, the costings, the chats, Lily had hopelessly – and unprofessionally – fallen for him.

She felt utterly ridiculous, like a schoolgirl with a crush, but she couldn't help herself. She felt like she'd found what she was looking for, her few previous relationships paling into insignificance. So positive was she that they were meant to be together, that the connection between them was so strong, she knew it was only a matter of time. Of course, she knew nothing could happen yet, not while work was so intense. For now, it was enough to know he relied on her.

James had indicated there were exciting opportunities for those who embraced change and worked hard. Lily felt herself being caught up in his excitement for the future, his ambition was contagious. Now that the integration was over and the dust settled, Lily knew the figures and was convinced the future looked bright. She had known it would just be a matter of time – and now, after this phone call, the moment was here. The *promotion* was here.

She pulled out the mirror she kept in the top drawer, the mere thought of seeing him sending butterflies racing to her stomach. Silently cursing the shadows under her eyes, she sighed. If the weather stayed fine this weekend, she'd definitely try to catch some sun so she didn't look so peaky – maybe sit in the park. Quickly, she applied some lipstick and fluffed up her hair. That would have to do.

She approached the desk outside James's room where his secretary sat guarding her boss with her usual Rottweiler tendencies. Lily was met with her customary frosty smile but for once she didn't care.

'Just go through, please.'

Opening the door with a deep breath Lily stepped into the room, the thick luxurious carpet softening her footsteps as she made her way to the large mahogany desk situated in the corner. James smiled and, ever the gentleman, rose to his feet when he saw her. She caught a whiff of his familiar expensive cologne as she sat down, returning his smile and nodding to Helen from HR seated beside him.

'I'd like to start, Lily by saying how much we appreciate the work you've done for Bremners over the past year. You've been an integral part of the smooth transition. Your professionalism and dedication have been second to none.'

'Thank you,' she replied feeling a warm glow of pride spreading through her. All those hours of hard work were about to pay off.

'However, moving forward we've had to take some difficult decisions.'

Lily looked up sharply, something about his tone ringing alarm bells.

'Looking to the future, we've decided to introduce some strategic reorganisations ...'

James's lips – the ones she had imagined tasting a thousand times – were still moving but suddenly Lily couldn't hear anything except the pounding of blood in her ears. Her mouth went dry with a sickly sense of what was about to come. She waited, hardly breathing, as he carried on talking. And then it came.

Termination of employment. The words seemed to land with a thud on the desk, in big bold letters, creating a chasm as wide as a desert between them. In an instance they were on different sides. Part of the team and not part of the team. Lily swallowed deeply, her mind rapidly processing what this meant, none of it good. She was totally dumbstruck. Not only had she assumed her job was safe, she'd actually thought they were promoting her. The dancing butterflies scurried away leaving a ball of fury in the pit of her stomach. She looked at him helplessly for confirmation. Her mouth opened and then closed again. She thought desperately for something to say. How had she got it so wrong? How could he do this to her?

'I – I didn't think there were going to be any more redundancies,' she stuttered.

'As you know, we managed to reduce costs with natural wastage and the initial round of redundancies was successful in achieving our initial targets but now we have to look longer term. This will be the final round of strategic cuts and losses will be kept to an absolute minimum.'

He nodded patronisingly as if he was explaining something difficult to a child when in fact, she knew everything about the state of the finances. And they were good. Obviously too good. The systems she had helped set up didn't need a team of accountants. She had effectively provided him with the ammunition he was now using against her.

Tears of humiliation stung her eyes. She felt so foolish – not just on a professional level but personally. All this time she had been working for him, had he known this was going to happen? Was he planning this all along? She'd thought they might have a future together … She felt light-headed and sick. All she wanted was to get out of there, and fast.

'I'm very sorry, Lily, you know it's not personal.'

God, she really wished he hadn't said that. Because that was exactly what it was. Work had consumed her every waking moment. If she wasn't at work, she was thinking about it. About him. Everything in her life from the moment she woke up until she collapsed exhausted into bed late at night, was based around her work.

She knew the way he operated; this was final. Now Helen from HR was reaching over the desk, handing a letter.

'These are the terms of your notice, I think you'll find them very generous,' she said smugly. As if that would make a difference.

Lily took a deep breath. As much as she wanted to unleash the torrent of words thrashing abound in her head – and possibly hurl his laptop across the room for good measure – she knew they would stay in her head. She had never deliberately drawn attention to herself or caused a scene and she wasn't about to start now.

Her pride kicked in. No way would she let him see her humiliation. So she blinked away the tears and, mustering every scrap of dignity she could, stood up on shaky legs. James stood up too, following her to the door.

'I know this must be a shock, Lily. If there had been any other way, I promise …' His voice was low and beseeching, almost as if he meant it.

He held out his hand for her to take but unable to bring herself to touch him, she turned and walked away.

Chapter 2

Lily was lying in bed on Thursday morning. She wasn't sure of the time but there seemed to be little point in getting up. Everything had become a huge effort, a strange inertia settling over her.

Earlier she'd listened to the flurry of noise and activity, doors opening and closing, as her neighbours left for work. Like her, they were mostly young professionals but unlike her, they all had somewhere to go. Now everything had fallen eerily silent.

Lily shifted her position, trying to escape the trail of crumbs lodged uncomfortably against her skin. Eating crisps in bed last night in a vain attempt to soak up some of the alcohol probably hadn't been her best idea.

The weekend had passed in a daze of disbelief and self-recrimination, punctuated by copious amounts of comfort food, caffeine and alcohol. Her anger and disappointment at losing her job, and her feelings for James, were twisted into one angry knot of resentment. Her career and dream of a relationship had been wiped away in one cruel blow.

She could feel flames of mortification simmering within her as she tried to work out how she'd misread the situation so badly. All those times he'd looked at her, holding her gaze a fraction longer than necessary, the compliments and conversations that had peppered their working relationship. How sad that she'd somehow manoeuvred her life into a position where she'd been so desperate for his attention, reading something into it when all he'd been doing was being friendly.

Leaving the office on Friday already felt like a lifetime ago, although seeing six years of work reduced to the contents of a cardboard box wasn't something she'd forget in a hurry. Spare tights, a couple of mugs, aspirin and a few photos weren't much. She'd taken a final look around, swiping a box of gold paperclips and several pens in a final pathetic act of defiance. Technically stealing but given all the holiday she was due, she felt it was the least she was owed.

On Monday morning, she woke early out of force of habit. An initial euphoria at her newfound freedom gave her a burst of energy. *Take a few days and be kind to yourself after redundancy* had been the online advice. Who was she to argue?

So over the next few days, she'd done exactly that. She did all those things she'd always wanted to but never had time. She had the most expensive, luxurious facial Edinburgh could offer which had soothed her tear-induced blotchy skin, but had done little for her damaged self-esteem. She sat in the warm nook of a little cafe with a gigantic mug of coffee and read an entire novel. She stayed in her pyjamas all day watching films, only heaving herself off the sofa to take delivery of pizza. She joined the swarm of tourists for a tour of the castle, immersing herself in the glories and gore of the Scottish monarchs.

She came home from the supermarket laden down with every conceivable cleaning product she could lay her hands on, and scrubbed her flat from top to bottom. And she discovered that even if she did have all the time in the world, she still wouldn't use her gym membership.

It all felt unreal. She was playing truant and any moment someone from work would call, demanding she return to the office. Time and time again she checked her phone for messages or emails, anything to show she was missed, that she was still needed. She tried to put a positive spin on it, to see it as an opportunity. But the only opportunity she could see was going slowly insane.

The flat had always been her refuge at the end of the day. Now, in the silence of the day it felt claustrophobic, the walls closing in on her. She paced about, looking for something to do.

Apart from the dubious decor and temperamental heating, it was a nice enough flat. Lily hadn't intended to be there much longer, her interest already registered in *an exciting new development of high-quality contemporary apartments*, ideal for professionals like her. She'd enjoying visualising her new fat; a place of white walls, clean lines and understated elegance – ideally resembling a Swedish furniture catalogue. But she knew losing her job meant that wasn't going to happen now.

What she was supposed to do – the next piece of advice – was remind herself of her capabilities and make a plan to get back out there. At the moment, getting out of bed was a task too much. The weather was annoyingly warm and sunny, which didn't suit her mood at all. At least if it was cold and raining – entirely possible in Scotland in June – she'd feel more justified in burying herself under the duvet.

She'd got as far as updating her CV, noting with grim satisfaction that she looked impressive on paper, even if in reality she was a snivelling wreck. How things had changed in a week.

She'd told herself not to wallow. But then rationality would fail her and she would slump again, despondency taking over. She was *redundant*. The word seemed to hang in the very air around her so that there was no escaping it. She had been disposed of. Surplus to requirements. One day she had somewhere to be, belonged somewhere, people waiting for her input. Then, nothing.

The crumbs had somehow shifted again, biting into her flesh. Worried she might actually lie there forever, Lily was finally provided with the impetus to move by the soft thud of mail landing on the door mat.

Several moments later, she sat on the edge of her bed with an open letter lying in her lap, wondering if strange forces were at work. It wasn't so much the contents of the letter – she'd received ones like it before – but the timing. She scanned the words again embossed on the thick creamy paper from Bell & Bain Solicitors.

Mr Bell was writing regarding her late mother's estate, specifically the property in Loch Carroch. Taking into account that the property had been lying empty for several months, and mindful of current market conditions with a view to achieving the best price should she wish to sell, Mr Bell was politely enquiring if Lily had reached any decisions or would like to arrange a meeting to discuss the matter.

Lily sighed, casting the letter aside. No, she wouldn't actually. It had nothing to do with the current market or achieving best possible price and everything to do with finally facing the things she'd become an expert at avoiding.

She remembered the first time she'd met Mr Bell, the day still painfully scored into her memory. She'd sat on one side of his massive dark wooden desk covered in mounds of paperwork, shocked to her core after the death of her mother. It had felt utterly unreal to be talking about her in the past tense. In life, her mother's casual attitude to financial matters made discussing them now even more unreal..

But it seemed for once, Patricia Ballantine (or Patty as she'd preferred to be called) had thought ahead and done the grown-up thing. Mr Bell explained that after the recent death of her own mother, Patty had put her affairs in order and made a will.

'Makes things so much easier,' he'd said kindly. Lily had sat in stunned silence, staring at a small tuft of grey hair on top of his bent head as he patiently and meticulously made his way through various documents.

'And of course, there was the shop with the flat above it that

14

she'd recently purchased in Loch Carroch.' He'd regarded her over the rim of his owl-like glasses. 'Perhaps you'll want to sell, do you think?'

Lily had looked down, fiddling with her bracelet. She knew she'd have to go one day to face the small shop that her mother had bought in the north of Scotland. But selling it would be to acknowledge that her mother really was gone, and Lily simply wasn't ready to do that. As long as it was there, she still had something of her mother's but she wasn't sure she could explain that to Mr Bell. 'Not yet,' she had stated simply.

Time was meant to be a healer but Lily knew it wasn't. You simply found ways of dealing with it. You learnt to swallow the tears, forced yourself to think of something else. And in Lily's case that had meant focusing on her job. Work had always been important to her, it was her routine and her security. After Patty had died and all the changes had started in Bremners and James had arrived, it became even more so.

Lily sighed, opened the drawer of her bedside table, and pulled out a photograph, holding it in between her fingers. Beautiful and carefree, her mother's laughing brown eyes smiled out at her. She used to look at the photo all the time, talk to it sometimes. She'd bought a silver frame for it but then it had all become too painful. The frame lay empty and Lily rarely looked at the photo now; it been hidden in the drawer, rarely brought out or scrutinised – much like her feelings.

She exhaled deeply and tucked the photo away, feeling the familiar stab of guilt knowing she should have gone by now. Instead she'd left it all to Iris.

Iris lived in Carroch and had been part of their lives ever since Lily and her mother first visited there when Lily was a baby. It had been Iris who had helped arranged Patty's funeral in the same church in Dunbar where her own parents' – Lily's grand-parents' – funerals had been held. Other than that, Patty's only stipulation had been that her ashes be scattered on Loch Carroch.

Iris had taken the ashes back to Carroch with her and reassured Lily she'd keep an eye on the flat and shop in the meantime. 'Come when you're ready,' she had said.

Lily had fully intended to go up and deal with everything. But then tomorrow had become next week and now months had gone by. She had almost convinced herself she was waiting for the right moment, but deep down Lily knew there would never be one.

She'd gone straight back to work the day after the funeral. There had been no extended compassionate leave. No time to dwell. There had been only one occasion during a particularly long meeting when she'd had to rush to the ladies', taking a moment to compose herself at the sudden threat of tears. Other than that, it had been business as usual, channelling everything into her job so that if she thought of her mother, she buried it away and focused instead on the figures in front of her, masking her pain behind balance sheets and numbers.

Now, without her so-called glittering career, there was nothing for Lily to hide behind. She knew that was why the redundancy had been so devastating. It wasn't simply about losing her job; it had brought about this moment, the one she'd been afraid of. Now she had no excuses not to make the journey and sort through the life her mother had left behind. And although Lily knew she'd never be fully ready, she also knew she couldn't put it off any longer.

Chapter 3

Lily woke with a start. The warmth of the carriage and the hypnotic motion of the train must have lulled her to sleep. Edinburgh had been grey and drizzly when she'd left and now as if by magic, she'd been transported to another world. She blinked a few times as her eyes focused on the wild beauty of the Scottish Highlands outside the window.

Earlier she had taken a final look around her flat, reassuring herself she'd be back soon. Mrs Robertson on the ground floor had kindly agreed to take a set of keys and keep an eye on it. After that, there was really nothing left to do and so with a heavy heart, Lily had wheeled her case along the capital's cobbled streets towards Waverly station.

She rubbed a hand over her face now and stretched out her cramped muscles just as a crackly voice announced Inverness was the next stop. She remembered all the times she'd made the train journey with her mum, how it had always felt interminably long to Lily who wished for once they could go somewhere that wasn't a damp caravan in the north of Scotland.

Life with Patty Ballantine was never predictable but one thing that never changed was their annual holiday to Carroch. Lily would listen to girls at school returning from their Mediterranean holidays with tans and tales of boys on the beach. The only thing that Lily came home with was pale skin covered in midge bites. Lily's over-riding memory was of there not much being much to do and she could never really understand why her mother was always drawn back to the same place year after year. But Patty claimed it to be her spiritual home and had continued to visit long after Lily stopped coming, so perhaps there'd been an inevitability about her mother eventually going to live there.

It would be good to see Iris again, Lily told herself, rolling up her unread magazine and stuffing it back into her bag. And it would probably only take a matter of days to sort through everything and get it ready for selling. But despite her attempts at self-bolstering, Lily knew her memories of her mother were so entwined with Carroch, there was going to be nothing easy about facing it without her.

Lily stood up when the train slowed down and came to a halt, pulling her bag from the overhead space as other people in the carriage also started to move, hauling rucksacks and collecting bags. The doors of the train slid open and Lily stepped onto the platform watching as the train rumbled away. She took a deep breath of the fresh tangy air, suddenly engulfed by a sense of isolation.

She stood still for a moment before giving herself a shake and picking up her bag. She fell into step behind the other passengers making their way to the taxi rank. The thirty odd miles from the station to Carroch made the choice of a taxi an extravagant one but for once she ignored her instinctive frugality and took her place in the small line of people waiting. Besides, she highly doubted there'd be any buses this late in the day.

The taxi driver was cheery enough but thankfully not chatty, only interrupting the silence to comment on the few days of warm weather they were currently enjoying. Lily gazed out at the passing scenery until glimpses of the loch appeared through the trees and she knew they were almost there. She'd forgotten just how beautiful the loch could look, especially now at twilight when the dark shimmering water converged with a soft violet sky on the horizon. But even in the face of such beauty, Lily felt dread clutching at her stomach at what she was about to face.

They continued on the road which swept around the west side of the loch until finally they reached Carroch's small main street. A small, picturesque village, it sat in a sheltered bay and was surrounded by towering mountains and hills. Lily's heart quickened as she saw the familiar row of shops and neatly painted cottages which decorated the curve of the bay facing the water.

'Here we are then,' the driver announced, pulling up outside the shop. Lily nervously bit her lip as she quickly scanned the property that now belonged to her. It was the last in the little row of shops, a two-storey building painted white, with three small windows on the first floor and two latticed windows on either side of shop door on the ground floor. Lily vaguely remembered the shop being the post office when she'd last been here. It had sold a hodgepodge of sundries and she recalled being allowed to choose an ice-lolly from a chilled cabinet at the back of the shop which was crammed with frozen chips and fish fingers. Now the paintwork was flaking in places and the lettering above the door faded to the point of be indiscernible.

After paying the driver Lily climbed out of the car and walked round to the side entrance. She rummaged in her bag for the keys, her fingers suddenly clammy and clumsy as she fumbled to unlock the door. Inside the hall was dark but she managed to find the switch for the hall light, relieved when it came on even though she knew Mr Bell had arranged to keep paying the utility bills.

Facing her was a door which presumably led to the shop and to her right was a staircase. Deciding to head straight upstairs to the flat, she lugged her case up the narrow rickety stairs where four doors led off from a square, wooden floored hall.

The kitchen was positioned at the back of the house beside a small bathroom while the living room faced the front with views to the loch. She opened each door in turn, quickly scanning the rooms as if she'd find her mother in one of them. But of course, her absence was shatteringly real. Finally, she opened the last door to her mother's bedroom which Lily quickly closed again; that was simply too daunting to face tonight.

Instead she returned to the kitchen. Dominated by a large wooden table surrounded by mismatched chairs, the pale blue units appeared rustically charming more from their age than design. A recess of shelving was crammed with colourful crockery and an ancient stoneware cooking pot sat on top of the oven. Lily's mother wasn't always inclined to cook but when the mood took her, she never bothered with a recipe. Instead she'd simply throw in whatever was to hand, concocting slightly unusual tasting soups or casseroles.

A wicker shopping basket sat on the floor, a bamboo wind chime hung silently at the window. There were touches of her mother everywhere and Lily could picture her here so clearly, almost as if she'd walk through the door any moment. If only she would. Lily sighed silently, closing her eyes briefly.

The living room was quite large but as a result of their frequent moving and Patty's reluctance to acquire possessions, it didn't contain much furniture. Lily's eyes roamed the room, recognising the two brown sofas and the small walnut coffee table. There was a pretty fireplace and a shelved alcove lined with books. Patty always left half-read books lying around as if she'd lost the patience to finish them. Moving over to the mantelpiece, Lily picked up a framed photo of the two of them taken at the loch years ago, their heads close together smiling in the sunshine.

Lily had no memories of her mother in this house and if she'd hoped that might make it easier, then she was mistaken. She swallowed down the lump in her throat with the realisation this was going to be more difficult than she ever could have imagined.

As Lily silently roamed the house, it was clear Iris had been

20

keeping the place polished and clean. Not only that, but Lily was acutely aware that Iris had taken care of the house in the immediate aftermath of Patty's death, sparing Lily the devastation of seeing her mother's last movements unfolded and she felt a wave of gratitude and guilt wash over her.

Suddenly she couldn't stand the silence. She needed to do something, anything to fill the emptiness. She'd make a cup of tea – that's what people did to make things feel better. But she didn't want tea. What she really wanted, she realised, was alcohol.

She unzipped her suitcase where, protected deep within the folds of clothes, were a few staples she'd brought for her first night; a jar of coffee, teabags, a packet of biscuits and a bottle of wine. Bringing a glass through from the kitchen, she poured from the bottle, imagining the deep plumy taste of the silky red wine soothing its way into her bloodstream. She raised the glass to her mouth and froze.

Someone was unlocking the front door. With shaky fingers she laid the glass down, her ears straining to hear. Then she remembered – of course, it would be Iris. She hadn't told her she was coming but perhaps she'd seen her arriving?

Except the footsteps coming up the stairs didn't sound like that of a lithe 60-something woman. Some logical part of her brain was telling her burglars didn't have keys but that didn't stop her heart hammering uncomfortably in her chest. She'd almost stopped breathing when the door opened and the silhouette of a large man filled the doorway.

Definitely not Iris.

There was a moment of stunned silence as they stared at each other until Lily managed to find her voice. 'Wh-who are you?' she stuttered.

The man hitched his hands into the front pocket of his jeans, seemingly in no hurry to explain himself. When he did, his voice was deep and drawling. 'I could ask you the same thing.'

Lily opened her mouth and then closed it again, not seeing

21

why she should explain herself to this intruder. Or maybe he was a squatter – he did look a bit scruffy. But a squatter with keys – was that even possible? One thing was for sure, she should never have left the place as long as she had. Taking a step closer, she drew herself up which admittedly didn't make much impact on their height difference.

'Why don't you go first – who are you?' she demanded, amazed her voice sounded normal.

'I'm Jack Armstrong.' He leaned against the doorframe, folding his arms. 'And you must be Patty's daughter?'

'That's right.' Seriously, who was this man?

'Iris said you'd be here sometime.'

Slightly placated on hearing Iris's name, Lily still found his presence extremely unnerving. Maybe because in the semi-darkness his features were shadowed so that only the contours of his cheekbones and strong jawline were visible. Other than that, the only thing she could see was how obviously broad and tall he was. And she still had no idea what he was doing here.

'So um, why are you here?'

'I'm here to feed Misty.' His tone implied this was something she should know.

Lily blinked. 'Misty?'

At which point, a black and white cat miraculously appeared and began purring and rubbing itself against the man's legs. Lily frowned. This was all starting to feel quite strange. The man lowered onto his hunches, and Lily watched his hand run along the length of the cat's black fur. 'Hello girl,' he murmured gently.

Lily suddenly felt exhausted, feeling incapable of understanding anything right now. 'Sorry but why is there a cat here?' she asked.

He straightened up. 'You didn't know there was a cat here?'

'Evidently not.' Her voice was sharper than she'd intended but the unexpectedness of finding this stranger looking after a cat she knew nothing about had thrown her.

He let out a small sigh. 'Misty was a stray in the village. I used to feed her now and again but Patty let her come and live here with her. With the place lying empty, we weren't really sure what to do with her. Thought she might leave of her own accord but she seemed intent on staying and since I live nearby Iris gave me a set of keys. I've been keeping an eye on her.'

There was an awkward pause, Lily unsure of what to say next. Although she couldn't see them in the dark, she felt his eyes on her, assessing her in some way. 'So,' he said eventually. 'Now you're here, you can take care of Misty?'

Lily wasn't sure she liked the insinuation that she'd simply breezed in on a whim. She also didn't really like cats. 'Um, yes … of course.'

'You're sure?' he checked, not sounding too convinced.

'Absolutely.' *What on earth was she going to do with it?*

'Okay.' He gave a shrug. 'Well, in that case her food is under the sink and the litter tray is probably needing emptied.'

'Litter tray?'

'You know, for her—'

'Yes. Of course,' she snapped.

'I'll leave you to it then, I'm sure you have things to do.' He looked like he might be about to add something, but Lily didn't give him a chance.

'I do actually,' she agreed, making a move towards the door. 'And er, thank you.'

'Not a problem.' He paused for a moment, his voice softening. 'Patty was a lovely lady. I'm sorry for your loss.'

'Thank you,' she replied quietly.

He bent down to give the cat a final stroke and then with a brief nod in Lily's direction, he was gone.

Lily waited to hear the door close and then grabbed her glass, gulping a mouthful of wine. She gave herself a small shake, feeling well and truly rattled after that little encounter. If Jack Armstrong was a taste of what was to come, then the sooner she sold the shop and returned to Edinburgh the better.

Chapter 4

Lily was woken by a strangely heavy sensation on her chest. Her eyelids fluttered open to find a pair of jade-green eyes staring at her. She bolted upright with a shriek as a flash of black fur shot away in disgust, clearly not too pleased at the disruption. Feeling dazed, Lily perched on the edge of the sofa letting her heart rate settle as the room came into focus and her brain processed where she was and why a cat had been sitting on her.

Last night she'd ended up putting on her PJs and settling herself on the sofa. She had briefly considered sleeping in her mother's room but the truth was she'd been afraid, as if shadows and echoes from the past would come to haunt her. She doubted she'd get much sleep anyway so it didn't really matter. Instead, Lily had unearthed a patchwork quilt that she remembered her mother, in a rare moment of domesticity, had made years ago and wrapped it around her body. As she had feared, sleep hadn't come to her until the early hours when her body had finally given way to exhaustion.

She hadn't drawn the curtains last night and now early morning light trickled in through the window, the blue sky beyond promising a beautiful summer's day to come. Under other circumstances she might have been full of energy, tempted to explore her

24

surroundings. But today she felt shrouded in a sense of the past, of having to deal with things she didn't want to.

She supposed she'd better feed the cat, which was now sitting in front of the fire licking itself in unmentionable places. Lily grimaced, looking away. Rising gingerly from the sofa, she shuffled her way through to the kitchen where she successfully managed to locate two bowls, filling one with fresh water and the other with biscuits.

With her cat duties out of the way, Lily's thoughts turned to a hot shower although she wasn't holding out much hope. In the bathroom she switched on the shower, waiting with trepidation. There was a good amount of clunking and clanking from the pipes as the system came to life but to her relief, hot water finally spluttered out. It worked far better than she'd dared hope and after standing under the spray of hot water for several minutes, she stepped out feeling sufficiently galvanised for the day ahead.

Dressed in jeans and a soft grey jumper, she went about filling the kettle and finding a mug in the kitchen. She looked out of the window and down onto the back garden. It was more of a courtyard really, with wooden tubs full of colourful flowers sitting on paving stones and dark green ivy snaking its way along a trellised wall at the bottom.

Recalling the taxi driver's remarks from last night about the warm spell of weather, it was obvious from the vibrancy of the plants that someone had been watering them. Unless the cat man from last night had been watering the garden as well as feeding Misty, it must have been Iris. Big-hearted, kind Iris; Lily dreaded to think what she'd have done without her.

She and her mother had been kindred spirits, their shared passion for the Edinburgh festival one of many things the two women had bonded over and every year they would go together to experience the exuberant chaos of the live acts and street performers.

It had been last year on their annual pilgrimage to the festival when Patty had become unwell. Lily had been due to meet them for dinner later until Iris had rung to say Patty had been taken to hospital after collapsing. By the time Lily had reached the hospital, a cerebral aneurysm had already tipped her mother's body into a coma.

Lily had sat by her bed, somehow knowing her mother wouldn't linger. Being prodded and poked by doctors and nurses in a hospital bed wasn't her style at all. It wasn't just the indignity of it, it was simply far too boring. She would have hated people to see her like that, to be surrounded by sadness and tears. Lily could almost hear her voice; 'Must be going now, darling.'

This way her body would never be ravaged by months of sickness and even with life ebbing away Patty still managed to radiate beauty. Her dark chestnut hair held a rich hue despite a sprinkling of grey. Lily had brushed it gently, willing her mother to open her eyes but they remained resolutely shut. Lily had watched her intently, breathing every breath with her.

Theirs hadn't been the easiest of relationships but Lily had loved her mother. Seeing her like this, when she was usually so full of life and energy, was the worst and most difficult thing she'd ever had to do and despite Iris being there, she'd never felt so alone.

Lily had never met her father and knew little about him – only that he was French and part of a theatrical touring company in Edinburgh for the festival. According to her mother, Lily was the result of a passionate short-lived love affair. She didn't talk about him much, but Lily suspected her free-spirited mother found it all quite romantic. But whatever romanticised notions she may have had, the reality was that Lily had been brought up alone by her mother so now she had no other family member to share the same grief.

And so Lily had sat in the hospital holding her mother's hand, talking quietly about anything and everything until finally there was nothing left to do except thank the hospital staff and be grateful that she'd been with her at the end.

The world had suddenly felt a very different place; cold and dark. It didn't seem right that everything should be going on as normal. Somehow, she'd stumbled her way through the next few days, Iris constantly by her side. Lily didn't know how she'd have got through that time without her. She suddenly couldn't wait to see her.

It had taken Lily a while to calm down the night before after her unexpected visitor in the large, unsettling shape of Jack Armstrong. Not sure why it had irked her so much, she'd replayed their conversation over in her head, hoping but failing to see it in a more positive light. Eventually she'd given up and turned her attention to phoning Iris.

Lily hadn't told her in advance she was coming for the simple reason she feared she would change her mind at the last minute. After receiving a mild scolding for not telling her, Lily had to stop Iris coming round there and then. Instead, Iris told her she'd be there this morning.

Aware she'd be arriving soon, Lily finished making her coffee and carefully negotiated her way down the staircase, passing the door to her mother's bedroom. Sorting through her mother's personal things was for another day. She'd need a mountain of courage for that which she simply didn't have, at least not yet.

She stopped for a few seconds before entering the shop, filled with a sudden apprehension. Taking a deep breath and mentally squaring her shoulders, she opened the door and stepped into the shop.

Bright daylight poured in through the windows as if to welcome her in so that instead of the cold emptiness she'd braced herself for, she experienced an unexpected warmth. The air was a little musty and a fine film of dust coated the surfaces but it could have been much worse considering the shop had been empty for all these months. Despite the slightly neglected air, there was something immediately appealing about the shop. Leaving her mug on the wooden counter Lily crossed the floor

27

to the large front windows where outside people were wandering along the main street, the sparkling loch providing the perfect backdrop. She savoured the view for as long as she dared and then, worried she might be seen, turned away from the window to survey the shop.

The black and white tiled flooring was in need of a good clean, but complemented the pale green walls perfectly. Rows of wooden shelves lined one of the walls while an old distressed dresser formed the focal point of another. There were a couple of free-standing display cabinets, and stacked rather precariously in one corner was a pile of cardboard boxes and a mound of various parcels and packages which, by the looks of things, remained unopened.

A friendly looking old-fashioned till sat on the counter and Lily ran her hand over the cool metal wondering where her mother had unearthed it from or if it had always been there. She couldn't help smiling when she saw a messy pile of papers and a couple of notebooks scattered about behind the counter – her mother was never one for orderly piles. But there were also sheets of coloured tissue paper, boxes and bags in different shapes and sizes and pretty swathes of ribbon, ready for gift wrapping.

As she moved around, Lily was unexpectedly comforted by how much she could feel her mother's presence. How easily she was able to picture her here, floating about in one of her quirky ensembles with clashing colours and patterns that she somehow always managed to make look stylish.

Lily gave herself a small shake. A plan, that's what she needed. Organisation was her first, last and middle name. Thinking about where to start first, she swallowed the last mouthful of her coffee just as she heard the sound of a key in the side door and then Iris's voice drifting through from the hall.

'Lily?'

'Through here,' she called, rushing to meet her. And then suddenly, Iris's kind face was there in front of her.

'Iris.' It came as a half-sob.

'Come here,' Iris soothed, dropping a massive yellow canvas bag onto the floor and wrapping Lily in a warm hug.

Until that moment Lily hadn't realised how much she'd been holding herself back, how uptight she was. Iris eventually released her, holding her at arm's length with an appraising look. 'Goodness, there's a lot of tension in you.'

It was true, she had a knot of tension the size of a small boulder between her shoulder blades that seemed to have lodged itself there recently. 'I'm fine,' Lily assured with a watery smile.

'Hmm, perhaps you've arrived just in time,' Iris said, sounding rather enigmatic as she picked up her bag and followed Lily through to the shop.

Lily looked at Iris affectionately, marvelling at how she never seemed to age. It occurred to her she didn't know exactly old how Iris was, but it seemed somehow irrelevant because she never changed. Her blue eyes were as vibrant as ever and she still wore armfuls of bangles, her hennaed hair styled in a loose bun, her smile never far away.

She still lived in the same cottage near the caravan park where they'd first met her all those years ago. She'd been a music teacher before retiring, travelling throughout the Highlands and Islands to different schools. She'd been married two – or was it three – times but had never had children of her own.

She had been more of a permanent fixture in Lily's life then her own grandparents whose strained relationship with their only child meant she'd seen more of Iris over the years than she had of them. Lily felt a rush of emotion for her. 'I'm so sorry I haven't been before. Leaving you to deal with all this.'

Iris waved away her apology. 'You have nothing to be sorry for. Patty was my friend, of course I wanted to help any way I could. Besides, I didn't do much. Just a bit of dusting and tidying.' She paused, taking Lily's hand. 'I have the ashes at home with me, I didn't want to leave them here. So, whenever you think the time is right we can take them to the loch.'

Lily nodded mutely, blinking away the sudden tears clouding her eyes. She knew it was something that had to be done but it wasn't something she could easily contemplate at that very moment.

Iris continued. 'I left her bedroom for you, all her personal bits and pieces are there. I know it's going to be difficult for you but its part of the healing process. A stage of mourning and letting go that you have to go through but once it's done I think you'll find it will help you.'

Lily remained silent as Iris carried on, her voice brighter. 'I knew you'd come when the time was right. Did you finally take some holidays?'

'A bit more than a holiday. I was made redundant.'

'Oh. I'm sorry to hear that.'

'I certainly didn't see it coming,' Lily said sagely, trying to keep the bitterness from her voice. The last thing she wanted was to unload her woes onto Iris. She'd already done enough without having to provide a shoulder for Lily to cry on.

'And last we spoke it was going so well,' Iris remarked.

'These things happen, I suppose.' Lily shrugged.

'Quite. But you know, perhaps some time away won't do you any harm. And you're certainly in the right place if you want to unwind for a while.'

'I'm not going to be here long,' Lily responded quickly, perhaps too quickly. 'I'll be selling.'

Iris gave a kind but knowing look. 'You must do what you think is right. But there's no hurry is there?'

Lily looked around, as if looking for a reason but failed to find one.

'I don't suppose so, no.'

'Is there someone waiting for you? A young man, perhaps?' Iris's voice tinkled as she shrugged off her jacket revealing a long floaty skirt and white tunic top.

It was so far from the truth Lily could have laughed. Nothing and no one was waiting for her, she thought dismally. An image of James's handsome face drifted in and out of her mind, pretty much the way he'd done in her life. She shook the image away, helping Iris to lift her bag onto the counter. 'No one waiting,' she replied lightly.

Her personal dreams might be lying in tatters but she always had her career to fall back on despite this current setback. She was good at her job and she missed it. Even here, far from her usual environment, she still had to fight a nagging feeling that she should be at her desk, starting a day's work. The redundancy had indeed been generous so financially at least there was no urgency but even so, she decided there and then that finding another job would be her priority as soon as she sold the shop.

She glanced at her iPhone on the counter, her only link to the outside world and her only chance of looking for another job. Frustratingly, she'd only been able to get a sporadic connection.

'Do you know if there's somewhere I can go for Wi-Fi?'

Iris flapped her hand dismissively. 'I don't really know about these things but I've heard people mention café in the activity centre has a place you can go. Although you know a digital detox might do you good.'

Lily couldn't help but laugh, recognising it as something her mother would have said.

'I've brought you a few things,' Iris said, rummaging in her bag. 'Some incense sticks – chamomile and jasmine, very good for calming the mind. And this,' she declared holding up a small brown bottle, 'is my herbal remedy. Ingredients are secret but I can guarantee it'll make you feel better if you're having an off-day.' She laid the items on the counter before digging into her bag yet again, this time producing a ceramic dish wrapped in foil.

'Shepherd's pie which you can reheat later, and don't take this the wrong way but it looks like you could do with a bit of sustenance.'

Lily could only smile her appreciation, well aware she wasn't exactly looking her sparkly best.

'Talking of which,' Iris said, 'when was the last time you took a holiday?'

Lily pursed her lip.

'Just as I thought.' Iris shook her head. 'Why don't you just take some time for yourself? Time to just be, time to think – that's what you need and Carroch is the perfect place.'

Lily nodded blandly. That's what she'd been avoiding; the thought of empty time terrified her.

'You could always come for a swim.' Iris turned to her with bright eyes. 'Do you remember how you used to love it?'

Lily vividly remembered. Swimming in the loch was one of the few things she'd actually looked forward to in Carroch, her mother having passed on her love of wild swimming. Patty had never taken Lily to girl guides or dance lessons or any of the other activities girls in her school had gone to, but one thing she'd insisted on was teaching Lily to swim from an early age. Although she deplored the chlorinated, characterless heated swimming pools, she had endured them each week to teach Lily to swim.

'There's a group meet every morning around eight, down by the jetty. I go most days but you can just turn up.'

'Perhaps.' Lily replied noncommittally but she didn't dismiss the idea totally. She was touched that Iris had included her and felt suddenly lifted by her presence. 'Thanks for coming today, Iris,' she said gratefully. 'Although you didn't have to rush around today.'

'I was coming to the shop today anyway.'

'Oh?'

'I didn't tell you on the phone but I would have been here today for the knit club.'

'Knit club?' Lily echoed in surprise. Her mother wasn't exactly the tea and knitting type.

'Your mum didn't knit but it was all her idea. One of the ladies in the village your mum was friendly with had recently moved into sheltered housing a few miles away. Patty used to go and visit her and she became friendly with several of the other women living there too. She came up with the idea to use the back room here as a knitting club, somewhere they could come for a change of scenery and bit of company each week. She arranged the transport and everything.'

Lily followed her through a door to what she had assumed was some sort of storage space but was in fact a bright room with a window looking out onto the small back garden. A large trestle table sat in the middle of the floor surrounded by an assortment of chairs and there was a small sideboard piled with tea making things next to a small sink.

'It had only been running a few weeks and after your mum … well, we carried on. It seemed a shame to stop it when the ladies enjoyed it so much. I hope you didn't mind?'

'Of course not.' Lily hadn't known about the knitting club but was hardly going to turn up now and start objecting. She looked down suddenly, feeling a brush of something against her leg to see the cat had sauntered in, looking for all the world as if she owned the place. Which now she came to think about it, she kind of did.

'Hello Misty,' Iris chirped.

'I didn't know Mum had a cat?' Lily watched Iris bend down to briefly welcome their feline visitor.

Iris wrinkled her forehead. 'Ah, did I not mention that? She and your mother, well they sort of adopted one another. I would have taken her but I'm terribly allergic and so we decided to let her stay here. Jack lives nearby and very kindly agreed to help out. She's quite clean though, don't worry. We took her to the vet's and had her all checked out.'

'I met him last night – Jack. Gave me a bit of shock, I can tell you.'

'Yes, I imagine he would have,' Iris chuckled. 'I don't suppose he'd have been expecting you either.'

Lily hadn't thought of it like that and it occurred to her now she may have appeared rude last night. But for some reason she couldn't work out, their brief encounter unnerved her. Maybe it was guilt, knowing she should have been the one helping out, not him. Or maybe it was because there'd been something about his physical presence – almost a vague familiarity – she'd been too aware off.

'I'm very grateful to Jack, I can tell you. With everything he's got on he still took time to help with Misty. He's an absolute gem – you'll see that once you get to know him.'

Lily bit her lip realising she'd probably overreacted last night. But given that she had no intention of getting to know Jack Armstrong better anyway, she kept her thoughts to herself and changed the subject.

'What can I do to help?' she asked, glancing around.

'Putting the kettle on would be a good place to start.'

Lily let the water run for a few seconds, trying to recollect the shop from her previous visits. 'Who owned the shop before mum bought it?'

'For years it was the post office, you'll probably remember Mrs Mackie running it. She was a bit of a character,' Iris reminisced fondly. 'There was more gossip passed over that counter than anything else. But when they closed the post office down she decided to sell up and sold it to a couple from London.'

Iris shook her head. 'It was all very sad. Alice and Robert were high-flying lawyers in London and this was their retirement dream. They had great plans for the place and they'd had the shop all fitted out with shelving and storage. But then Robert's health began to deteriorate. He had a long illness and Alice nursed him but of course the shop was closed all that time. After he passed away, she couldn't bring herself to open the shop.'

'That's so sad,' Lily sympathised. 'So what happened?'

34

'Alice wanted to sell the shop but wasn't interested in the money. I think for her it was more important who bought the shop. She and your mum had become friendly and so that was when Patty decided to buy the shop from her – it never went on the open market. Your grandparents had passed away so she was in a position to be able to make an offer. I do know she insisted on giving Alice a good price though – said she wouldn't buy it otherwise.'

Lily knew that to be the case from Mr Bell. More or less everything Patty had received from the sale of her parents' house had gone into buying the shop. 'So do you know exactly what Mum was planning to do?'

Iris puffed out her cheeks, thinking. 'We spoke a bit about it, she had ideas. She saw it as an adventure more than anything. She didn't have a business plan or anything like that.'

Lily hesitated, then gently asked, 'Do you think she was really serious about it all?'

Iris sighed with a sad smile. 'You know your mum. I think she was more interested in the people who would come in and the spirit of the shop. She wanted it to be a happy place.'

Lily nodded. She could certainly imagine her mother doing that. Patty had never cared about any outward signs of success or prosperity or been driven by money. She'd also never been particularly focused on anything not had a job for any length of time before becoming bored and moving on.

Lily had never heard her mother sound as excited as when she told her she'd bought the shop with a small flat above and hoped with all her heart she had finally found what she was looking for. She'd been surprised when her mum had called to ask her a few questions about stock and pricing but had happily answered all her questions, managing to bury the little nag of doubt that it was just another adventure that wouldn't last.

Lily had fully intended to come up and visit her mother but it had been a crucial time at work. Dunn Equity had just taken over Bremners and Lily had started working closely with James – but her mum hadn't minded.

'Wait until I have it all organised then you can come up for the grand opening,' she'd said excitedly. Now regret raged through Lily that she'd never made it. Forcing her thoughts back to the present she asked Iris about the boxes she'd found this morning.

'It was all the stock she'd bought,' Iris stated matter-of-factly.

Lily's eyebrows lifted in surprise, not realising she'd got as far as actually buying stock.

'Where did she get it all from?'

'I know she'd registered with a couple of wholesale suppliers and then there was the trade fair we went to—'

'You went to a trade fair?'

'Oh yes, it was all quite good fun. She placed a few orders and everything arrived but she hadn't got round to unpacking anything yet. I stacked it all the corner and put a sheet over them. I hope that was all right?'

'Of course,' Lily rushed to reassure her. 'You've already done too much.'

The redundancy might be the reason she was here now but Lily knew it wasn't an excuse for her not coming sooner. And she knew if anyone understood why she hadn't come before now it would be Iris but that wasn't providing her with much consolation. 'I'm really am sorry I didn't come before.'

Iris shook her head. 'Don't give yourself such a hard time. You're here now and that's all that matters. Take your time and do what you have to and don't worry about folk talking.'

Lily's eyes widened. 'Are they?'

'Och, you know what people are like in a small place.' Iris shook her head. 'I think there's been a bit of sniffing about what with the place lying empty, especially now that the village is busier.'

Lily chewed her lip, having difficulty associating the term busy with Carroch. But even so, she hated the idea of being the focus of speculation and it notched up another reason to sell up and leave again.

'It's your inheritance and only you can decide the right thing to do.'

Bizarrely, Lily had never viewed the shop and flat as her inheritance before, not even when Mr Bell formally read out the details of her mother's will. To Lily, it was something that belonged to her mum, almost nothing to do with her. But of course, it was hers now and she had to deal with it. She also knew the only right thing to do was to sell. What use was it to her?

And as much as she was grateful and thankful to Iris she couldn't afford any sort of emotional attachment. She was here to sort through her mother's belongings and leave. A sense of goodbye, she needed that and then she could get back to Edinburgh and her life there.

Both women turned their heads at the sound of tapping on the shop door.

'That's them now,' Iris announced. She opened the door to a small army of elderly ladies, the average age of which had to be eighty and all of them brandishing knitting needles.

'Hello ladies, in you come.' They trooped in regarding Lily with interest as Iris introduced them and explained Lily's presence. Mary, a sweet-faced lady with powdered cheeks and wispy white hair clasped her hand, peering closely at her. 'You're very like your mother.'

Lily simply smiled at the comment she'd heard so many times before; her dark brown hair, full mouth and high cheekbones had always been strikingly similar to that of her mothers. Her vivid blue eyes she could only assume came from her father.

'We all loved Patty, she was a lovely lady.'

'Thank you,' Lily croaked, a sudden lump forming in her throat.

'She was so kind to us, letting us use this room. It's such a pity the shop never opened, we were all very excited about it,

37

you know, looking forward to seeing all the wonderful things she was going to sell.'

As the ladies began to settle themselves at the table, arranging cushions behind their backs Lily became aware that she was expected to sit with them. Fearing an interrogation was imminent, she quelled her instinct to run; besides, she really had nowhere to go. And so she took her place at the table, surrounded by faces sparkling with interest.

Tea was poured from a large brown teapot, beautifully moist lemon cake was unwrapped and cut into slices, and plates passed around. Lily's stomach rumbled in hunger, a soggy train sandwich and a few crackers last night now a distant memory.

Lily didn't normally do cake, choosing instead to power through the day on a super-green smoothie which supposedly enhanced mental performance. She shuddered thinking of it now as she popped the final bit of cake into her mouth, washing it down with a mouthful of tea.

And so with the clacking of needles and the voice of Ella Fitzgerald quietly serenading them in the background, Lily found herself sitting in a sea of kindness, watching withered and gnarled fingers weaving together shades of pinks, blues and greens.

Somehow Lily found herself spilling out the last few months of her life. She was tempted to gloss over it, say how she was taking a planned career break. But what was the point in lying? Redundancies happened and she was sure these ladies had all seen their share of heartache. The only part she didn't reveal in full was how she'd fallen for James.

They listened, nodding and tutting sympathetically. They certainly saw her future in a more positive light than she had managed, the general consensus being that she was young and it would all work out. 'Sounds like you're burnt up, that happened to my niece,' said one of them, patting her hand.

'You mean burnt out,' tutted Mary.

Some of the ladies remembered the famous Bremners department store from years ago and Lily was enthralled by their memories as they told her apparently it was the place to buy a handbag or to be seen shopping on a Saturday. Much to Lily's delight one of the ladies had worked there, explaining how they only employed refined young ladies considered to be of good breeding. Lily listened, fascinated. Comforted by their presence and kindness, she was disappointed when Iris announced their lift had been arranged and it was time for them to go.

Cardigans were pulled back on, spectacles and bags collected and then Iris and Lily saw them to the door as they left with waves and cheery smiles. 'See you next week,' they chorused.

Lily turned to Iris looking alarmed. She didn't want to think about next week and what would happen to the knitting club.

'Don't worry about it just now,' Iris calmed her. 'You'll likely still be here next week anyway?'

Lily supposed that was reasonable to assume but even so felt her heart plummet. She really hadn't expected any of this.

Iris stayed for a while, and only left after checking that Lily didn't want to come home with her. Everything suddenly felt very quiet. Lily drew in a deep breath, determined not to give into the sudden sadness that enveloped her. At that moment she'd give almost anything to sit and have a conversation with mother, the way she'd just done with those women. Her head felt as if it could explode with a thousand questions she had for her. Suddenly desperate to clear her mind, Lily decided she needed fresh air.

She ran back upstairs and studied her reflection in the mirror. The ladies from the knitting club had all looked so colourful and lively. Lily on the other hand was dismayed at how pale and tired she looked, only a scattering of freckles saving her from looking a total wash-out. Hastily she applied some tinted moisturiser, ran a brush through her hair and headed out.

Chapter 5

In her memory, for some reason Carroch was always dull and muted, absent of any colour. But strolling along the main street now Lily could see tourists milling about, cyclists and hillwalkers with rucksacks hitched to their backs. Everything looked lively and vibrant and she realised the village of her recollections was very different to how it looked today.

Whitewashed cottages with gardens in full bloom adorned the shoreline and wooden benches were dotted along the banks of the loch. Everywhere she looked, flowers burst from window boxes and planters, clusters of pink petunias and tiny white flowers spilling over the rim of hanging baskets.

She passed a bakery, its window crammed with sugary short-bread, plump fruit scones and warm pastries. The pub looked newly painted, its chalkboard menu boasting fresh seafood and vegetarian options and Lily was also surprised to see an art gallery displaying a range of prints and colourful landscapes by local artists.

Only now did it occur to her the impact of having an empty shop in the village. She hadn't given it much thought – if anything she had thought it might be difficult to sell a little shop in a remote sleepy village. But putting together Iris's earlier comment with what she could see now, perhaps that wouldn't be the case at all. At least knowing the shop would sell easily was one less thing to worry about.

As Lily left the main hub behind and approached the loch, memories of their holidays tumbled into her mind. She swallowed deeply, taken back to another time. A time of dipping toes into freezing water, of scrabbling over rocks and taking turns with the other kids for the single swing and rickety slide in the caravan park. And the most special times – now the most poignant to remember – when Patty used to take Lily down to the loch to watch the sunset. They'd sit huddled together and for those precious few moments Patty seemed at peace with herself and the world.

Lily had been a teenager the last time she'd been here, her head full of plans to go to university. Her future was laid out before her, somehow golden and full of hope. Now, she wasn't so sure about things, a feeling that something intangible was escaping her.

Lily continued to walk, passing under a canopy of Birch trees where mosses and lichens clung to the trunks and carpeted the roots, making the earth damp beneath her feet. Bluebells and primroses lined a rough path which sloped downwards and then meandered along the shoreline. Now Lily was able to see the loch in all its glory, she let out a small gasp. The nine-mile stretch of sea water, surrounded by mountains and thick woodland, shimmered in the sunlight and looked breathtakingly beautiful.

Recalling a walk she used to make with her mum, she decided to see if she could retrace their steps and headed towards the north end of the loch, following a path through the trees and over a boardwalk bridge where she could see glimpses of the river. Her walks to and from work every day meant she wasn't totally unfit but even so she had to stop a couple of times to catch her breath. Finally, she was able to stand for a few moments, the reward for her aching calf muscles and burgeoning blister now being able to see the enchanting waterfalls as the river made its way towards the loch.

Finding a secluded bay with a small gravelly beach she sat down to face the loch. She listened to the water gently lapping on the shore and lifted her face to the sun, breathing in deeply.

Iris's words circled around in her head. *Just be.* But she didn't have a clue how to do that. She knew how to keep busy. Although if you did want a place to sit back and forget the world, you wouldn't find a better place than this, she conceded.

Lily stared out at the water, surrendering herself to its vastness and allowing herself to feel small and insignificant. A view like this made you think, made you reflect. And that's what she'd been afraid of. The silence. No emails or no phones, no deadlines to meet.

All the usual parameters of her life had been removed and she suddenly felt adrift. Her mind flitted to what she'd normally be doing at this time; every minute of her day was usually planned and she thought longingly of her desk, letting out a sigh. She really wasn't very good at not having a structure to her day or not knowing what she was going to be doing next week. Her mother's nonchalant attitude to life and disregard for any sort of routine had left Lily with a need for security and routine, both of which her job had provided.

They had moved around a few times – a spell in Glasgow, a few months in Dundee, a year in Newcastle. Lily always sensed a restlessness from her mother as various jobs and relationships came and went, as if each time they moved she was looking for something.

When Lily left school, Patty had made it clear she wanted her daughter to live her own life and had encouraged her to spread her wings, probably imagining a rucksack and a one-way ticket. But Lily, studious and with an aptitude for maths, knew exactly what she wanted to do. To study accountancy and get a job. To be settled and secure and be able to provide for her and her mother in the future. Her whole life Lily had lived with a vague feeling something would come crashing down and when it did she wanted to be in a position to help her mum, at least financially.

Never interested in academic achievements, Patty had regarded her daughter with bemusement on hearing her plans. 'Accountancy? Really?'

When Lily had started her course at Edinburgh University, her mother had gone abroad for a while, only returning to move back in with her parents where they lived in the small town of Dunbar in East Lothian. Patty had never had an easy relationship with her parents. Seen through their well-meaning, safe suburban eyes, their only daughter becoming a single mother was disappointing if not scandalous. But calling a truce on their uneasy relationship, Patty had moved in to help look after her father who was now in the wretched grip of dementia.

By this time Lily had started work at Bremners and was loving every minute of it, not least because of the security and sense of belonging it gave her, something she'd never experienced before.

Lily was rudely jolted back to the present by the realisation she was under attack from a swarm of midges. The slight breeze from earlier had disappeared, making her exposed arms a prime target. She furiously batted them away, aware it was time to move.

She stood up quickly, dusting down her jeans and began to retrace her steps, deciding to head in the direction of the jetty to see if she could find the old boating place she remembered.

As she drew closer, Lily was surprised to see it had been totally transformed. What had once been basically a wooden hut with a few small boats for hire was now a fully-fledged activity centre. A large single-storey timber-framed building stood with huge full-lengths windows at the front facing the loch. There was an information board and an enormous map of the loch in a glass display case surrounded by people with bikes or in walking gear planning their day.

A sign by the front door bearing the name Carroch Activity Centre listed the range of activities available including kayaking, canoeing and windsurfing. To one side there were now parking bays and a pretty café with table and chairs outside was bustling with people coming and going.

Lily's step faltered as she recognised the prowling cat man from last night. Close to the water's edge, he was working on a small upturned boat, engrossed in his task. Lily watched him, transfixed by the way the muscles on his arms and shoulders flexed as he moved. She narrowed her eyes, again a vague sense of familiarity tugging at her memory. And then in one heart-stopping moment, it came rushing back to her.

***

She was sixteen again, and it was the last summer she'd been here with her mother. Her skin had turned golden under the rays of a rare, long Scottish summer. She'd discovered that a little mascara brought out the blue in her eyes and that she liked the pretty pink sheen from her cherry lip gloss. Now that she was old enough, she would stroll down to the loch on her own. And hopefully she would see him, the good-looking boy who worked at the boats.

Lily had reckoned him to be a couple of years older than her; he exuded a worldly confidence and physical presence she'd found thrilling. Not to mention he was easily the most handsome boy she'd ever seen. Pretending to read a book, she'd sit and watch him from afar, never brave enough to go and speak to him. Not like the other girls who'd hang around him, giggling and flirting. Lily desperately wanted to go and speak to him but her heart would pound and her mouth turn dry long before she went anywhere near him. Instead she retreated to the caravan park and at night, thoughts and images of him would make her stomach swirl in a way she'd never felt before.

She hadn't thought of him in all that time and she could hardly believe he was still here, still doing the same thing.

The intervening years had certainly done him no harm. His body had filled out from that of a teenager to a fully formed – and extremely muscular – man. With a certain amount of dismay, Lily noted how ridiculously handsome he still was.

He was wearing an old T-shirt, dirt-streaked jeans and his jaw was shadowed by stubble. Clearly he didn't pay much attention to his appearance although she supposed he pulled it off – if you liked that sort of thing. He turned his head and caught her gaze before she had a chance to look away. Lily's heart starting thumping for some reason, and she fought her instinct to turn and run away.

He straightened up and, after wiping his hands on an old rag, walked towards her. Based on Iris's obvious high opinion of him and knowing she might have appeared slightly ungracious at their first meeting, Lily thought she should make an effort to appear friendly.

'Hello again.' He smiled tentatively at her and as their eyes met, Lily felt something in her response which surprised her. She was a grown professional woman now, not a gauche teenager with a crush on him.

'Morning.'

'You've been for a walk?' he asked.

She nodded her head. 'To the waterfall and back.'

'That's a fair walk,' he commented before lifting his eyes skywards. 'Looks like you made it back just in time.'

Lily looked up. Sure enough, a massive black cloud loomed over them and she could actually feel a few specks of rain. She shook her head at the fickle climate. 'Rain and midges,' she muttered, rubbing at her arms. 'Pretty much just as I remember.'

'Kind of goes with the territory.'

His eyes, which really were very green, travelled down Lily's arms where all her earlier clawing had left unattractive red welts on her skin. 'That looks quite nasty. Hold on, I'll get you something.'

'No, its fine—' Lily started to object but in a few strides his long legs had already almost covered the distance to the centre where he disappeared through the door. Lily stared after him and fiddled with her hair, suddenly feeling self-conscious. Returning a couple of moments later, he handed her a tube.

'Here, this should help cool your skin. We always keep a supply.'

'Thanks.' Lily rubbed some cream into skin, appreciating its instant soothing effect, and handed it back to him.

A little silence descended over them, and Lily searched for something to say. 'So er, you look busy,' she tried.

'Yeah, I'm just helping out today with the boats although I'm usually more behind the scenes these days.'

'The place certainly looks different from how I remember,' she commented.

His eyes roamed her face and she wondered if he remembered her, which was silly. Of course he wouldn't. 'When were you last here?' he asked.

Lily lifted her eyes, calculating. 'Over ten years ago. Before that though my mum used to drag me here every year until I was eighteen..'

His mouth quirked. 'Not your favourite holiday destination then?'

'It was okay when I was younger, I suppose. But by the time I started university I'd only ever been to Carroch on holiday so I couldn't wait to stretch my horizons, see different places.'

'So where'd you go?'

She shrugged. 'Inter-railing around Europe, spent a few weeks in Asia when I was a student ...' Her voice trailed away, distracted by the intense way he was looking at her.

'Sounds good,' he said. 'It depends what you're looking for I guess.'

'Suppose it does.' It dawned on Lily now that she'd never found that one place in her heart that had made her want to return to, the way her mother had done here.

'And you've not been back since?' he asked, sounding surprised.

She shook her head. 'Not until now, no.'

'You'll see a big change then.' He threw a glance over his shoulder and then brought his gaze back on her again. 'I hope I didn't startle you too much last night?'

'No. Well, perhaps just a little,' she admitted.

He looked at her evenly. 'So how are you getting on with Misty?'

'Um, okay, I guess.'

'You're coping with her?' he asked, a hint of amusement in his voice.

'I'm managing,' she assured him although she shuddered inwardly remembering the contents of the litter tray this morning. 'Um, does it ever go out?' she asked hopefully.

'Not much. Occasionally she'll make an appearance at my place but she seems happy to stay indoors.'

Lily nodded silently. He was clearly fond of the cat, knew her habits – perhaps it could live with him. 'I don't suppose you'd like to take it?'

'Misty, you mean?' He looked a little incredulous.

'Yes, Misty.'

'I've been happy to help out but I'm not sure I'd want to take her.'

Lily sighed. 'It's just all a bit of an inconvenience, that's all.'

'An inconvenience?'

She cringed inwardly at how that sounded. 'I—'

'Perhaps if you'd come earlier it wouldn't be an issue,' he interrupted dryly.

Lily frowned. 'I just meant my flat in Edinburgh isn't really suitable for a cat. But I'm sure I'll find somewhere for her before I leave.'

'You're not hanging around then?'

47

'Here?' She didn't mean to sound quite so horrified by the idea. 'I've got work to get back to.' At least she would have, once she'd got a few interviews lined up. 'So I'll be selling the shop as soon as possible.'

His mouth tugged down at the corners. 'Good for you. I'm sure you'll get a good price for it.'

'What? It's not about the money—'

'If you say so.' He shrugged.

'I do say so,' she said, exasperated. God, he was infuriating.

He turned his head on hearing someone call him and waved to acknowledge them. 'Looks like I've got to go. See you.'

Lily stood agog as he sauntered off, smiling briefly at two women as he passed them, much to their obvious pleasure.

Oh please. Lily rolled her eyes. He might not have moved on with his life but she certainly had. She shook her head, wondering how in the two times she'd met Jack Armstrong, both times he'd succeeding in getting under her skin quite so much.

She turned to leave, furiously scratching at her arm again, not understanding why she was so upset. She couldn't believe he thought she was just here for the money. She didn't need to explain or defend herself to him and why should she care what he thought? What did he know, anyway? Tinkering about with boats all day.

She reached the main street, her eyes scanning the shops. Up ahead she could see the sign for a general store and made a beeline for it.

The smart interior was a far cry from the sad-looking shop she vaguely remembered. The shelves were well-stocked and attractively presented and Lily stalked up and down the aisles half-listening to the conversation taking place at the till which seemed to revolve around the weather. She was surprised to see the shelves laden with fresh produce and grabbed a few things to keep her going over the next few days – milk, soup, free-range eggs, organic bread and tomatoes. Finally she added some more midge repellent and spotting some cat biscuits on offer, popped them in too.

She felt a stab of annoyance as she approached the counter, the interminable conversation about the weather still ongoing. A knot of anxiety twisted in her stomach and she tried to ignore the feeling of having to be somewhere or do something. Taking a deep breath, she forced herself to relax. She wasn't in a hurry, was she?

Distracting herself she looked around, her eye caught by a section of outdoor clothes and water sports accessories obviously there to cater for all the outdoor activities. She ambled over to where there was an impressive array of waterproofs, fleeces and outdoor gear. She remembered Iris's offer to go swimming and found herself rifling through a selection of wetsuits until she found what she reckoned would be her size. On an impulse she put one in her basket and made her way back to the counter.

Chapter 6

Lily still hadn't been able to face her mother's room and had spent another night on the sofa. With everything she needed to hand she was beginning to feel like a little bird building itself a nest. She'd unpacked her clothes into neat piles and was working her way through a couple of paperbacks she'd found – if she ignored her aching back, she was comfortable enough.

Although it hadn't slept on her chest again the cat was always there, its watchful gaze fixed on her. It didn't seem to ever leave the flat. Wasn't it supposed to be out catching mice or something? Lily had never given much thought to what cats did all day and now knew it wasn't much – at least, not this one. She was the very essence of mindfulness and Lily wished she had an ounce of her serenity.

Lily fed it now, noting with grim satisfaction that it seemed to like the new biscuits she'd bought. After enduring the horror of emptying the litter tray she headed downstairs. She passed the door to her mother's bedroom which remained closed. She knew it probably wasn't helpful to keep putting it off but she simply wasn't ready to deal with it yet. Instead, today she'd decided to tackle the shop.

She opened the door to the shop and stepped inside with a

little shiver. Outside the day was gloomy, giving off little light, and the air felt chilly. Lily flicked on the light switch, a warm glow illuminating the space and immediately making it appear warmer.

Lily stood in the middle of the floor, her mind automatically switching to professional mode as her eyes made a sweep of the shop as a retail space. Although her work in Bremners had confined her mostly to her office, after James arrived she would often accompany him on walkabouts as he talked to all the different departmental managers, listening intently while they explained their roles. Of course, beneath all the chat and charm he was ruthlessly calculating – finding out how they operated, where costs could be saved. She remembered how people responded to him, more than happy to explain what they did and show him how they run their departments.

Her thoughts slid back to those times, at her newfound confidence beside him, how she loved the feeling of the two of them working as a team and how close they'd become. Or so she had thought.

Forcing her thoughts back to the present, Lily tried to picture the shop once all the stock was in place and to be honest it didn't take much imagination. The shop held such warmth and character, there was no doubt in her mind that her mother would have been able to turn it into a thriving small business.

Breaking her reverie, Lily reminded herself what she was supposed to be doing and moved over to investigate the pile of boxes stacked in the corner. She reached up and pulled the dust sheet off, fine particles catching the back of her throat and making her splutter. Bundling the sheet into a ball, she took it to the front door where, after saying good morning to a young couple and waiting for them to safely pass, she gave it a good shake.

Back inside, Lily felt a flutter of anticipation as she lifted down the first box, kneeling on the floor to open it. Her fingers delved into a mass of packing chips where she found pretty decorative pebbles made from white stoneware clay. She studied them for a few moments before moving onto the next box where nestling in bubble wrap she found Caithness glass paperweights and tea light holders.

A few boxes later it was beginning to look like Christmas morning. Lily sat back on her heels, slightly dazed by how much stock there was. She hadn't even opened everything yet and already she'd found Harris Tweed purses, a selection of enamelled jewellery and some beautiful cashmere scarves in shades of muted blues and forest greens.

She'd seen similar items before in Bremners and other shops in Edinburgh. They were all good quality products and she was sure they would sell here in Carroch, particularly as there were no other gift shops in the village. Lily wondered how her mother would have gone about displaying and selling it all, and felt an ache of sorrow that she would never now have the chance to do it.

Lily smiled ruefully, imagining her mum getting her head around the difference between profit and turnover, or how much stock to buy. She would have asked Lily to go through it all for her eventually and Lily would have loved to have helped her.

Lily didn't like how unfinished it all felt. She'd need to go over it all properly and see if she could find invoices for everything. She couldn't imagine her mother keeping strict records but knew there must be some paperwork somewhere. She rooted about behind the counter and found a couple of notepads, some random pieces of paper and a folder stuffed with invoices. As Lily suspected there was no discernible system or order to them and her accountant's brain itched to go through it all.

Taking one of the notepads she started to list everything down, not helped by Misty who kept either disappearing into the boxes or attacking the wrapping paper in quite a vicious manner. It was only when she looked up to give her eyes a rest that Lily noticed a large white unopened cardboard box in the corner. Not sure how she'd manage to miss it, she lifted it onto the counter and opened the lid, surprised to find an envelope with her mother's name on it.

She held it in her hand for a moment. The poignancy of a letter addressed to Patty that she would never open made Lily's heart heavy. It almost didn't seem right just to tear it open but equally, leaving it unread didn't seem right either. Lily sat down on the stool behind the counter and carefully opened the envelope to read the letter inside.

Dear Patty

It was so lovely to meet you and it's so exciting that we're both starting our businesses at the same time.

As discussed, here is your first order. I know you said you weren't in a hurry but even so it has taken me much longer than I thought – sorry!

As agreed, let's see how they sell before we discuss further orders or price. I'm really keen for any feedback you get and I can't wait to see how they sell – hopefully well!

I know this is new to us both and I'm so looking forward to us working together.

Beth Brookes

Taigh-na-bruich Cottage

Lily stared at the flowing handwriting as she mulled over the contents of the letter. She placed it down and then gently started to lift the contents out of the box. Wrapped in white tissue paper she discovered a range of bath and skin products made from essential oils.

Tilting her head, she studied the various brown jars and bottles. The packaging was simple but effective, the name *Highland Aromatics* printed in a handwritten font on cream-coloured labels. Lily felt her senses implode simply reading the list of ingredients; bergamot, lemongrass, lavender, peppermint, rosewood and ginger, all made into balms and lotions designed to relax, revive, sooth and calm.

53

Unable to resist, Lily prised open a jar of body oil and breathed in its delicate herbal aroma. It was divine, the scent seemingly wrapping itself around her. She felt something stirring within her, instinctively knowing there was something special about them. Clearly they were a quality product but there was also a charming, natural cottage-industry feel about them.

She understood from the letter it was a new business which explained why she hadn't seen the products being sold anywhere else before. Intrigued, she picked up the note and scanned the words again. She wondered if this Beth lady knew Patty had died. Surely, she couldn't still be waiting to hear from her after all this time. The thought unsettled her and she felt an overwhelming need to respond to Beth, an obligation not only to her but to her mother.

Lily looked up on suddenly hearing a noise and noticed a shiny BMW pull up outside the shop The driver clearly wasn't too concerned about parking restrictions or the fact they were effectively blocking the pavement.

A man climbed out, carrying a file under his arm. Immaculately groomed and wearing a smart suit, Lily knew she'd be able to smell his expensive cologne from ten paces away. Her eyes followed him as he walked round the car, his appearance and businesslike manner making him look incongruous amongst the tourists and hill walkers. He paused briefly, his eyes squinting against the sunlight as he looked up at the front of the shop.

Lily braced herself, aware she was about to have a visitor. She moved quickly, scooping up and shoving the things she'd unpacked back into their boxes. For some reason she didn't want anyone seeing them, not until she'd figured out where all this stuff had come from and what she was going to do with it all. A moment later she heard a tap and the door opened. Lily turned and smiled tentatively, her mild irritation at being interrupted tempered by curiosity.

'Can I help you?' she asked, notes of cedar and musk proving she'd been right about his cologne.

'Good morning.' His smile revealed teeth almost as dazzlingly white as his shirt. 'I'm Finlay Reid from Thornton's commercial property.'

She took his extended hand, his appearance now making sense.

'Obviously I keep my ear close to the ground and I'd heard someone had moved in. I was in the area and thought I'd take the opportunity to introduce myself.'

His eyes flitted around the shop. His ear must have been very close to the ground to have found out so soon. But Lily supposed that was his job – to be out and about, making contacts.

'You're intending on opening soon?' he enquired politely.

'Oh no.' She gave her head a little shake. 'I won't be opening. The shop belonged to my mother but she passed away.'

'I'm so sorry,' he sympathised.

'Thank you.'

He left a respectful pause before speaking. 'Have you made any decisions about what you're going to do?'

She wasn't sure why she hesitated; it wasn't as if it was a secret. 'Only that I'll be selling.'

He nodded in a slightly imperiously fashion implying this was clearly the sensible option. 'Luckily Thornton's have offices all over Scotland and our fee structure is very competitive.'

Lily didn't think there was anything lucky about having to sell due to her mother's death but that small detail seemed lost on him. Oblivious, he carried on. 'We have a team of experts and years of experience in selling commercial properties.'

Lily wasn't sure she was ready to discuss selling yet, it all felt a bit soon. But there didn't seem to be any stopping him, he'd already taken a couple of steps in, casting assessing eyes around the shop and giving Lily the benefit of his expertise.

'Clearly it's a bit tired around the edges and of course you won't be selling as a going concern so you won't have any accounts to show profit and turnover or seasonal variations for potential buyers to see.'

'Do you think that will be an issue?'

His mouth tugged down at the corners. 'Could be with some buyers but I really don't think so.' He continued breezily, 'But you can leave all that for us to deal with, you wouldn't even need to stay around. Simply leave us keys and let us get on with it. Where is it you've come from?'

'Edinburgh.'

'I love Edinburgh,' he gushed. 'Went to university there.' He lowered his voice in a conspiratorial tone. 'You must be finding this place a bit different. Bet you can't wait to get back.'

Lily muttered something vaguely in agreement. She thought of her neat, quiet flat in Edinburgh where everything would be waiting for her just as she'd left it. Then her thoughts drifted upstairs to the cluttered little flat. She imagined it would be nice knowing it was there at the end of a day working in the shop. Giving herself a small shake, she turned her attention back to Finlay.

He flashed her another smile. It was a business smile and one she'd seen a thousand times before. She doubted it held much genuine warmth but even so, Lily allowed herself to be reassured by it. Admittedly Finlay had been quick off the mark, but she was grateful to have someone who knew the local market. There was no room for sentimentality. Business was business and she owed it to her mother to get the best price she could. Perhaps she could make a donation of some sorts to the sheltered housing where the knitting ladies lived.

'There's a few things I need to sort through first,' she told him. 'I'll need a bit of time but after that we could discuss getting it on the market.'

'Of course, I'd be delighted to. Perhaps I could come back in—'

'Hello.' A deep voice came from the door.

Lily turned, surprised to see Jack at the door. She frowned, wondering what on earth he was doing here. Simultaneously, her stomach did a strange little flip at seeing him. She really should have remembered to lock the door.

He smiled briefly at Lily before shooting a look at Finlay which was nothing less than arctic.

'Jack.' Finlay spoke in a tight voice, his smooth demeanour momentarily dented. Jack glared back at him in silence. Lily didn't suppose it was that surprising they knew each other; what surprised her was the sudden chill in the air that had nothing to do with the weather outside.

Lily couldn't help noticing the glaring differences between the two men. Where Finlay was all sharp suited and groomed, Jack was rugged and outdoorsy, wearing an old shirt and pair of jeans that had clearly been washed a hundred times.

Luckily the little impasse didn't last long with Finlay apparently deciding it was time to leave. He handed Lily his business card. 'It was a pleasure to meet you Lily. Call me if you have any questions.'

Lily had no intention of going for a drink with Finlay but something about the way Jack had taken a couple of steps, almost as if deliberately manoeuvring himself between her and Finlay had irritated her. 'Thanks, I will,' she said pointedly.

She took the proffered card just as Misty decided to join proceedings, strolling in and releasing a rather vicious hiss in Finlay's direction. As Lily led Finlay to the door she saw Jack out the corner of her eye bend down to Misty. 'Good girl' he murmured.

She closed the shop door and turned to face him, hands on her hips. 'Can I help you?'

'This is for Misty, in case you need to take her somewhere' He held up a cat carrier and then placed it on the floor. 'Leave it here, will I?'

She stared blankly at it for a moment. 'Right, thanks.'

'Not wasting anytime getting the place on the market, I see.'

Lily bristled, wondering how he had the ability to make her

feel so judged. She narrowed her eyes at him. 'Not that it's any of your business but he just showed up, I didn't invite him.'

Jack held up a hand. 'You're right, it's none of my business.'

Remembering his acerbic remark about getting a good price for the shop, Lily wasn't prepared to let it go so easily. 'You seem to have formed the impression that I've turned up simply to sell for as much as I can when that's not the case at all.' Feeling oddly fired up, she tilted her chin defiantly. 'Let me assure you I am not here just to see how much money I can get. I know I should have been here before now but well, it's complicated.' God, she hated saying that. It sounded like a get-out-of-jail-free card, an excuse for not dealing with things. But in this case, it really was true.

He was looking at her, wide-eyed.

'I'm grateful to you for looking after Misty and I'm sorry if that inconvenienced you in anyway.'

'It didn't.' He shook his head. 'I was happy to do it and you have every right to do what you want with the property.' He let a moment go by. 'I'm also really sorry about the circumstances that brought you here – none of this can be easy for you.'

She just about managed to keep the huff out of her voice. 'Thank you.'

He ran a hand around the back of neck. 'I guess I was trying to say don't rush or agree to anything you're not happy with.'

'Trust me, I won't. All I want is to sell and go and I'm perfectly capable of handling it.'

An uncomfortable silence descended. Jack dug his hands in his pockets, casting a glance at the various packages and boxes scattered around. 'So, do you need a hand with anything?' he asked awkwardly.

Lily shook her head. 'I'm just sorting through the stock my mum had bought.' Absently she picked up one of the cashmere scarves lying on the counter, feeling its softness between her fingers as her eyes landing on Beth's letter.

Glancing over at Jack, she figured she may as well use his local knowledge. She picked the letter up and pointed to the address at the bottom of the page. 'Would you be able to tell me where this is?'

He came to stand beside her, close enough for Lily to breathe in his woody masculine scent. He scanned the page. 'That's one of the cottages on Dallochmore Estate.'

'Dallochmore?' she repeated, liking the sound. 'Is it near here?'

'About twenty miles north of Carroch.' He leaned against the counter as he continued. 'It's one of the largest estates in Scotland, been in the same family for hundreds of years which is quite unusual these days. But they've had to work hard and diversify to make it viable. There's a few cottages which were originally built for estate workers but now they're a mixture of holiday accommodation and longer lets. Taigh-na-bruich is one of those.'

Lily listened with interest. Her mind's eye pictured Beth making her creams and lotions in a little cottage and she felt her curiosity piqued. There was no phone number but Lily thought she'd like to try and see her. Clearly a lot of time and effort had gone into making the products and she'd at least like to return them to her or else offer to pay for them.

'Thanks.' She nodded thoughtfully. 'How long would it take to drive?'

'About half an hour.' His forehead creased. 'You're planning on going there?'

'Possibly.' She shrugged, thinking out loud. 'I'll see if I can borrow Iris's car.'

Jack's expression changed. 'It's not the easiest of places to get to and you don't know the roads.'

'I'm sure I'll manage,' she replied dryly.

'There's a lot of single-track road and there'll be a lot of caravans this time of year.'

'I'll keep that in mind.'

He shook his head, sounding almost irritated. 'I'll take you, I'll be going that way anyway in a couple of days.'

As offers went Lily wouldn't exactly call it gracious and if it was his attempt at being friendly, then it was too little too late as far as she was concerned. 'I'll manage on my own, thanks,' she said firmly, making a point of checking her watch. 'Now if you don't mind, I have things to do.'

'Suit yourself.'

He opened the door to let himself out and Lily locked it behind him, dragging her eyes back inside to stop herself watching as he walked away.

Chapter 7

The water looked dark and unforgiving and Lily wondered if she was mad before acknowledging that of course she was. You had to be slightly mad to go swimming in a loch in Scotland, no matter what the time of year or how good the weather. She slipped off her jacket and rolled it up along with her towel and bag. She found a spot under one of the trees a little distance from the jetty where Iris had told her the swimming group met.

She was glad she appeared to be the first person here. She had arrived deliberately early, not only to compose herself but to give her time to make a hasty escape if she suddenly decided to chicken out which, she had to face it, was entirely possible.

She'd woken early that morning, filled with an energy she didn't know what to do with. After feeding the cat and drinking a cup of tea, her eyes had settled on the wetsuit which she'd left lying on the back of the chair. Along with Iris's offer to join the swimmers echoing in her head, it seemed to tempt and dare her.

She thought of all the times she used to paddle in the shallows of the loch, then as she had grown older, venturing out further and deeper. She remembered the thrill of the ice-cold water, the feeling of putting her body in extreme conditions. She knew she

61

would never forgive herself if she came to Carroch and didn't experience that sensation again.

It wasn't just the physical act of swimming. What really appealed to her was forgetting everything. It was impossible to think of anything except surviving in the water. Loch Carroch was a seawater loch and not as cold as freshwater lochs. But although the shallows warmed up during summer, Lily knew it would still be cold enough for hypothermia to be a real danger.

Lily's eyes scanned the shoreline which was still quiet, with only a few fishermen in the distance who no doubt wouldn't be pleased if the swimmers chased away their catch. A small break in the clouds allowed for some sun to filter through and feeling warmer now, she removed her leggings and top, creating a neat little pile on top of her towel. Earlier and not without a struggle, she'd wriggled her way into the wetsuit and now she could feel it mould to every inch of body as she kicked off her trainers.

'Going for a swim?'

Lily spun round at the deep voice. Of course it had to be him. Her pulse quickened at the sight of Jack Armstrong looking at her, his expression suggesting he found the idea surprising.

He was dressed in waterproofs and his hair was damp. The smallest of smiles played on his lips and for a moment it was as if she couldn't see anything except the shape of his mouth which looked incredibly sensual. Lily almost jumped back when she realised she was staring.

'That's right.' She flicked her hair over her shoulder, aiming for a haughty nonchalance she certainly wasn't feeling. The thought of the freezing water was already making her insides roll about uncomfortably and now his presence was making it decidedly worse. His eyes did a quick skim over her wetsuit making it feel even tighter than it already was.

'I didn't know you were a swimmer.'

'There's a lot you don't know about me,' she quipped.

'True,' he acknowledged. 'Perhaps I'll find out more in time.'

'I think we've established I won't be here long enough for that to happen. I'm here to sell the shop and leave, not to get involved,' she said rather primly, wondering for whose benefit she was saying that.

He nodded, studying her for a moment before speaking. 'You've swum in the loch before?'

She rolled her shoulders. 'My mum used to go swimming and she'd let me swim in the shallows with some of the other kids. We'd jump off the old jetty.'

He smiled, remembering. 'There were only a few boats then, that was my Saturday job when I was at school.'

'I used to see you at the boats.' Lily had no idea what possessed her to say that, especially as he was regarding her now, his expression full of curiosity.

'You used to watch me?'

'I wasn't watching you,' she clarified, squirming slightly. 'And as I recall you were usually surrounded by a fan club,' she said dryly.

'Occupational hazard,' he chuckled before looking at her again. 'You weren't ever tempted to come over and say hello?'

'No,' she lied.

'Didn't think so.'

'Why not?'

His eyes sparkled and he held her gaze. 'Because I would have remembered you.'

Lily felt her cheeks flush pink, and she was unsure how to respond. 'What are you doing here anyway?' she huffed, wishing he'd go away. It really was quite irritating the way he looked so pleased with himself.

'I've been out on the loch canoeing with a bunch of kids early this morning so I jumped home for a quick coffee.' He inclined his head to where Lily could just make out a stone building through the trees.

'That's where you live?'

63

He nodded. 'I bought it a couple of years ago – I don't think anyone else wanted to take it on as it was fairly dilapidated but it's perfect for me being near the centre. I'm in the middle of doing it up.'

'Nice commute,' she commented, wondering if he lived there alone.

'Sure is.' He smiled, his eyes crinkling. 'Can just roll out of bed if I want.'

Lily tried to blink away that particular image, beginning to feel jittery. Her mind seemed to be confusing her with her younger, immature self who used to go weak-kneed at the sight of him. She was not that person anymore.

'You okay? Not having seconds thoughts, are you?'

Uncertain if she'd imagined the challenge in his voice or not, Lily felt something ignite within. Suddenly she knew she definitely wanted to do this, to prove to herself – and him – that she *could* do this. It seemed so long since she'd done anything spontaneous or carefree and she felt all her earlier misgivings evaporate. She met his gaze full on. 'Of course not.'

Just at that moment, Lily heard voices and swivelled her head round to see Iris waving at her, beckoning her over.

'I need to go.'

'Enjoy your swim. Oh – and I'm one of the lifeguards so take care out there otherwise you'll be seeing me sooner than you think.'

The quick smile he gave her didn't quite reach his eyes but still managed to turn Lily's legs to jelly despite their tight encasing, forcing her to take a moment to compose herself before moving to join the others.

A group of them were wind-milling their arms and stretching as Lily made her way over to them. Iris's face was lit up with delight as she came bustling over to Lily. 'I'm so glad you decided to join us, Lily! You won't regret it.'

Lily could only look on in awe as Iris stripped down to her

swimsuit. A hardened outdoor swimmer, she shunned a wetsuit. 'Going for the full sensory experience, I see?'

'Nothing quite like it.' Iris smiled beginning her warm-up routine. 'I see you were talking to Jack.'

'Uh-huh.' Lily replied, her teeth beginning to chatter.

'All this stunning scenery to look at and him too,' she said with a teasing wink.

Lily kept her features neutral. Tall, powerfully built and probably far too handsome for his own good, she couldn't really dispute Iris's assessment of Jack.

Iris sighed wistfully. 'I might be an old lady but I can still appreciate a good-looking man when I see one.'

Thankfully, she stopped singing any more of Jack's praises and took Lily by the arm, gently propelling her towards a man also preparing for his swim. 'Ah, there he is now. Come on, there's someone I want you to meet. He and your mother were good friends and I know he's keen to meet you. Angus, this is Patty's daughter, Lily.'

He was a bear of a man, tall and solid. His face was handsome and weather-beaten and his pale grey eyes beneath a shock of white hair regarded Lily intensely. His voice when he spoke held a strong Highlands lilt. 'It's good to finally meet you, Lily.'

He took one of her hands in two of his, appearing to study her for what felt like a long time.

'Patty spoke about you often.' Even the twinkle in his eyes couldn't disguise the sorrow Lily saw in them when he mentioned her mother.

'It's lovely to meet you too.' Lily didn't recall Patty mentioning Angus – not that she would have expected her to – but something about him and the way he continued to look at her gave Lily the impression he knew her mother well.

'She's decided to join us today, Angus,' Iris explained.

Lily gave a small laugh through her chattering teeth. 'Although right now I'm trying to work out exactly why. I'm freezing and I'm not even near the water yet.'

'Do you remember what we always used to say?' Iris coaxed. 'From the outside looking in, you can't understand it. From the inside looking out, you can't explain it.'

Lily smiled, remembering their old mantra.

A strange sense of trepidation and purpose seem to hang in the air as everyone made their way to the water, along with the question; why on earth would anyone do this?

'Remember,' Iris encouraged, 'block out your fear – just think of all those endorphins.'

Lily turned with a silent nod and made her way to the water. She didn't jump like some of the swimmers did. Instead she sucked in a deep breath and stepped forward, letting the water make contact with her feet. Fighting her body's instinct to jump straight back out, she forced herself to take another few steps, wading in deeper until the water reached her waist, the water feeling like a hundred small electric shocks against her skin.

She started to swim immediately, frantically kicking her legs to keep her core temperature up. Her senses shot into overdrive, every nerve end in her body screaming as the freezing water clawed at her limbs.

She gulped several times, her breathing ragged, and panic almost took hold but somehow she kept going, forcing herself to swim, pushing and pulling her arms and legs against the water until her breathing started to settle and then thankfully, mercifully, endorphins kicked in.

Everyone stayed close together, looking out for each other until cold, shaking and exhilarated, they emerged from the water. Her fingers numb and her jaw shivering, Lily wrapped a towel around herself, rolling off her wetsuit and piling on the extra layers she'd brought with her.

All the swimmers made their way to a sheltered spot and huddled round as a flask with coffee was poured into cups.

Lily shared a grin with Iris and took a sip of the steaming liquid; coffee had never tasted so good. She glanced over and saw Jack at the shoreline. He bent down to pick up some oars and Lily tried not to notice the way his wet clothes clung to the shape of his body. Turning suddenly, he caught Lily's gaze and she felt goose bumps prickle her skin. She quickly averted her eyes, taking another sip of coffee. She hadn't felt so alive in years.

***

One hour and a hot shower later, Lily was munching on some hot buttered toast, scrolling through some jobs when she heard a knock from the downstairs door. She quickly wiped her hands and went to open the door, surprised to see Angus, the man from the swimming standing at the door.

'Oh, hello.' Lily smiled.

He was holding his hat, looking awkward. 'I hope you don't mind my dropping by?'

'Of course not. Would you like to come in?' Lily offered.

She led him through to the shop and inside, he suddenly appeared much larger. He was wearing brown corduroy trousers and a checked shirt under a thick fleece jacket. There was a quality about him that Lily instantly took to; she instinctively knew he was a good man, solid and dependable.

His fingers worked the rim of his cap, his feet shuffling and Lily realised, whatever the purpose of his visit, it wasn't proving easy for him.

'Would you like a tea or something to drink?'

'I'll not keep you, lass,' he replied with a shake of his head. 'I'm heading home for a rest after the swim, it doesn't get any easier,' he joked. Lily strongly suspected he was fitter than most men half his age.

'Where is it you live?' she asked.

'One of the cottages by the caravan park, only been there a few years, mind.'

Lily remembered the lochside cottages, she and her mum had been regular visitors at Iris's. 'So you're close to Iris?'

'Next door but one.' He smiled fondly and paused for a moment. 'I moved there after my wife died.'

'Oh, I'm sorry.'

'We had thirty-five happy years, more than a lot of folk get and for that, I'm grateful. After she passed away, well, I was just about to retire anyway so I decided to move. Not sure someone my age can make a new start but I wanted to be somewhere different. So I moved here a few years ago and that was when I got to know Patty.'

Lily sensed his hesitation, as if he was considering carefully what to say next. 'I just wanted you to know that your mother meant a great deal to me.'

'You and my mum were close?' she asked gently.

'We were. I didn't seek it or expect it but we became good friends and were very fond of each other. And I hope this doesn't sound odd or anything but I wanted you to know that I was there for her. I'm not sure why I'm telling you or if it will make any sense. I certainly don't want to make things more difficult for you.'

When she'd been younger Lily had sometimes wished her mother had someone in her life, someone to share things with. She'd been aware of a few relationships over the years but had never been introduced to anyone and as far as she knew, there had never been anyone serious. Patty herself had never given the impression of needing or wanting anyone, she'd always been supremely self-contained but of course that hadn't stopped Lily worrying at times.

Neither was Lily surprised that Patty hadn't mentioned Angus to her – that wouldn't be something she would do. It was just one of the things she had grown to accept; her mother lived her own life and never felt the need to tell Lily things or share things with her, it wasn't the way she worked.

Now with Angus standing in front of her, Lily felt as if she was beginning to gather pieces of her mum's life. Things she hadn't known about. But far from feeling he'd made things difficult for her, she was comforted and touched by what he had just told her and sought to reassure him. 'I'm very happy you've told me – and it does help.'

He seemed to visibly straighten, as if a load had been lifted from his shoulders and he gave a gentle smile, inclining a hand around the shop. 'Is there anything I can help you with?'

'That's kind of you. But I think it's just a case of working my way through everything.'

'Patty used to talk about it, she wasn't in a hurry though,' he said. 'Iris mentioned you were selling.'

'Yes.' Lily rubbed a patch of skin on her wrist hoping she'd imagined the disappointment in his eyes.

'You must do what's right for you,' he told her, repeating Iris's words. 'Now, it's time for me to go before I fall down,' he joked. He turned to her. 'You'll be here for a wee while yet?'

Lily swallowed. 'A little while, yes.'

She saw him to the door and as she watched him walk away, Lily couldn't help wondering if he had said all he had come to say.

Chapter 8

It was Friday morning, the sun was shining and the journey had started well. Lily and Iris were heading to Dallochmore Estate, trundling along in Iris's ancient Mini. When Lily had explained about finding the Highland Aromatics products, Iris had been on board with the idea of going to visit Beth on the estate and as she had nothing else to do, had suggested she drive with her. Lily had been happy to have her company.

They hadn't even left the village when Iris's ancient Mini appeared to slow down of its own accord. The engine emitted an ominous sound and the car came to a spluttering stop.

'Oh dear.' Iris frowned.

Lily and Iris both got out and looked helplessly at the car as if somehow their desperate stares could magically fix whatever was wrong. Lily was just wondering what on earth they would do now when she heard the sound of a vehicle approaching. She turned to see a battered Land Rover pull up on the road behind them. Jack Armstrong jumped out, his eyes quickly running over the car. 'Trouble, Iris?'

'Oh, thank goodness,' Iris breathed in relief. 'I'm glad to see you, Jack.'

Lily didn't know if she was glad to see him or not. The image of him at the loch yesterday had been lodged unhelpfully in her mind and watching him now as he opened the bonnet and leaned over the engine was doing nothing to dissipate it.

'Looks like the alternator,' he said knowledgeably. 'I'll phone Billy at the garage for you. Do you need a lift somewhere?'

'We were heading to Dallochmore,' Iris told him, before launching into an explanation of the reason for their visit.

Jack looked between them then lifted an eyebrow at Lily. 'I'm on my way there now to the distillery. My offer still stands.'

'You offered already? Well, that's ideal then, isn't it?' Iris exclaimed.

Jack gave Lily a told-you-so look and she felt her stomach drop. She hadn't wanted to accept his lift the first time round and nothing had changed. Except now there were two pairs of eyes on her, waiting expectantly. 'I can go another day,' she muttered, knowing she sounded truculent.

'But you were so keen to meet Beth. Let Jack take you,' Iris insisted. 'I don't want you missing out.'

Lily hid her sigh. She'd had her heart set on seeing Beth but suddenly it felt like a distraction she didn't need – and she had the feeling Jack Armstrong could be very distracting which she definitely didn't need.

He smiled at her now and despite herself, she felt some of her doubts disappearing. He'd helped Iris in looking after the cat and had rushed to get her cream when she'd been in danger of being eaten alive by midges so clearly he wasn't all bad. She returned his smile with a conciliatory shrug. 'Okay. Thanks, I'd appreciate it.'

Within minutes Jack had the situation under control and they didn't have long to wait until a pick-up truck had come, taking Iris and her beleaguered car to the garage, leaving Lily and Jack alone.

He opened the passenger door for her. 'Sorry about the mess,' he apologised with a mild grimace, his eyes darting to the back seat which was covered in mounds of paperwork and a laptop. 'This place tends to double up as my office and I keep meaning to sort it all out.'

Lily took her seat, briefly wondering what paperwork he needed for fixing boats. She felt her fingers fumble with the seatbelt, suddenly far too aware of his proximity as he took his seat beside her at the driver's wheel.

'You all set?' he asked after waiting for her to settle.

'Yes, thanks.'

As Jack checked the mirror and pulled away, Lily found herself wondering if he was always this relaxed. He looked as if there was nothing life could throw at him that he wouldn't be able to handle. Some people were like that she supposed, negotiating their way through life without much angst.

Lily on the other hand, wasn't relaxed at all. She could feel her pulse racing and she was oddly uncomfortable with this whole situation. It didn't help that Jack appeared to have smartened himself up today, his clean-shaven jaw and swept-back dark hair only managing to make him look more attractive. She found herself thankful they had nothing in common otherwise she suspected those looks were quite capable of reigniting her old crush which really wasn't what she needed right now.

She sat rather primly with her hands in her lap, her mind flitting back to the last time she'd been in a car with a man. Then it had been with James. Gliding along the motorway in his company car on their way to a meeting with suppliers, she'd felt very much at home in that situation – quite smug if truth be told, in her new charcoal-grey suit and pale-blue silk shirt. The meeting had been at a clothing manufacturer's in Manchester, James determined to reduce costs and negotiate a better deal for Bremners – which of course he had.

They had stopped for dinner at a small restaurant on the way back. It had been ludicrously expensive and they didn't have a booking but James had handled it – on account obviously –

securing them a table which just happened to be an intimate table for two discreetly tucked in the corner.

He'd had to take a few business calls during the meal – it was difficult for him to ever switch off – but James had talked that night about the new growth markets and the possibilities of opening up a Bremners store in the Far East to capitalise on their love of all things Scottish. Lily had envisaged herself being involved in a secondment to China or perhaps a role working with James in Dunn Equity. After all, she knew how the company operated, she had been a team player, embraced all the changes. It didn't really matter what the role was, either way she and James would be together. Lily almost cringed now thinking how none of it had materialised, how it had all been in her head and she felt the familiar twist of disappointment in her stomach thinking about it.

Jack's voice filtered into her thoughts, keeping his eyes on the road as he spoke. 'So what are your plans for today?'

A good question and not one she had a ready answer for. 'I don't really know.' She explained the situation briefly to him about finding the stock. She thought it all sounded somewhat random, a bit of a wild goose chase. 'I don't even know if she'll be there.'

Jack shrugged, indicating it was no big deal. 'Just play it by ear. Sometimes that's the best way. It's a good place to visit anyway. There's a castle, gardens and a café so there's plenty to do.'

Lily nodded vaguely. Playing it by ear wasn't how she usually operated. She much preferred to have a plan and stick to it. But today, hurtling through the Highlands with a virtual stranger on her way to meet someone she didn't know, she thought it was fair to say she didn't have a plan.

Last night she'd gathered together all the scattered paperwork and for three hours she had forgotten everything else, losing herself in the numbers and figures, meticulously making her way through the invoices. All the stock had been bought and paid for which certainly made life easier and she reckoned the value of the stock could simply be included in the sale of the shop.

The only complication appeared to be all the products from Beth at Highland Aromatics, none of which had been paid for and she hoped today she would at least be able to tie up that particular loose end.

They had left the village behind now, their surroundings growing ever more remote as they drove through valleys and glens, the heather-clad purple mountains roaring up to the sky, looking simultaneously imposing and beautiful at the same time. Lily had never seen such space, even the sky seemed huge.

She tried not to think about what would happen if the car broke down but then decided Jack was more than capable of fixing an engine. He had that look about him, she thought, glancing surreptitiously at his hands which were broad, tanned and strong-looking. He drove with concentration but steered the vehicle with ease, seeming at one with his wild, rugged surroundings.

Lily reckoned she'd probably be hopelessly lost by now if she'd ever attempted this drive by herself. And while Jack Armstrong had this strange ability to make her feel oddly ruffled, she supposed she was at least grateful for him stepping in to help today.

'Thanks for doing this.'

He glanced over with a smile. 'As I said, I was going this way anyway.'

'You said you were going to the estate?' she asked.

He nodded. 'To the distillery actually, to see my friend.'

Lily remembered when Bremners had decided to expand their range of whisky and whisky products and she'd worked alongside the buyer. With impeccable taste and effortlessly stylish herself, Arabella's job was to research and evaluate the products that would ultimately end on Bremners' shelves. Lily had enjoyed helping her do some background research into the whisky industry and found it fascinating.

She'd read about the process and art of blending whisky, how wooden casks that had once held port or rum affected its flavour and how only whisky made in Scotland could be called Scotch whisky.

There was a romanticism to whisky, something about holding a glass in your hand knowing the passion and history behind it, which people found beguiling. And although it was a multimillion-pound industry with a huge market it was also a very competitive and challenging one, with over a hundred distilleries in Scotland.

'Which distillery is it?' she asked.

'Dallochmore. It's a relatively small operation.'

Lily hadn't heard of it but was interested. 'Is it on the estate?'

Jack nodded. 'It's owned by the Montgomery family – they bought the land and outbuildings from the estate years ago. Jock's been at the helm for years but he's retired now and it's his son Adam who's taken over – we grew up together.'

A shadow crossed Jack's features but it passed as quickly as it came. 'He's been in Canada for a while but he's back now and taken over the running. He's keen to get involved with this whisky festival event coming up and for some reason thinks my brains are worth picking.' He gave a self-deprecating smile.

Lily recalled visiting one of the distilleries in the area years ago. She'd been too young to truly appreciate the experience and definitely too young to taste any of the whisky but something of that day had always stayed with her. 'Whisky festival sounds like fun,' she said.

'Should be,' Jack agreed with a quick smile. 'Plus my sister works at the distillery so I'll see her and that'll earn me a whole load of points with my mum.'

'Your family live around here?'

He nodded. 'I grew up in the village next along from Carroch with my parents, three sisters and a brother.'

'Sounds busy.'

'Chaotic at times,' he admitted with a low chuckle. 'Only my youngest sister still lives at home now so my mum's always thinking up ways to get as many of under the same roof at the same time. Christmas, birthdays, days ending in a y – any excuse will do.'

Lily smiled but felt the familiar pang in her chest. She never dwelled on not having all those family occasions but that didn't stop her imagining what it would be like. A family of her own one day was a dream she held deep within her, to have what other people had and so often took for granted. But she rarely allowed herself to picture it – what was the point? Fate, chance, luck or whatever it was might see that it never happened for her.

'And you?' Jack's voice filtered through. 'Do you have a large family?'

'No. It was just my mum and me.' She turned to look out of her window, speaking in a matter-of-fact manner that hopefully conveyed it wasn't an area she wanted to elaborate on.

Thankfully, Jack seem to pick up on it and waited a couple of moments before moving on. 'So what's your job then?'

'My job?' she echoed.

'You said you had to get back to it.'

'Oh yes. Well, actually I'm between jobs,' she told him. 'But I've got a few things lined up,' she lied, thinking back to last night when she'd managed to find something not quite right with every job she'd seen. Perhaps she just hadn't been in the mood.

'What is it you do?'

'I'm an accountant.'

He nodded thoughtfully but remained silent.

'I worked in Bremners department store for the past six years, dealing with their financial matters.' For some inexplicable reason she wanted Jack to know how much she'd loved her job, how much responsibility she'd had and for the next few minutes heard herself babble on about profitability and growth, controlling expenditure and the intricacies of taxes and audits before stopping

76

herself. She was beginning to sound like she single-handedly ran Scotland's finances.

'Sounds like a lot of pressure,' he commented.

'Well, some jobs are more stressful than others I guess,' she responded rather waspishly.

He glanced over at her. 'You were happy?'

'Of course I was.' Lily frowned. It seemed a strange and personal question to ask someone you hardly knew. Besides, her career was about much more than happiness. It gave her independence, security, the sanctuary of routine. But she wouldn't expect him to understand any of that.

'That's all that matters then,' he nodded. 'I tried all that corporate stuff.' He sounded contemptuous, waving a hand dismissively. 'Guess it's just wasn't for me.'

That didn't surprise Lily in the least. She certainly had difficulty picturing Jack moving in business circles or being tied to a desk all day.

As they had continued to travel, the road had started to curve inwards and Lily could see Highland ponies and sheep grazing amongst the grasses and rocky moorland. The wilderness was quite spectacular but the Land Rover made easy work of the terrain as they rattled over cattle grids and then over a stone bridge which crossed a burn tumbling down from the hills. After a while they turned off the main road and Lily became aware Jack had shifted gears and was slowing down.

Her pulse quickened. Oh my God, he was stopping in the middle of nowhere.

He stopped, cutting off the engine. He turned and looked at her, his face breaking into a grin. 'Don't look so worried. I want to show you something. Come on.' He swung open his door and raced round to her side.

She stepped out, still unnerved. They were literally miles from anywhere. Lily didn't have any choice but to follow him as he strode ahead, clambering over a few rocks to a raised ridge of land. Her trainers weren't really designed for this sort of thing and she almost lost her footing. Slightly out of breath, she came to stand beside him.

'Look,' he said.

Lily trailed after his gaze as he stared into the distance. The scenery was certainly impressive but no different from the miles they'd just driven through – if anything it was just more remote and she couldn't help thinking it was a fairly desolate spot to stop.

Even on a summer's day like today, the landscape held a certain bleakness and despite the sun, Lily shivered, impatient to move. But Jack didn't seem to be going anywhere. He stood still, seemingly with all the time in the world.

Suppressing a sigh, Lily loosened her shoulders, forcing herself to try and relax. She inhaled deeply and the air was so fresh and tinged with such sweetness she could almost taste it. Soaring high above them two birds of prey swooped by in an elaborate display of dipping and diving. She scanned the distance again, this time more slowly. And then she saw it.

A solitary tree on the moor. Bent and windswept, it was clinging onto the crags.

On first appearance it looked withered, almost dead. But as Lily continued to study it, she realised it was alive, somehow managing to survive in these harsh surroundings. There was something so beautifully rugged and wild about it, Lily could hardly tear her eyes away from it.

'It's extraordinary,' she said, not sure there was a right word to encapsulate its raw beauty.

'I must have driven this way a thousand times,' Jack said. 'Head down, eyes on the road. One day a deer suddenly appeared out of nowhere. I don't know who got more of a fright – him or me. I was shaking so I got out and walked around for a bit. And then I saw the tree.' He pointed to it. 'I stayed for a long time, just thinking. About how short and precious life is.'

Jack stared into the distance. His expression was inscrutable but Lily could see something hidden in the depths of his eyes which suggested there was more to Jack Armstrong than she'd thought. She certainly hadn't been expecting this moment of quiet reflection.

'I promised myself that day that I'd never drive by here without stopping. I decided there and then that I always wanted to be able to take time and appreciate what I had around me.'

Lily knew he was right, of course; how easy it was to rush around, never stopping to appreciate something simple. She knew she was certainly guilty of it. It was so peaceful here, the silence reminding her just how much she'd been on autopilot over past few months – rushing around, climbing to some elusive point. But then it must be easier to catch peaceful moments in a place like this, far from crowds, buildings and noise.

'How does it survive in these conditions?' she asked him.

'Probably because of its elevated position - it means sheep and deer can't get to it.'

'What kind of a tree is it?'

'A rowan tree. They say they're magical trees. They're supposed to symbolise courage, wisdom and protection. People plant them close to their houses to keep away evil spirits.' He waggled his eyebrows. 'Tourist like that stuff.'

'And you don't?' she smiled.

'Not so sure about the magic bit,' he replied with a grin. 'You look cold, let's get you back inside. The estate's not far from here.'

Jack started up the engine again and Lily fastened her seat-belt trying to work out how she felt. For those few moments, she'd felt so far removed from reality, almost as if she'd slipped into some alternative universe. For a moment she had felt totally free, something she hadn't experienced before. It was strange to think of Edinburgh now, only a few hours away. Pavements packed with people, buses and taxis and trundling along roads and the constant noise and movement. Lily thought of her life there. On some levels it seemed like an empty existence. No family, no friends she saw regularly. And a relationship with a man that had been a fantasy in her head. She hadn't regarded herself as lonely but deep down she knew she had been.

Lily sat back in her seat as Jack drove away and felt an unexpected core of calmness within her. She was suddenly very glad Jack had stopped today and hadn't chosen to drive by just because she'd been there.

The road started to flatten out and as they drove along the estate road, Jack pointed in the direction of the formal gardens and castle where Lily could just see the grey ornamental turrets visible through leafy green foliage of the trees. Jack turned the land rover in the other direction along a road lined with bright yellow daffodils and then drew up close to a group of small cottages. He cut the engine and turned to her.

'Hope it all goes okay.' He seemed to sense her sudden nerves. 'I can come with you if you like?'

'I'll be fine. But thanks.'

They agreed where to meet again in a couple of hours and Lily made her way towards the cottages. Stone-built and picture perfect, they were clustered around a courtyard and separated by small front gardens. Lily scanned each of their wooden name plaques until she found Taigh-na-bruich.

She walked up the path and was met by the scent of the honeysuckle which wound its way up and round the side of the house. Taking a breath, she rapped the brass knocker against the red painted door and then stood back, feeling the heat of the sun on the back of her head.

There was a window to the side of the door and Lily could see a large white cat sitting on the sill, its cool disdain reminding her of Misty, who she'd left this morning basking in her own spot of sunlight. Purring contently and with her small white paws tucked neatly under herself, she had showed no signs of moving

80

anytime soon but Lily had left her some extra biscuits just in case she was delayed for any reason.

Perhaps she hadn't knocked hard enough. Either that or no one was here and it had been a mistake to just turn up unannounced. Lily knocked again and to her relief, after another few moments the door was opened by a woman.

She was wearing jeans and a loose shirt, her thick dark hair tied in a loose ponytail. Slim to the point of thin, there was an air of wariness about her, almost a fragility. Her face was pale and dark circles marked the skin beneath her large brown eyes, but Lily could see the fine bone structure of a beautiful woman.

She wore a quizzical expression and Lily realised she wasn't likely to get many passers-by here. She tried to smile reassuringly. 'Beth?'

'Yes,' she replied cautiously.

'Hello. My name is Lily, I'm Patty Ballantine's daughter.'

There was a pause. Lily could see her making the connections and then she drew in a breath.

'Oh, of course,' she said, her frown easing slightly.

Lily wasn't sure what to say next, she didn't want to suddenly blurt out that her mother had died. Sensing her hesitation, Beth regarded her with concern. 'Is everything all right?'

'I wondered, could I come in for a moment?'

'Yes of course, sorry,' she flustered, widening the door.

Lily followed her down a narrow hallway which opened up into a kitchen at the back of the house. 'I tend to live in here,' she told Lily who immediately understood why. Two plump sofa chairs sat either side of a wood-burner, a pile of logs stacked up to one side. An oak table covered with books and magazines sat in the middle of the room and there were several shelves crammed with pottery and framed photographs. Lily thought it looked wonderfully cosy and cluttered.

Before she said anything else, Lily thought she had better explain right away why she was here. 'I'm so sorry to have to tell you, but my mother passed away.'

81

'Oh.' The lady lifted a hand to her mouth and for a terrible moment Lily thought she might cry. 'I'm so sorry ... you must be devastated. What happened?'

Lily explained about the aneurysm, how Patty had been in Edinburgh at the time and how Lily had only come to deal with the shop now. 'I found the delivery with your products along with your note and I wanted to speak to you in person.'

Beth looked thoughtful and indicated for Lily to take a seat. 'Would you like a coffee?' she asked.

Lily, who had been awake since 5 a.m. couldn't think of anything she'd like more. Especially when she spied the shiny, silver coffee maker in the corner, looking at odds with the rest of the kitchen.

'I live frugally but this is my one luxury.' Beth smiled softly. Lily watched as she made the coffee. Her hands were red and chapped but moved deftly, pouring beans into the machine. Soon, the room was filled with the most heavenly aroma of coffee. She set down two cups and joined Lily at the table. 'When I hadn't heard from your mother, I did wonder,' she frowned. 'I thought perhaps she'd changed her mind.'

'Oh, I'm sure she wouldn't have done that. The products you made – they're amazing.'

Beth flushed, her eyes widening almost in disbelief. 'Do you really think so?'

'Really.' Lily was touched she appeared to have no sense of how good they were. 'Who else have you sold to?'

The question seemed to surprise her. 'No one else. I did go to a trade show but I'm afraid I found it all quite daunting. Lots of people showed interest – and a few people took my details but somehow I left without any orders.' She looked down with a shrug of her shoulders. 'I love making the products, but I'm afraid I'm not very good at the business side of things.'

'So where do you actually make everything?'

'Would you like me to show you?' she asked tentatively and

seemed almost surprised when Lily said she'd love to. 'Finish your coffee and I'll take you.'

A few moments later Beth had led Lily out of the back door and down a path winding its way down a narrow and surprisingly long garden. 'Looks like you're embracing the good life,' Lily remarked, passing a vegetable patch and narrowly avoided tripping over a few chickens pecking the ground.

'Trying to,' Beth answered ruefully.

They came to an impressive looking double-door wooden workshop painted green with three large windows. Stepping inside was like entering a different world, an intoxicating blend of sweet florals and warm exotic fragrances permeated the air.

Lily could see all the tools of her trade laid out on the various work surfaces; digital scales, thermometers, measuring jugs and various whisks and saucepans. Natural light flooded in through the windows and it was immaculately clean, reminding Lily of a science lab.

'Wow,' she exclaimed.

'I can lose myself for hours in here. I've been working on a new line – would you like to see?' Beth asked, removing the lid from a white tub for Lily to smell. 'I've been experimenting with sandalwood.'

'It smells heavenly.' Lily raised her eyes appreciatively at the warm, sweet, woody aroma.

'I'm going to mix it with lemon. Sandalwood oil has all sorts of therapeutic properties; it's anti-inflammatory so really good for skin conditions and it can help you to relax,' she explained replacing the lid.

'So how did you start all this?' Lily asked, waving a hand to encompass the room.

Beth released a slow breath before speaking. 'It was after my husband died.'

'Oh, I'm sorry. I didn't mean to pry.'

'You haven't, please don't worry,' Beth reassured with a small

83

shake of her head. 'I'm not really used to speaking about it which probably isn't very healthy. It's been just over a year and some days I'm fine. Other days it feels as brutally raw as if it happened yesterday.'

Lily nodded sympathetically.

'I was so devastated, didn't know what to do with myself at all. I couldn't bear the thought of staying where we had lived together, trying to carry on without him. I just knew I had to do something totally different. So I packed up everything, gave up my teaching job, sold our home in York and moved here. My grandfather was Scottish and I used to come here as a child, so something seem to draw me here. I took a long-term lease on this place and decided to embrace my solitude. For now, anyway.' She finished with a watery smile.

'That can't have been easy.'

'No.' Beth paused for a moment. 'Anyway, I was always interested in aromatherapy and the use of natural oils and organic products so I thought I'd see if I could make a proper go of it. I did a few courses and there's been a lot of trial and error. I know you can buy creams and lotions so easily and cheaply these days but I thought there might be a market for handmade, organic products. People are so aware these days aren't they – of what goes into the products they use.'

'Definitely,' Lily agreed.

'I was really at the stage of setting up and experimenting with a few ideas when I met Patty on the estate one day. She was here visiting the gardens and we got chatting.' She smiled, remembering. 'She told me about the shop in Carroch she'd bought recently and I told her about my ideas. She was so enthusiastic about what I was doing. In fact, I'm grateful to her because that spurred me on. Otherwise I fear I'd never have got organised enough to actually make an order. That's what took me so long.'

As Beth locked up the workshop and they walked back to the

house, Lily was thoughtful. In the warm kitchen, she gathered herself together, dreading what she had to say now.

'The thing is, I'll be selling the shop. So I'm afraid I won't be needing your products.'

'Oh. Of course, I understand.'

Disappointment flitted over Beth's features, giving the impression she was a woman accustomed to disguising her feelings and Lily felt terrible. She hated to think she was letting her down and rushed to speak. 'I'll arrange to have all the products sent back to you and I'll pay you for them also.'

Beth shook her head. 'There was nothing formal between us, no contract. We hadn't negotiated terms. Really, you don't owe me anything.'

'Please, I insist. You've lost all this time,' Lily said, well aware she should have been here sooner to let her know. 'This way, you'll be able to sell them to someone else.'

Beth's brow creased. 'I'm not sure. Maybe it was all a bit ambitious. Perhaps I should think of something else, I could always go back to teaching.'

Lily was horrified that Beth was ready to give up, feeling responsible in some way. 'Please, you mustn't do that. I have some experience of working in a retail environment and I'm sure I'd be able to help you, give you some contacts and a few pointers in the right direction. I really don't think it would be too difficult to establish yourself.'

'I'm really not sure,' Beth replied doubtfully. 'My idea was always to keep things small and based here, I don't want to do anything on a large scale.'

'You don't have to. Keep it small and local with a strong Scottish element – that could be your unique selling point. You're using high-quality, organic ingredients and other businesses are usually keen to support start-ups. These are all big positives. I'm very confident you'll secure a contract.'

'I'm sorry, it's all sounds like a different language to me.'

85

Beth was beginning to look overwhelmed. Lily had wanted to make her feel better but had the feeling she was doing the opposite. 'The main thing is you've got a fantastic product,' she began gently. 'Listen, I'll be here for a little while longer. Perhaps we could meet somewhere one day – you could come to Carroch if you like?' she suggested. 'That'll give you time to think about things and I could get some contacts for you.'

Beth clasped her hands together nervously. 'I don't really go out much these days, I'm afraid I've become a bit of a recluse.'

'I could come back here if you like?' Lily offered.

A few seconds passed, Beth's features suggesting some sort of inner dialogue was taking place. Finally she spoke, sounding more decisive. 'No. I'll meet you. It'll do me good to get out. I keep meaning to visit some of the villages and I'd like to see Carroch.'

With an arrangement made to meet in a few days, the two women made their way to the front of the cottage, Lily's mind busy. She hadn't been sure what to expect today but she'd taken to Beth instantly and hoped there was some way of helping her. It would be a terrible shame if her venture came to nothing.

Beth was perhaps several years older than Lily but there was something about her that she could easily identify with, recognising the look of someone who was perhaps a little bit afraid of life at the moment. It was sad it had been such tragic circumstances that had brought Beth here but Lily hoped she'd be able to find happiness again.

Lily stepped out into the front garden, admiring the lilac bushes and geraniums bordering the small front lawn. As settings went, Lily couldn't think of anywhere more idyllic, the type of place you might imagine living one day with a loving husband, perhaps children. Having said that, the silence and remoteness felt peculiar to her senses which were more used to the city. She imagined it would take some getting used to.

'Do you ever feel isolated living here?' Lily wondered.

Beth's brow puckered as she thought about it. 'I think I've

learnt the difference between solitude and loneliness. And I've found out I'm quite self-reliant. And I have Snowy here to keep me company.' She picked up the white cat who had appeared at her feet. 'A local farmer offered her to me. I was almost thinking of getting another one but then thought I might be in danger of turning into a mad cat lady.'

Lily laughed. 'I know what you mean. I seem to have inherited a cat that my mum had adopted. I'm not sure what I'll do with her but the worrying thing is I'm kind of getting used to having her around.'

'They can be easier to deal with than some humans that's for sure.'

The two women shared a smile of understanding and Lily left. She glanced at the time. She still had some time before she was due to meet Jack and so she set off, looking forward to exploring the estate.

Chapter 9

The estate had been enchanting. From the Baronial castle sitting on the banks of the river to the remote bothies where people could literally escape from the world, Lily had been charmed.

She remembered Jack telling her the estate had diversified and they appeared to be doing it very successfully. Obviously she hadn't been able to see it all with her own eyes, the scale of the estate was massive, but she'd seen a range of accommodation including luxury private Victorian houses and small charming cottages. There were all sorts of opportunities for spotting wildlife and sporting activities and she'd spent a very pleasant hour walking around the castle admiring its interior, brimming with works of arts, tapestries and antiques, not surprised to learn it was a popular destination for private functions and corporate hospitality. It was all quite impressive.

When Jack had collected her, he'd been interested to hear how she'd got on with Beth, listening as Lily told him how she was hoping to help her by giving her some contacts for selling her range of products.

In turn Jack had told her about the upcoming whisky festival, Lily becoming quite caught up in the idea of tastings and tours and masterclasses. By the sounds of it, the visitors expected from all over the world were in for a treat.

After that, they'd lapsed into a companionable silence. It hadn't felt awkward. In fact, so relaxed and with tiredness catching up on her, Lily had closed her eyes and was slightly dazed when a gentle squeeze on her arm awoke her. She opened her eyes to find Jack had already parked outside the shop and was looking at her.

His mouth had curved into that easy smile and for one mad moment she'd actually considered inviting him in before giving herself a sharp mental kick. She'd enjoyed his company more than she'd expected and the thought of prolonging it was tempting, but she was pretty sure Jack had something else more important to be doing and no way was she going to risk making a fool of herself – she'd done enough of that recently. So she had thanked him and quietly let herself into the flat, making her way up the stairs to find Misty sitting waiting for her.

After supper, she'd settled herself on the sofa hoping sleep would find her quickly but instead she'd been restless and reflective. The last few days in Carroch had taken her by surprise, her aim of slipping in and out quietly and quickly not exactly going to plan. Angus, the knitting ladies and now the drive with Jack and meeting Beth had all been on her mind, thoughts of them spinning around her head and spilling into her dreams last night.

This morning, she felt determined to take control of things, to get things back on track. And so, at an insanely early hour this morning she'd set about scouring the job market, the internet connection testing her patience and making it a long and tedious process. Until that point, she'd been fairly confident that there would be plenty of work for an experienced accountant but she'd been disappointed, any hopes of easily finding her new dream job quickly extinguished. There wasn't a huge choice of jobs, certainly nothing that screamed out as her as something she really wanted to do.

She'd sent her CV to a recruitment agency specialising in finance and accounting and had found a couple of jobs that didn't look too mind-blowingly boring which she applied for, allowing herself to feel a little buzz of excitement when the acknowledgements popped into her inbox.

After that, Lily knew there was only one thing left to do. So much of her life in the last year had been about avoiding this moment but today the time had come to finally sort through her mother's personal possessions.

She thought back to yesterday, to stopping at the rowan tree with Jack and how she'd felt for those few moments. They might have been standing in one of the most remote parts of the world but the moment had felt strangely intimate. Jack's words came back to her about life being short and precious. Lily realised now that whatever her life might hold in the future, she needed to start by doing this today.

Armed with a mug of tea and Misty by her side, she made her way to her mother's bedroom. But standing at the door, her feet suddenly felt rooted to the spot, her body paralysed with fear.

It wasn't just about the practical matter of sorting through her mother's things, it was about facing up to the woman Patty Ballantine had been – perhaps that was what frightened Lily most of all. Patty had been a free spirit. Captivating and beautiful, everyone had loved her. But for Lily growing up, at times that could be difficult to embrace.

As a young child, Lily knew no other life. She couldn't remember the exact moment she became conscious of her mother not being like other mothers, there hadn't been a specific moment or event, just a growing consciousness that their nomadic lifestyle wasn't the same as everyone else's.

There had been no traditional birthday parties, no bedtime stories, no pennies left by the tooth fairy. There had been no strict rules or times to come home. Nor were there twenty questions asking where she was going or who with. Not that Lily went out much or needed to test her boundaries. At times she had felt like the adult, the one who remembered to buy milk or do her homework.

After being introduced as the new girl yet again, Lily learnt to keep her head down and work hard. Not only had it paved the way for Lily's self-reliance, it also meant she didn't make friends easily. But on the odd occasion when she did feel comfortable enough to invite friends home, they'd all loved Patty and wished their own mothers could be more laidback like her.

Conversely, Lily had sometimes wished her mother to be a different person, someone who would wrap her up in a warm motherly embrace and tell her everything was going to be all right. But she never had. Instead, Lily had constantly anticipated her mother announcing they were moving again, and she had lived with the uncertainty that everything might change at a moment's notice.

Her mother had always provided for her, she'd never been cruel or neglectful and Lily was never ungrateful. But Patty's laissez-faire attitude to parenting and disinclination to praise Lily or openly show affection had left Lily with the deep-rooted, unsettling notion that somehow she'd been an intrusion into her mother's life.

It wasn't something Lily chose to dwell on but every now and again it surfaced, that vague sense that because she was the result of a brief affair, perhaps Patty had never really wanted her.

Other than the necessary facts, her mother had never talked much about Lily's father and Lily had come to accept that or at least push it to the back of her mind. After all, there probably wasn't much to say about a relationship that lasted a few weeks. But now Lily wished she'd pressed her mother for more, asked more questions so that she at least had more of a picture who her father was and the time her parents had spent together.

But of course, it was all too late now, and she'd never have the chance.

Lily let out a long breath, glancing down at Misty who was sitting patiently, almost expectantly, and knew there would be no magic wand, she simply had to get on with it. 'Here goes,' she whispered and then slowly opened the door.

She placed her mug down on the bedside table and switched on the lamp, a flash of panic almost taking hold as she wondered where on earth to start. Normally she was a methodical person but for now all her organisational skills deserted her.

Her eyes flitted around the room, landing on the old rocking chair that she immediately recognised. A long forgotten memory surfaced of her swaying to and fro, a ragdoll sitting on her lap and the image of it somehow managed to calm her.

She recognised the old dressing table too, placed in front of the window with her mother's favourite jade green beads with the shell flower clasp beads hanging over the oval mirror. But the whitewashed bed and wardrobe must be new, something her mother had bought more recently.

It was a pretty room, Lily realised. The walls were painted creamy-white and cherry print curtains framed the window which had the most perfect view overlooking the trees and hills. She and her Patty had stayed in several houses and flats over the years — none of them had been truly awful but this was by far the nicest place her mother had lived in and Lily was happy that this had been the last place she had lived.

And so she began. By many people's standards Patty didn't have a lot, just everyday items. Books and trinkets, a few bags, different pieces of jewellery, photos and cards. But each time Lily found something, a different memory surfaced, snatches and snippets of her life. Finding things not just from mum's life but the things that had made up Lily's life too.

Several times she faltered and would head to the kitchen for more tea – she'd never drunk so much of the stuff – or something to eat even though she wasn't hungry. Or simply just to wander around the flat aimlessly, each time steeling herself to carry on.

Several hours later she had managed to work her way through all of it, creating a couple of bags for charity and another full of things she knew she could never throw out.

Opening the last drawer, Lily let out a little gasp on finding her mother's favourite dove-grey wool jumper. She held it up close, feeling the softness of it on her cheek, sure she could still smell her mother's scent on it.

And that was when she finally let go, something seeming to tear at her inside so unbearably painful.

She hadn't cried before, not properly. Not like she did now, great gulping sobs that seem to come from deep within her. She covered her face with her hands and she knew then just how much she'd been holding onto her grief. Now it was as though a full-beam light was shining on it and she could feel the full ferocity of it. She knew this was why she had put off this moment. There was such a finality about it, the inescapable reality that her mother was no longer here, and she was on her own.

She wrapped her arms tightly around herself as if she could shield herself from the pain, rocking herself to and fro. Swamped by grief, love and regret, she cried for her mother and for herself until her throat was raw and her eyes painfully swollen.

As her tears eventually subsided Lily unfurled herself, stood up slowly and went over to the window. Opening it, she felt a little breath of air caress her cheek and she closed her eyes, the crystal wind chimes dancing in the gentle breeze. 'I love you, Mum,' she whispered.

Iris had been right about the process of sorting through her mother's possessions being cathartic. By facing up to her grief, Lily had also faced up to the relationship she'd had with her mother. And while she might not go so far as to say she'd come to terms with everything, she had at least come some of the way and was left with a feeling of somehow being closer to her mother. For now, that would have to be enough. She turned from the window and for the first time felt the smallest glimmer of hope, a flicker of light on her horizon. Maybe everything would be all right.

It had grown dark now and Lily was exhausted, spent on every level. In the kitchen she refilled Misty's water and tipped some biscuits into her bowl. She paced about, opening and closing drawers, not sure what she was looking for. More than anything she was so, so tired. Not sure her spine could take another night on the sofa, she thought of the bed in her mother's room and wondered if she could finally bring herself to sleep there.

After rummaging in the cupboard and finding a still-in-date tin of hot chocolate, she heated some milk in a saucepan. She returned to the bedroom and snuggled up in the bed with her hot drink and the paperback she was almost finished. Misty, who had stayed by Lily's side the whole day, was curled up asleep on the end of the bed and looked so at home Lily wondered if this was her usual sleeping place. If she didn't know better, she'd guess Misty had been keeping her company in the living room these last few nights. Lily stroked her gently, grateful for her company.

Chapter 10

Lily opened her eyes to see daylight creeping its way around the edges of the curtains and knew she'd slept much later than usual. Long peaceful sleeps had eluded her for so long but glancing at the time on her phone Lily was shocked to see she'd been asleep for a solid seven hours. Not only that, but it had been in her mother's room. In the end, nothing about it had felt strange or scary and after finishing her hot drink she'd fallen asleep surprisingly quickly.

She stretched and rose from the bed, her limbs feeling pleasantly heavy after their long slumber. In the kitchen she waited for the kettle to boil and looked down onto the garden. It was such a pretty little space and she was pleased and more than a little relieved to see her diligent watering appeared to be keeping the daisies and busy lizzies alive and flourishing.

Patty had always had a way of making things grow. Even when they'd lived in a flat in Glasgow, she had window boxes filled with flowers. And then when they had moved into a house which had a garden she would spend hours there. Lily recalled the afternoon she'd helped her mother, horrified when she'd managed to spill muddy earth all over her clothes. She'd thought her mother might be angry at the mess but instead she'd simply laughed and told her it didn't matter.

Lily stood for a few moments absorbing the peace. She was glad yesterday was over. She had done the thing that she had put off for too long and perhaps now she could start to move on. But it was odd, every time she thought of the future, it was like shutters coming down – almost as if now she had stopped she couldn't start again.

She sloshed boiling water over a teabag and contemplated the day ahead, puzzled that her thoughts were pulled towards the shop. Shouldn't she be doing more on the job front? Her career had always been important to her. Some of her work over the years had been repetitive, some of it outright dull, but she'd always got on with it and it had never occurred to her to do anything else. Yet here she was, for the first time in her adult life without a job.

She felt as if facing the death of her mother and now facing her own future were inexorably linked. Feeling the full force of her grief had in turn made her reflect on her life, particularly the last year. And the uncomfortable truth was that without work she didn't have much. She had neatly packaged and projected her job and James into her future and now that had been taken from her, she was left with nothing.

She wasn't sure if she liked the person she had become in the last yar. Everything had been about work. Striving to achieve a promotion that didn't happen. When had she last really laughed, or done something that wasn't work-related. She decided there and then, whatever she did next, she wouldn't let it take over the way she had let her last job. And she definitely wouldn't fall for her boss.

After showering and feeding Misty Lily headed downstairs and entered the shop. Something felt different today. There was an air of expectation, as if the shop was waiting for something to happen. For a moment she stood feeling utterly lost, not sure what to do. She cast her eyes round and a small scratching sound catching her attention. She glanced down to see Misty clawing at the door of the room where the ladies had held their knit club.

'You want in here?' She opened the door, choosing to ignore the fact she had just spoken to the cat. Misty immediately jumped up onto the window sill where sunlight flooded into room. The air felt warm and stuffy so Lily opened the window, having to use a little force.

As she turned her eye caught some items propped against the far wall. She went to investigate, not sure how she'd missed them before. Bending down, she discovered what look like a dream job for a DIY enthusiast; several new white shelves with all the fittings, a corkboard still in its wrapping and an Anglepoise lamp. There were also paintbrushes and a tin of paint which Lily lifted up. 'Buttercup yellow,' she read aloud.

She held the tin in her hand and as she looked around, taking in the grubby cream walls, she realised that her mother must have intended to paint the room. Not only that, but put up shelving and some task lighting, presumably to enable the ladies to see better when they were knitting.

Lily bit down on her lip, fighting the tears which suddenly burned behind her eyes. She'd have thought after yesterday there'd be none left, but that wasn't the case.

It was the same as when she found the stock – Lily felt unsettled by how unfinished everything felt. She thought about the women turning up for their next knitting meeting. She thought of all the life and vitality reflected in their eyes and how much she'd enjoyed their company. Then her heart dropped, thinking what would happen when the shop was sold. It was ludicrous but she found herself wondering if she could sell the shop with a clause to keep the knitting club going for the ladies.

Lily paced about the room feeling restless, an idea forming in her mind. Perhaps there was something she could do. Putting up shelving was perhaps beyond her capabilities but the tin of paint was sitting there. How difficult could it be to paint a room – surely she could do that?

She knew she'd be selling but she'd be here for at least another week, perhaps slightly longer. After all, there was no rush to go back to the city, was there? No matter what else happened, there was one thing she could do; she could have the room the way her mother had intended for the ladies next week.

One part of her brain questioned what she was doing but it was too late, the other part was already up and running with the idea. Anyway, she reasoned, it certainly wouldn't do any harm to have the room looking better when it came to selling. Really, it made sense.

Fuelled by her idea Lily felt a little surge of energy and five minutes later, she was dressed in jeans and an old oversized shirt she'd found, her hair twisted into a ponytail. With the radio on and Misty watching proceedings from her little pool of sunshine on the window sill, Lily set to work. Armed with a cloth and a bucket of hot soapy water, she began washing down the walls and the skirting boards.

There was more dust and grime than she'd realised and she refilled the bucket several times, using the stool from behind the counter and reaching rather precariously to remove the cobwebs lurking in the corners. It didn't take too long before she could see a difference. Soon the walls and surfaces were clean, the floor was swept and – having budged Misty out of the way – even the window was now gleaming.

Lily had never painted a room before and as she prised open the tin of paint, she felt out of her comfort zone. But she was on a roll now and felt her spirits lifting, pleased to be doing something practical. She'd do the lower parts of the wall first and then figured she could use the stool for the higher parts.

A couple of hours later she straightened up, blowing a loose strand of hair from her face, and stood back to examine her handiwork. She rolled her shoulders and arched her back, deciding caffeine in some shape or form was needed. She was pleased with the progress she'd made and was disappointed when she heard a jaunty rap on the shop door. Somehow, she wasn't surprised to see Jack at the door.

Opening the door, Lily didn't know what was more worrying; the fact he seemed to look more attractive each time she saw him or that she felt so inexplicably pleased to see him. Not only that but he was holding two cups of coffee as if he'd managed to read her thoughts.

'I thought you might be appreciate a decent coffee.' He handed her a cup.

The thought he'd come over just to give her coffee made her feel a little odd. She took it from him, suddenly feeling very conscious of her grimy appearance. She eyed the coffee suspiciously, wondering where he'd got it from. She hadn't seen any evidence of coffee that smelt this good being sold in the village. She took a sip. Rich, smooth and perfectly textured, it totally hit the spot and she couldn't help the small sigh of pleasure escaping.

'It's good,' she admitted with a small smile. 'Where's it from?'

'The café at the activity centre. You should go in sometime – does some pretty nice stuff.'

His eyes swept around the shop then landed on her with a questioning lift of his eyebrow. 'You seem busy. What are you up to?'

'Er, not much.' She knew she was being evasive but wasn't sure if what had seemed a reasonable idea in her own head a few hours ago now appeared slightly mad.

Jack stood at the doorway of the room where her morning's work was laid out and it occurred to Lily she hadn't exactly been neat about it. He took a mouthful of his coffee, regarding her over the rim of his cup. 'You've managed to make quite a mess for not doing much.'

She let out a small breath. There suddenly didn't seem much point in hiding what she'd been doing, plus she was pretty sure she had splats of paint on her face. She explained about the knitting club and all the things for painting she'd found.

'I thought it would be a good idea to give this room a clean and a lick of paint. Obviously it'll help for selling.'

He glanced around, his eyes settling on the stool with a frown. 'Please tell me you haven't been standing on this?'

'It's fine,' she replied airily. 'I'm careful.'

'I'm sure you are but promise me you won't use it again?'

His face creased with such concern, Lily didn't have any choice but to give her word. She should be able to find some step-ladders somewhere.

He regarded her thoughtfully for a moment. 'Let me help.'

Taken by surprise, her response was instant and instinctive. 'I don't need help, thanks, I can manage.'

'It wouldn't take much. All the fittings are here – and it'll give me an excuse to use my toolbox.' He lifted his eyebrows.

He was like a one-man crusade, Lily thought, always ready to offer assistance. Was he always so helpful? She stalled for time. 'Don't you have to be at work?'

He shrugged, indicating it was nothing. 'They can manage without me for a while. That's the beauty of being your own boss, it means if something comes up, I can go.'

It felt slightly alien to Lily to hear someone be so casual about their job. She respected that his priorities were different from hers and probably the boats weren't that demanding but even so, his casualness only succeeded in making her feel more uptight and uneasy.

'Why would you want to help?'

'Why wouldn't I?' He shrugged, in a way that Lily couldn't work out if it was annoying or not. 'We're practically neighbours so it's not so odd to help out, is it?'

She looked around uncertainly, not sure this was a good idea. It felt like another step in a direction she shouldn't be taking. It wasn't so much accepting help as accepting it from him. She was beginning to suspect it could be quite easy to be charmed by Jack Armstrong and she heard a voice cautioning her to keep her distance.

He looked at her curiously. 'You don't accept help very easily, do you?'

'There's nothing wrong with being self-reliant.'

'Of course not,' he agreed. 'But it's still okay to take help sometimes.'

There he went again, confusing her, being all reasonable and helpful. She couldn't help thinking life would be easier if she could relegate him to smug and arrogant. Perhaps she was over-thinking things? Reading far too much into what was a simple offer of help, the same way he had helped with Misty who, Lily noticed now, had come to sit in-between them.

'Sorry, you're right. And as long as you don't mind, then I'd be really grateful.'

He drained his cup. 'Right, let's get started.'

After ten minutes (during which Lily dashed upstairs to make sure her face wasn't actually covered in paint which thankfully it wasn't, although her cheeks were decidedly flushed) Jack had returned with his toolbox. He lifted one of the shelves, running his fingers along the grain of wood in an expert manner and then held it up against the wall for Lily to judge the position.

'What do you think of here?' he asked, a pencil between his teeth. 'You should still be able to reach things and then I can put the others below it?'

'Looks about right,' Lily agreed. Despite being broad and tall, he moved with agility and Lily watched his movements, trying and failing not to notice when his T-shirt hitched, revealing his taut midriff.

After marking the spot on the wall Jack got to work with a spirit level and there didn't seem to be much for Lily to do at this stage except watch him – which wasn't too much of a hard-ship. He focused fully on the job and looked as if he was thoroughly enjoying himself.

'You enjoy DIY?'

He nodded. 'I've learnt loads since I started doing up my own place – improved my skills no end.' He grinned, or at least as much as the pencil between his teeth allowed.

'How long have you lived in your house?'

'Almost three years – I moved in after I split with my fiancé.'

'Oh. I'm sorry.'

'All water under the bridge now.'

She shot him a curious look but his expression gave nothing away.

'What about you?' he asked, fixing her with a look. 'Is it just the job you need to get back to or is there someone waiting for you?'

Iris had asked her the exact same thing except coming from him, it sounded and felt very different.

'No, just the job,' she replied. 'In fact, I've registered with a recruitment agency and I'm waiting to hear back about a couple of positions I applied for.'

Suddenly she was inordinately pleased she had done so. Something about the way he had just looked at her made her glad she had them to anchor her to reality. She wondered when she'd hear but wasn't holding her breath, these things could take a while.

She picked up a cloth and absently wiped the counter, wondering how in the space of a few days she'd gone from scrutinising numbers to scrutinising Jack's physique. She seemed to have no control over her eyes which kept sneaking their way over to him as he drilled a bracket into the wall, skimming the line of his dark hair along the back of his tanned neck, over his broad shoulders and all the way to his long muscular legs …

'You look miles away,' Jack's voice broke in. 'Head back in the city – missing those balance sheets?' he teased.

Lily cleared her throat, giving herself a brisk shake. 'Something like that.'

Hopefully she'd hear back soon about those jobs. That was real life, she reminded herself. Not this.

Chapter 11

Lily's spirits nosedived when she saw Finlay's face through the glass of the shop door. Standing behind the counter, she'd been totally absorbed in sorting through the pieces of jewellery, studying the exquisitely pretty silver pendants she'd found in one of the boxes. Along with the enamel necklaces and the handcrafted rose drop earrings, they made a stunning collection. She'd also discovered small jewellery dishes made from fused indigo and purple glass which she thought would make perfect gifts alongside the jewellery.

Lily wondered if he just happened to be passing again, given that it was only a matter of days since he'd last been here. Physically they were different but something about him reminded her of James she realised. He'd want to discuss business and money, things she didn't want to think about right now. She briefly considered ducking behind the counter but it was too late, he'd already seen her. With a silent sigh, she opened the door. Without waiting for an invitation, Finlay stepped over the threshold leaving Lily little choice but to move aside and let him in.

He removed his sunglasses, turning to smile at Lily with a small courteous bow of his head. 'Good morning, Lily.'

The charm he'd displayed so readily on their first meeting was still very much in evidence but Lily detected a slight change in his demeanour today, a more determined air and businesslike manner. 'How are you today?' he asked, his eyes flitting to the jewellery laid out on the counter and then back to her.

Lily took a couple of quick steps to lean her back against the counter, a futile gesture given that he'd already had an eyeful of the jewellery.

'Good, thanks,' she replied breezily. 'I wasn't expecting to see you so soon.'

There was a fraction of hesitation before he appeared to decide to cut straight to the chase. 'I wanted to see if you were ready to discuss putting the place on the market yet?'

Clearly he wanted to try and secure the property on his books, she understood that. She also knew how easy it would be for her to say the word and Finlay would take care of it all. The irony wasn't lost on her that her mother had probably bought the property without too much thought to its value or the profit it could make but now that Lily had seen how busy the village was, she knew the shop would be an attractive proposition to many people looking to run a small business.

Lily knew she could leave Carroch today if she really wanted, she could be on a train and back in Edinburgh within a few hours. But somehow it didn't feel as simple as that. All the stock felt like a weight around her neck, a symbol of how unfinished everything felt, as if her mother had started something and now she needed to finish it.

Suddenly she wasn't in the mood for this conversation. What she wanted was to get back to what she'd been doing. Some of the jewellery had come with velvet display trays and she'd love to see how the pieces of silver and enamel would look in the display cabinet.

'The thing is,' Lily started. 'I don't want to rush into anything—'

'Of course,' Finlay interrupted, his tone slightly condescending.

'But its best to strike while the iron's hot and I do have clients who are interested. And of course, it's really not ideal to have the property lying empty for too long, especially with the winter season ahead of us.'

Lily nodded, knowing she had no argument against what he was saying. She tried to ignore her unease as his eyes roamed the interior almost if he was calculating the square footage and how much it would be worth.

Thinking about the story of Alice and how her mother had come to acquire the shop from her, the money side of things seemed to poison the air in some way. She felt as if she was letting everyone down in some way – she knew that was silly she knew, it was bricks and mortar. But even in the short time she'd been here, Lily had learnt so much more about the shop and her mother's life and she knew she was beginning to feel differently about it. She could no longer deny there was an emotional attachment. It wasn't just the business side of the shop. There was a feeling, one she couldn't easily put into words, but it felt like some sort of connection to her mother that she hadn't expected.

Even the shop looked different. The hobby room, as she had taken to calling it, had undergone a small transformation. Now all freshly painted, the shelves were up and lights fixed – all things Jack had helped her with – so that it was a bright and functional space and she couldn't wait for the knitting ladies to see it.

She faltered, beginning to feel uncomfortable, not least at Finlay's presumption that she would sell with him. She hadn't had the chance yet to consider other agents nor had she spoken to her solicitor, Mr Bell in Edinburgh. Her head was swimming slightly and she massaged her temple. Perhaps it was the paint fumes lingering, or was it Finlay's aftershave? Either way she was beginning to wish he would just leave.

'I could give you a valuation, take some measurements and photos,' Finlay pushed, misinterpreting her silence as acquiescence.

Lily glanced up at the sound of laughter as people passed by the shop, her heart beginning to thump at what she was about to say. She realised now that an idea had been circling in her head for a while, growing on some subconscious level but now that she was about to articulate it, she hoped she sounded more confident than she felt.

'Actually I've decided to stay on for a while and open the shop for a short time so I won't be selling immediately.' She blurted it out quickly, the words almost seeming to form themselves.

He gave her an astonished look. 'Your idea is to actually open?'

'Only for a little while. There's enough stock to make it viable to open for a few weeks and as you pointed out, I don't have any accounts to show.'

'Of course, but—'

On a roll and not giving him a chance to respond, Lily carried on. 'This way I'll be able to provide at least some figures, even if it's just a snapshot at what could possible in terms of trade. The village appears to be quite busy so I'm fairly confident I'd be able to catch the last of the summer trade.'

He seemed a little speechless and gave an odd sort of chortle. 'Well, I'll admit I certainly wasn't expecting that.'

There was an awkward pause. Lily was sure he was about to point out the follies of her plan wouldn't be difficult.

But instead, he dipped his head. 'Of course, it's entirely your decision,' he said smoothly. 'I'm not sure it's at all necessary but you know where to reach me.'

'Yes, of course.' She opened the door with shaky fingers. 'And thank you.' She closed the door with a sigh of relief, glad to be on her own to mull over what had just happened. But within moments of Finlay leaving, the door opened and Jack appeared, so that her solitude lasted no more than seconds.

She was getting used to his visits – perhaps too used to them – and although she could feel her heart do that little jump whenever she saw him, she really wasn't in the mood for company right now. She might have just told Finlay she was going to open the shop, but she needed to live with idea for a while, think it over properly. She wasn't ready to share her decision with anyone else yet.

Lily watched Jack close the door behind him, the shop instantly appearing smaller with him in it.

'See you had a visitor,' he said, throwing a glare in the direction of Finlay who was climbing back into his car.

Lily tilted her head, wondering what it was between those two. 'Not your favourite person, I take it?'

'You could say that,' he muttered darkly.

'Yes, well estate agents aren't on everyone's Christmas lists but they have a job to do,' she pronounced rather tartly. Okay, she'd admit Finlay might be a tad ingratiating but he was a professional and she of all people could respect that.

'Did he say if he had a buyer?' Jack asked.

Lily turned, surprised by the question. 'He didn't give me the impression it would be difficult to sell.' 'I bet he didn't,' Jack mumbled. 'Did you ask who his clients were?'

Lily frowned. 'No.'

Lily wasn't sure if she should be touched by his concern or annoyed at his interference. She had enough to sort through in her own head just now and while she was grateful for Jack's help, his barbed comments weren't helping her.

'I appreciate your concern but I think I might have more experience than you in dealing with matters like these so with all respect, please don't worry on my account. I'm quite capable of handling things.'

A muscle twitched on his jaw. 'I have no doubt you can handle yourself. Just be cautious.' He rubbed a hand round the back of his neck. 'Don't let him pressure you into anything, okay?'

Lily shook her head, feeling irritated. 'Look, if there's something you think I should know, perhaps you'd care to enlighten me?'

Jack studied the floor for a moment as if considering what to say and then lifted his eyes to meet hers. He let out a sigh and then spoke. 'You remember the old boat place – how it used to be when you came years ago?

'Of course,' Lily nodded.

'It was just a small set-up – Alistair had owned it for years. I'd helped out there since I was a boy, working at the weekends, taking tourists out and fixing the boats. For a few years after I left school, I did some labouring and bar work but I always carried on helping Alistair whenever I could. As long as I was near the water, I was happy.'

'Then for a couple of years I got an office job, working for an insurance company based in Inverness.' He paused, scoffing. 'Let's just say things didn't work out.'

Lily chewed her lip, listening carefully.

'I still went to see Alistair regularly at the old boat place and by now he was getting on a bit and struggling. Told me he might have to sell up.' Jack shook his head. 'I couldn't stand the idea. So I did a bit of research and it didn't take much to see the tourism sector in Scotland was really taking off. The new section of motorway to the north had recently been completed and believe it or not—' he flashed her a quick smile '—the mobile coverage had become much better. I could see there was a real opportunity for something more at the loch.'

He let out a long breath. 'Basically, Alistair and I went about setting up a whole new business. We got a loan and applied for grants. There was a tonne of stuff to get our heads round. We had to be fully licensed to operate, there was first aid certificates to deal with, rescue training, hiring staff. We applied for a grant for new equipment – canoes, paddle boards, mountain bikes and so on. I became a qualified instructor and soon we were able to employ four full-time and six part-time staff.'

Lily opened her mouth and then closed it, finding herself speechless. She was totally shocked. She'd had no idea that Jack

108

was behind the activity centre. He'd never said anything and to be honest, his laidback demeanour gave absolutely no hint of it.

'It was hard work but it paid off. Soon we were fully booked and doing so well we were able to give local kids free sessions. Then one day, Sonny Jim turns up.' He hooked a thumb in the direction of the door Finlay had recently exited. 'Says he has clients interested in buying over the boat centre and the bit of land that went with it. I did a bit of digging about and it turns out the clients were developers who wanted to build a retail and leisure development by the loch.'

Lily let out a small gasp.

'They tried to spin it saying it would become a major tourism destination with huge economic potential and provide hundreds of jobs … they started talking about a million visitors a year as if that was a good thing.' He shuddered. 'Can you imagine?'

'I don't think I'd like to,' Lily replied truthfully. She of all people knew that jobs and business were vital but not at any cost. 'Surely that would ruin the uniqueness of this place?'

'Exactly. If they had gone ahead, God knows what would happen to the ancient woodland, not to mention the pollution in the water.'

'So what happened?'

'We saw them off. Even when they started offering silly money, we refused to sell.' The casual shrug he gave belied the steely glint she saw in his eyes and left Lily in no doubt how much it all meant to him.

'And that's why the village is so much busier then,' she said almost to herself.

'Yeah, and it's good to see the place thriving. I'm not saying all business is bad, of course not. But it's about balance. For me, the loch and all this—' he swept his arm expansively '—isn't a playground for some rich developers. It's about allowing people to enjoy the loch but keeping the peace and tranquillity.'

109

'And do you think it's the same developers who would want to buy the shop now?'

'Probably not. I doubt they'd be interested in a small property like this. But when they weren't above resorting to a few underhand tricks, all of which our local estate agent friend was quite happy to be party to.'

'Why didn't you tell me – that you owned the activity centre?'

He shrugged. 'What difference would it have made?'

She swallowed. 'None. I just thought—'

'You thought?'

Lily lowered her eyes, not sure how to admit to herself or to him that she'd made assumptions about him that were way off the mark. What could she say? That he didn't look the business type, that she thought his skills started and ended with boats? Clearly, she was wrong on all accounts. In fact, she found it appealing that he was so astute and driven yet didn't have all the normal trappings that so often went with it. 'You surprised me, that's all.'

He was staring at her as if he could see her thoughts and she blushed. The moment lasted but then his face broke into a wide smile. 'I'll take that as a good thing then.'

Lily let out a breath of relief.

'Listen,' Jack continued, 'it's all history now and I know it has nothing to do with you. I don't trust him and my instinct was to warn you. Just don't let him put you under any pressure. Make the right decision for you.' His hand balled into a fist by his side. 'But it still makes my blood boil to think what might have happened. Every time I see him I want to punch his lights out.'

Lily pressed her lips together, trying not to laugh.

'Not that I would obviously,' he added sheepishly.

'Actually,' she said, a tentative smile making its way onto her lips, 'I have made one decision. At least I think I have.'

'Oh?'

'I was thinking of staying around for a bit.'

He regarded her. 'O-kay,' he said slowly.

Lily swallowed. 'That's what I just told Finlay – that I'm opening the shop.'

Now it was his turn to look shocked.

'Only for a couple of weeks at the most,' she hastily clarified.

'Isn't it a lot of bother to go to if you're going to be selling anyway?'

'Not really. It makes sense from a business perspective. There's all this stock lying around and hopefully I can catch the last of the summer season. I'd like to be able to sell Beth's products, I'm sure they'll sell easily.' She took a couple of paces. 'And Mum had clearly intended to do all these jobs so I wanted to finish them for her ...' Her voice faded on a wobble.

Jack was by her side in an instant. 'Hey, I'm sorry, I didn't mean to upset you.'

'No, no you didn't.' She shook her head, not sure where that had come from. There was no room for sentimentality, she reminded herself, clearing her throat. 'I mean, it's a business decision pure and simple. And it's only for a couple of weeks at the most.'

He touched her hand with a gentle squeeze and then let it go again. 'I think it's a great idea.'

Her skin tingled from touch and she tried to distract herself with practical matters, thinking about what she'd need to do. The place would need a good clean, a few decorative touches and it would be perfectly presentable for the public.

She became aware of Jack looking at her. 'What about your job?'

Her mouth tugged downs at the corners. 'I haven't heard anything back yet and as I say, it'll only be for a few weeks at most.'

Jack waited a couple of moments and then spoke, his voice hesitant. 'So if you're going to be here for a while, why don't we make the most of it?

Lily blinked. 'Sorry?'

'Well,' he began, 'how about we do something together – you and me?'

'You and me?'

'You don't need to sound quite so horrified.'

'Sorry, it's just …' She stalled, questioning the wisdom of spending time with Jack. 'I won't be here that long and I'll probably be quite busy.'

'Exactly, so why not make the most of it? I've not had a day off in a while. You know, all work and no play … It'll be nice to do something different for a change.' His eyes met her with a mischievous glint. 'And I can prove to you it's not all rain and midges.'

'You make it sound like a challenge.'

'I'm always up for a challenge.' He kept his eyes firmly on hers. 'And who knows, you might even fall in love.'

'Sorry?' Lily spluttered.

'With the place, of course.'

'Of course.' Lily gulped, her mind and body shooting into panic mode for some reason. She wondered if she could spend more time with Jack, her hesitation proving to her just how isolated she'd let herself become. But she felt something stir within her. Like swimming in the loch, she felt herself stepping out of the confines of her usual life. She had to admit she was beginning to relax more with Jack and he was being friendly, that's all – it wasn't as if he was asking her on a date or anything. Was it?

'But just to be clear, it's not a date. Just so there's no mixed wires,' she blurted out suddenly, feeling heat rise in her cheeks. 'I'm not really looking for anything … not that you are either.' *Oh God, shut up.*

Jack rubbed his jaw, looking amused. 'Not a date then. Now that we've got that cleared up, how about a boat trip on the loch? How does that sound?'

A boat trip sounded all right actually, and she did love the water.

'And this way,' he carried on, 'you can create some new memories of Carroch while you're here.'

The sentiment of his words caused a breath to catch in her throat. She looked into his eyes and thought how easy it would be to lose herself in them. He tilted his head with a smile, waiting for her answer.

Lily found herself smiling back at him. 'A boat trip sounds good.'

Chapter 12

Lily had arranged to meet Beth at the café in the activity centre. Now that she knew how good the coffee was, she'd suggested it as their meeting place. Lily had arrived first, the two-minute walk making it literally on her doorstep - something even Edinburgh's abundant coffee shops had never afforded her the luxury of.

The café itself didn't disappoint either. It was all very modern with chrome tables and chairs, background music playing and young, energetic staff buzzing around. They were sitting at a table overlooking the loch and had been served by a young boy who had brought them coffee and fudge brownies which Lily had managed to demolish hungrily in a few mouthfuls while Beth had only picked at hers.

She glanced over at the other woman, sensing her nervousness. Like the first time they'd met, Lily could see her grief etched on her face. She looked wary – even more so today as if being out was a new experience to her. Earlier, the clatter of dropped cutlery had almost made her jump out of her skin.

Lily had just finished explaining to Beth her idea to open the shop for a short time. She took a sip of her coffee and sat back, keen to hear her response. 'So, what do you think?'

'It's a lovely idea,' Beth replied tentatively. 'But you're not doing it just to sell my products? You don't owe me anything, honestly.'

'No.' Lily shook her head firmly. 'It makes sense for me to sell all the stock.'

Now that she'd had time to think about it she was sure opening for a time was the right thing. She reckoned it would take a couple of weeks for it all to sell, depending how busy it was. It would give her something to do while she waited to hear back from her job applications and give her time to apply for anything else that came up. In the meantime, she had decided to view this time as a bit of a working holiday. She rooted in her bag now for her notepad where she'd jotted down some ideas for pricing. 'You and Mum hadn't discussed costs or anything?'

Beth gave a little helpless shrug. 'Your mother and I had joked about how neither of us had business brains.'

Lily had spent a few hours researching similar products and combined with her own knowledge, had made some estimates. She flicked through a couple of sheets, asking Beth a few questions about her overheads which, as she had suspected, were reasonably low. Her priority was making sure Beth was paid a fair price and she showed her the figure she had in mind.

'You'll think they'll sell for that?'

Lily smiled at her surprise. 'Pretty sure.'

'I suppose it would be exciting to see how they sell.'

Lily saw something ignite in Beth's eyes, as if for the first time she'd allowed herself to think she really might have a successful business that could make money.

'There's something else I wanted to mention to you. I hope you don't mind but I had a chat with the buyer in Bremners who I used to work with.'

Lily had phoned Arabella who was still with Bremners and after they'd enjoyed a quick catch-up, she had explained about Highland Aromatics. The growing demand for organic, chemical-free products had actually made it a dream product to pitch to Arabella and in theory, she'd been very receptive to the idea. 'I used to work with her and I told her a bit about you and your products. She was really interested.'

Not wishing to bombard her with too much at once, Lily let Beth digest this for a moment. She hoped she hadn't been too presumptuous and watched the other woman's face closely, still seeing her doubt and hesitancy. 'Obviously you don't need to decide anything yet, it's just for you to think about in the future, when you're ready.'

Beth gave her head a little shake, appearing a little lost for words. 'I will,' she promised. 'I'll think about everything. And thank you.' She smiled, twisting the band of gold that Lily noticed she still wore on her wedding finger. 'When do you plan to open?'

'In a couple of days,' Lily told her. 'I just need to give the place a good clean and get all the stock ready.'

The café was busy as they made their out and it didn't look as if their table would be empty for long. Emerging into the sunshine, Lily blinked. There had been a cloak of mist hanging over the loch earlier but it had lifted and now the water shimmered under a brilliant azure sky. The shore line was full of life and activity, as if everyone was determined to grab every drop of sunshine, knowing that tomorrow could just as easily be cool and damp.

Had it always been this beautiful, Lily wondered. All the years she'd come here she didn't remember it having this effect on her. She supposed she'd been too busy with her own thoughts, probably with her head in a book, to pay much attention to the scenery. Her mother always used to say she'd been born with an old head on her shoulders. Perhaps she'd been right. Now it was almost as if she could hear her mother's voice again, except this time she was telling her to embrace life, not to be scared.

Jack had teased her about falling in love with the place and she had the slightly unnerving sensation that that was exactly what was happening – as if the loch, the hills and wild beauty of the landscape had awakened something in her. She was no longer sure about things she thought had been the cornerstones of her life and apart from a few calls to Mrs Robertson to check up on the flat, she was surprised how little she'd thought about her life in the city.

In the distance she could see different boats on the water, an elegant steamboat cruising by, and the spray of a speedboat slicing its way through the water. She was meeting Jack later today and Lily could hardly believe they'd be out there, just the two of them. She couldn't help wondering if they were crossing some invisible line. She gave herself a shake, determined not to overthink things. But as she went to say goodbye to Beth, she was unable to stop the little shiver of anticipation run through her.

***

Lily took hold of Jack's hand, his strong warm fingers steadying her as she climbed onto the boat. The bobbing of the boat made her sway slightly so that her hand landed on Jack's chest. She felt her stomach somersault but wasn't sure if it was due to the motion of the water or her brain registering the hardness of the muscle beneath her fingers. 'Sorry,' she mumbled.

'Not a problem.' Je smiled down at her.

Lily carefully lowered herself onto one of the padded seats, the small space suddenly feeling intimate and a small wave of panic washed over her as she thought about what she was actually doing here. She was aiming for casualness but on a boat with a man as gorgeous as this, it wasn't coming easily. She told herself there was nothing to be nervous about. She'd never been afraid of the water, she was a strong swimmer and she was in the company of a lifeguard. So that left only one other reason for the bundle of knots in her stomach: Jack.

She took a calming breath, tucking a strand of hair behind her ear. Without her regular blow dries there really wasn't any point in even trying to control it although she'd forgotten the way her hair could sit in waves beneath her shoulders the way it did now, without being straightened to within an inch of its life. This morning showering and moisturising had been the extent of her efforts and it was quite nice to feel her skin breathe and not worry about mascara smudging.

From behind her sunglasses Lily watched Jack concentrate as he started the engine and manoeuvred the boat away from its mooring, steering it away from the shore and further out onto the loch. As he fiddled with various dials and switches on the dashboard, Lily rummaged in her bag, her fingers feeling clammy. She'd realised she'd taken a risk wearing denim shorts and a pink vest top, leaving plenty of exposed flesh at the mercy of the sun and the midges but she wasn't taking any chances and had brought plenty of protection with her.

Jack was still standing, feet apart and hands on the wheel. He turned as she was massaging cream into her skin, his eyes skimming her bare shoulders. 'Putting on sun cream?'

'And midge cream,' she told him sagely, slathering repellent on top of the sun cream, not too sure about the resultant odour.

'We're heading to the eastern shore so there'll be enough of a breeze to keep them at bay.' He looked skywards. 'In fact, we've got the perfect day – a bit of patchy rain but that won't be until later in the day.' He stopped and his mouth crooked into a half-smile. 'Sorry, force of habit to recite the conditions.'

'I don't know how you keep up with it.' She shook her head, smiling. 'It's been like four seasons in one day since I arrived.'

Today though, she had to agree, was perfect. Pleasantly warm, the sun beamed down from a clear blue sky, a gently breeze rippled the surface of the water and in the distance heather-strewn hills were ablaze with light. There were a few other boats on the water and Lily could see a stunning display of wildflowers along the banks with ducks dabbling at the shore.

She took a moment to appreciate how idyllic it was, thinking how strange it was that she hardly noticed the weather in the city, unless it meant she had to think about whether to take an umbrella or not. A hot summer's day meant opening the office window, sitting on a bench to eat lunch and watch the open top tour bus go by. In winter she liked being able to wrap up in a warm coat and have an excuse to buy a new pair of boots.

But these mornings, the first thing she did was to look out of the window, captivated by the constantly changing colours of the loch and the landscape, the way the clouds moved across the vast sky, sometimes racing, other times drifting.

Her gaze fell on Jack. His back was to her, his top stretched tightly across shoulders making Lily imagine what was underneath. She dragged her eyes away. Clearly all the Highlands air was playing havoc with her sensibilities.

She'd never actually visited Loch Carroch in the winter and found herself wondering what it was like.

'Is it very different here in winter?' she asked Jack.

'It can be pretty quiet but winter's actually my favourite time.' He squinted his eyes against the sun looking into the distance. 'There's nothing like a winter landscape, when you see snow-capped hills above the water. The roads are much quieter without all the tourists, so at weekends I can get out on my bike for a long ride. Then home to warm up by the fire – my perfect Sunday.'

Lily blinked. To her, Sunday was simply the precursor to Monday at work. Very occasionally she'd meet friends for lunch or sometimes go for a stroll, do some shopping. But the way Jack had described it, made his version sound very appealing.

'What about the activity centre?'

'We try and keep most of the activities going. Won't let a bit of bad weather put us off,' he told her.

'I don't think I could go swimming in the winter, not even Iris manages that.' Lily chuckled before it dawned on her she wouldn't be here in winter, the thought causing a little dollop of despondency for some reason.

'You're enjoying the swimming?'

'Not those first few moments,' Lily admitted with a shudder. 'But then once I'm in and swimming, something else takes over, you know? It's like having a different perspective on the world and everything seems less important somehow.'

She felt a little self-conscious but Jack nodded. 'I get that.'

He slowed the boat to curve round what looked like a tiny wooded island in the middle of the loch. Lily thought it looked eerie, as if the sun somehow never reached it. 'Is that an actual island?' she asked.

He nodded. 'That's the Isle of Carroch. Legend has it that two lovers are buried there.'

'Really?'

'The Norwegians used to dominate this part of the West Coast and legend has it that there was a young prince who was Chief among the Vikings and he had a tower built for his princess who he was in love with. There was to be a big expedition which he was to lead and the Princess feared she would never see him again. They devised a plan – a white flag would be flown from his ship if he was alive and black if he was dead. This way the Princess would know if he was alive.

'The princess worried he would enjoy the excitement of battle and became plagued by doubts. When she saw his ship return with a white flag she decided to test his love for her. She boarded a boat and went to meet him. She lay down pretending to be dead surrounded by her maidens pretending to grief.Her plan worked – the prince was frantic and he killed himself. When the princess realised, she was convinced of his love and she too killed herself. They say their bodies are buried there.'

'Who'd have thought?' Lily said. 'Scotland's very own *Romeo and Juliet* here in Carroch.'

'I guess so, never thought of it like that,' Jack laughed. They carried on for a few more minutes until Jack found a small inlet to stop and then flicked a few switches to stop the engine.

'Look over there,' he said, handing Lily the binoculars. She lifted them to her eyes, adjusting them slightly as Jack gently guided her by the shoulders in the direction to look. It took a few moments to focus but then she saw them, grey seals playing in the water, hauling themselves over the small rocks, their whiskery snouts bobbing in and out of the water.

'I see them!' she exclaimed, delighted to have spotted them.

'Just behind where the seals are playing there's a track which you can cycle up and it takes you right into the forest – the views are amazing. And those mountains and crags up there? They're the perfect place for golden eagles to nest and if you're really lucky, you might get to see one gliding in the sky. It's an incredible sight.'

Lily spent a while longer enjoying the seals. Listening to Jack, it was impossible not to be caught up in his enthusiasm. Lily had that feeling again, the same one when Jack had shown her the rowan tree.

The scenery, and being on the water with Jack, seemed to be rubbing off on her in some way. She couldn't help relaxing as stresses seemed to melt away, for the time being anyway. When had she last felt carefree? She couldn't remember. But just for today, not to worry about the shop or selling or estate agents or finding another job, she was overwhelmed by a feeling of freedom she'd not experienced before. She felt the breeze brush against her skin and the sun warm her back, feeling a sudden burst of hope.

She blinked, realising she'd been miles away and lifted her eyes to find Jack watching her.

'Enjoying yourself?' he asked.

She nodded, surprised just how much, handing the binoculars back to him.

'Do you come out on your boat much?'

'Not as much as I'd like, just too busy these days. But whenever I get the chance, I take it. To me, this is perfect.' He pulled off his cap, running a hand through his hair and looked around, his love for his surroundings apparent. His head spun back to her. 'Of course, having the right company beside you makes it a whole lot better.' He replaced his cap, shooting her a quick smile. 'Would you like a drink?'

'Please,' Lily croaked, suddenly finding an urgent need to bury her face in her bag looking for more sun-cream. While Jack busied himself organising drinks from the cooler bag Lily took a moment to compose herself needlessly reapplying more sun-cream and then gratefully taking the glass Jack offered her.

'I've got orange, is that okay?'

'Sure, thanks,' she replied, touched at the effort he'd gone to. She sat back and took an appreciative sip of her cold drink as Jack folded himself into the seat beside her.

'So have you travelled much?' she asked.

'Did a bit after my engagement ended. Travelled round Australia and Asia for a few months. But I always knew I'd come back.'

He spoke quite matter-of-factly about his engagement and Lily wondered if he was good at hiding his pain. After all, he had intended to marry her.

'Your ex-fiancée,' she asked gently. 'What happened?'

Jack turned away, contemplating the depths of the water for a long moment and Lily worried she'd stepped over some line she had no right to. 'I'm sorry, I shouldn't have asked.'

'It's fine.' He brought his eyes back to her and paused for a moment before speaking.

'I was working on the boats when I met Jessica. It started as a holiday romance, she was here with her family. They lived in Inverness and after the holiday we kept seeing each other. It wasn't always easy with the distance but we managed, taking it in turns driving to see each other.

'It was all a bit of a whirlwind, we got engaged fairly quickly. Jessica seemed in a hurry for some reason and I found myself going along with it. That's the type of person she is, going through life taking what she wants. She comes from a wealthy family and I don't think her father was too impressed when she brought me home, even less impressed when we announced our plans to marry. So, I thought I should get a better paid, more secure job, save up for the wedding and our future.'

'That's when you got the insurance job?' Lily asked, remembering him telling her he'd worked in an office for a while before setting up the activity centre.

Jack replied with a wry smile in confirmation. 'That's when I tried to be something I wasn't.'

He rubbed a hand down his throat, almost as if the memory was choking him. 'It was a company specialising in farming insurance. Involved some driving around but mostly at a desk. I hated every minute of it.'

'Then one night I got a call to say Jessica had been involved in a bad car crash.' He gave his head a small shake. 'It was late at night and I couldn't work out where she'd been going. At first I thought perhaps she'd been coming to surprise me but it was the wrong direction. Plus I knew she wasn't that keen on driving, especially in the winter.'

Jack looked down, his forehead creasing. 'I raced to the hospital and the first person I saw when I arrived was Adam, my friend from the distilley. I couldn't understand it.'

Lily's hands were tightly clasped together and she felt them grow clammy.

'Turns out Jessica hadn't been driving at all. It had been Callum, the man she'd been seeing behind my back. They'd been out drinking for hours but it seems Callum thought it was all right for him to get in a car and drive.'

Lily gasped. 'Oh no, that's awful.'

Jack gave a short savage laugh. 'That was nothing. There were two cars involved. Jessica and her friend were fine, a few bumps and bruises – but the driver of the other car had been killed instantly. It was Adam's wife.'

Lily's hand flew to her mouth in shock. She was filled with such sadness for what Jack and Adam must have been through and wasn't sure how to respond. She would never have guessed that beneath Jack's easygoing manner, he had been dealing with such terrible pain and betrayal.

'I can't imagine how awful that must have been for you and Adam.'

Jack looked at her blankly for a moment before blinking. 'Me? As far as I'm concerned, I'm better off without her. But Adam ...' He paused, his frown deepening. 'They'd only been married a year. That idiot who'd been driving gets a ban but at least gets to live his life.'

He took a breath, letting it out slowly. 'I grew up in a large happy family. Suppose I took it for granted that one day I'd meet someone, have a family of my own. When I started having doubts about us, that it wasn't right between us, I couldn't bring myself to admit it. If I'd been brave enough to call it off she wouldn't have been sneaking about and none of this would have happened. I just can't help feeling responsible in some way, as if there was something I could have done to stop it.'

Lily reached over, laying a hand on his arm. 'You mustn't think like that. There was nothing you could have done differently.'

Jack's eyes swept the horizon of the loch. 'After that, I got my priorities sorted. I gave up the insurance job and it was soon after that I started the activity centre with Alistair.'

'Was it then that you saw the rowan tree?'

He looked at her for a long moment, recognition in his eyes. 'Yes.'

'Anyway, Adam's back now.' Lily heard the forced lightness in his voice. 'So hopefully he can start to rebuild his life.'

'I guess it won't be easy for him.'

'No. I understood why he needed to get away but the two years he was in Canada was difficult, I felt so helpless. At least he's home now and in the best place with his family and friends around him.'

Moved by his obvious concern for his friend, Lily couldn't help wondering about Jack himself. He must have his dark moments and she wondered how he'd dealt with it all, if he'd been able to find happiness again or even consolation with someone else.

'And since Jessica, has there been anyone?' she asked tentatively.

'Apart from a few meaningless causal things, no.' He shook his head firmly. 'I turned my life around for Jessica, trusted her. But it was all a sham.' For a moment anger blazed in his eyes and regret roughened his voice. 'These things tend to leave a bad taste. Let's just say I'm not in any hurry to go there again.'

Lily remained silent. A definite case of once bitten twice shy, she concluded, but it was easy to understand why. He certainly sounded quite adamant about it – not that it concerned her in any way but at least she knew where he stood.

Jack stretched over and into the cooler bag, bringing out more juice. 'And you?' he questioned. 'Has there ever been anyone special for you?'

Lily thought about it. There'd been dates, a couple of casual flings but she'd certainly never come close to being engaged or even having a serious relationship for that matter. 'A few relationships but nothing ever serious.'

Jack regarded her with an intensely searching look. He'd been open with her and now Lily wanted to be honest with him. 'There was someone at work,' she said eventually.

She told Jack about Dunn Equity's involvement with Bremners and how when she'd started working closely with James, she thought her career and personal life were both leading somewhere. 'Turns out I got it wrong on both accounts,' she said.

She explained how Dunn Equity had brought about some much-needed investment, but had also made some fairly brutal cuts and sweeping changes which had eventually affected Lily.

She told him how she'd busted a gut only to have it come crashing down when she was made redundant. Not only that, but James had been instrumental in it. 'We worked well together, grew close ... I thought there was something between us but I can see now there never was.'

Lily thought it all sounded a bit pathetic now. Nothing had actually happened between them, it had only ever been in her imagination. By concentrating on her career, she had provided herself with an excuse to keep people at a distance, avoid the risk of hurt. Perhaps that was why it had suited her to think there might have been something between her and James – because deep down she'd known it was never going to happen. James had been a one-sided, pseudo-relationship. It had all been in her mind, what she'd wanted it to be. She surprised herself by revealing as much as she had to Jack. It was as if it had all been sitting on the tip of her tongue waiting to spill out, and once she'd started she'd been incapable of stopping.

She let out a long breath when she stopped talking, feeling a weight lifted. Jack was a good listener, making the odd comment and Lily realised that being here on the loch had given her a different perspective on things, everything didn't seem to matter quite as much.

They sat in companionable silence for a while, each with their own thoughts until the driver of a passing boat called out to Jack in greeting. He waved back in acknowledgement and when he turned back to Lily, the tension she'd sensed from him earlier seem to have evaporated.

His face broke into a sudden smile. 'You hungry?'

Lily responded with a smile of her own. 'I am actually.'

Jack turned his attention to the cool bag and Lily lifted her face to the sun, taking a deep breath. No one had ever done anything like this for her before. Sitting here on the boat with Jack, she was almost frightened to admit to herself just how magical it felt. Like she'd stepped out of herself so that all her usual thoughts and worries seem to scatter in the breeze and for the first time in so long she had allowed herself just to be. She'd been unsure about today but she'd ended up feeling comfortable and relaxed, happy just to sit and talk with him.

Their picnic of French bread, chunks of cheddar and apples was delicious and afterwards when Jack had brought the boat back to the jetty, Lily was almost reluctant to put her feet back on solid ground. As they came ashore, Jack helped her off the boat and with his hands on her waist and her hands on his shoulders, it somehow became a small embrace which had lingered pleasantly and probably longer than was strictly necessary.

Jack looked deep into her eyes. 'Did you enjoy yourself?'

'It's been perfect,' Lily smiled up at him. And that was what terrified her.

Chapter 13

Swimming in the loch was proving to be quite addictive and Lily found herself going every morning. Even in the short time she'd been coming her fellow swimmers didn't feel like strangers, such was the camaraderie amongst them. She was struck by the sense of being together, everyone keeping an eye on each other in the water and it was a nice feeling.

The days were beginning to take a shape, starting with a swim first thing and finishing with a mug of hot chocolate and a book, Misty curled up at the end of the bed. She was beginning to feel the benefits of her healthier lifestyle, sure her skin and eyes appeared brighter, her body feeling that little bit sharper and more energised.

Iris was there every morning, Lily always conscious of her calm and gentle presence and aware of her watchful gaze on her. She saw her now arriving with Angus, clutching her bright yellow bag as usual. Lily waved over to them as she continued with a few warm-up stretches.

Plunging into the icy water was never easy but today more than ever Lily relished the chance to forget everything except not succumbing to hypothermia. In particular she wanted to empty her mind from one thing. And that was Jack Armstrong.

Since the boat trip a couple of days ago he had been creeping into her thoughts on an alarmingly regular basis. The last thing she'd expected was to have her thoughts occupied by a man but that was exactly what was happening.

She sensed something had shifted between them, an understanding that perhaps neither of them was what the other had first thought. Certainly, her first impressions of Jack Armstrong were long banished; to say he wasn't the person she first thought him to be was something of an understatement. She could now see a man comfortable in his own skin, not prepared to be someone he wasn't and someone who cared deeply about his environment. A man who'd been hurt and who she suspected would find it difficult to trust again.

They had opened up to each other and the closer Lily began to feel to Jack, the more she could see she'd never had anything real with James, it had all been in her head. Jack on the other hand, was beginning to feel very real. But that unsettled her, made her feel vulnerable.

While she might be having difficultly ignoring the connection she was feeling to Jack, she knew her real life was in the city. Not only that, but Jack had made it very clear he wasn't looking for anything meaningful so why she was even thinking like this was beyond her. With a deep breath and a final lunge and stretch, she determinedly pushed thoughts of Jack aside and made her way towards the water.

The swim was hard. Lily knew how quickly the weather could change but even so, it was startling just how fast conditions had deteriorated. They all ended up cutting the swim short. Looking forward to a hot drink she moved as fast as her numb fingers would allow. She changed out of her wet gear and layered up, gratefully hugging her jacket tightly around herself. She looked up at the sky, wondering if it was about to rain and then lowered her eyes to the shoreline. Jack and another instructor were bringing a group of children back to the centre, Lily unable to keep her eyes from following his wetsuited form as he passed. So much for emptying her mind of him.

He drew closer and their eyes met when a sudden commotion made them turn their heads in unison. It was difficult to see properly but in the distance someone appeared to be waving a paddle in the air, their kayak capsized beside them. The man was gripping onto the side but his body kept being buffeted by small waves.

Everything seemed to happen all at once. Lily heard Jack curse under his breath before he sprinted off. He swallowed up the distance easily, showing the sheer athleticism of his body and within seconds he'd reached the man. It became immediately obvious he knew exactly what to do, his training kicking in as he expertly dragged him from the water and back to shore. By this time other staff had arrived, and the man was covered in blankets and being checked over and given a hot drink.

Lily felt relief infiltrate her body and her heart rate settle, only to have it rocket straight back up as she turned to find Iris crouching over a body on the ground.

'Oh no!' she cried, seeing it was Angus

Jack had also seen and immediately ran over, Lily following behind him and dropping to her knees beside Angus who was horribly pale. Her stomach clenched in fear at how vulnerable he suddenly appeared. They helped Angus to sit up and then very slowly helped him to his feet.

'I'm fine,' he declared, looking embarrassed by all the fuss.

Jack was watching the older man carefully. 'You're sure, Angus?'

'I felt a bit faint, that's all. I'm—' He staggered suddenly, Jack catching him just in time.

'Afterdrop?' Jack asked Iris quietly as they carefully lowered Angus back down.

'Probably.'

Lily had heard the term before which basically meant Angus's core temperature was still plummeting and so likely was his blood pressure.

'We've got to get his temperature back up gradually but I'd be much happier if he was checked at the hospital. Jack, will you be able to take him?'

'Of course, it'll be quicker than an ambulance.'

Jack took off and Lily stayed close to Angus while Iris gave him a hot drink from a flask and found more layers to wrap around him. 'Can you go on with Jack and I'll follow in my car?' she asked Lily. 'That way I'll be able to bring Angus home later.'

'Of course.'

Within minutes Jack had pulled up in the Land Rover, as close as he could get and they helped Angus into the seat. Jack was standing at the side, beginning to shiver himself and Lily realised he too was cooling down. He changed quickly, peeling off his wetsuit and grabbing clothes from the vehicle but not before Lily caught sight of his perfectly toned torso. He wrapped a towel round his waist to deal with his bottom half, Lily practically leaping into the Land Rover beside Angus. Given the circumstances it felt wildly inappropriate to be so aware of Jack's body and the effect it seemed to be having on her.

***

Lily considered how you could be in any hospital waiting room in the world and somehow it would look and feel the same. Sterile white walls, the odour of disinfectant and trepidation hovering in the air and the obligatory vending machine sitting in the corner. Garish-coloured plastic seats stood lined in neat rows and despite the oversized clock hanging on the wall, time seemed to stand still.

Jack came over and handed Lily a polystyrene cup. 'Sweet tea.'

He sat down, his bulk spilling over the seat so that she could feel the warmth of his thigh touching hers. She didn't move, the contact was comforting.

'Are you okay?' he asked.

She shrugged. 'Just hospitals, you know.'

131

'Yeah, I do,' he agreed with feeling. 'Never usually a good place to find yourself.'

'Certainly not how I thought the day would turn out.'

He gave a rueful smile. 'The inshore waters are ideal for learning which is great, but you'd be surprised the number of incidents there are. Thankfully none of them usually end up with anything too serious. The guy who fell off his kayak was lucky today, though if he'd been in the water much longer it could have been a different story.'

'And Angus – do you think he'll be okay?'

'I doubt it's anything serious, try not to worry.'

She only wished she could. She sipped her tea, the tepid taste somehow reminding her of all the time she'd spent waiting with her mother for those last hours.

Lily tried not to revisit that time in the hospital. Iris had constantly reassured her that Patty had been happy and laughing right up until the last moment, that there was nothing anyone could have done and that it had only been a matter of time before the bulging blood vessel would rupture. But today, the memories seared painfully into her mind.

It wasn't just the flashbacks of her mum in hospital making her feel so uneasy. It was the realisation of how scared she'd been today. She hadn't known Angus for long but she'd grown fond of him. She looked forward to seeing him at the swimming each morning and to their little chats. She knew it was stupid and pointless but over the last few days she'd even imagined what it would be like to have had him as her father.

Now the thought she might not get the chance to know him properly sent a shudder through her body.

Lily wasn't aware she was trembling until Jack took the cup from her hand. He put it on the floor and took her hand in his. 'You're shaking. Are you warm enough?'

'Yes. It's just – sorry.' She gave her head a small shake. 'Being here reminds me of when my mum was in hospital.'

'You want to talk about it?' he asked gently. His eyes held such sincerity that Lily was suddenly tempted to blurt it all out. To describe to him the darkness of those hours at Patty's bedside which still haunted her. How alone she'd felt and that there were still times she wasn't sure she was really dealing with any of it and that sometimes she was floundering from day to day still trying to come to terms with her death.

But as comfortable as Jack was beginning to make her feel, he was probably only being polite and if she started talking, too much would spill out and he'd get more than he bargained for. No, this wasn't the time or place to lose it. She mustered a small smile, replying, 'It's okay but thanks.'

His eyes stayed on her for a moment as if checking that really was the case and Lily was suddenly grateful to have him beside her. And as she recalled the events from earlier, she reckoned they were all incredibly lucky he'd been by the water earlier and had been so reassuringly in control. 'You were very calm today,' she commented.

He shrugged. 'You get used on high alert, especially with kids about.' He yawned, rubbing a hand tiredly down his face. 'Sorry, early start catching up with me.'

Lily guessed he'd used up a good amount of adrenaline today. His body was undoubtedly fit and healthy, she'd seen plenty evidence of that today. But he appeared exhausted now as he rested his head back against the wall, one hand still holding hers and closing his eyes for a few moments.

Lily watched the rise and fall of his broad chest, tempted to lean against it. Seeing him off-guard only proved how strong he usually looked, always with that air of energy around him and Lily couldn't help thinking about what it would feel like to experience that energy in other ways …

Jack opened his eyes slowly, his gaze lingering on hers for a long moment.

'You tired?' she asked, trying to dispel her previous line of thought although his sleepy eyes weren't exactly helping.

133

He gave her a quick smile, straightening in his seat. 'Yeah, must be. Sorry about that,' he said without releasing her hand.

'No need to apologise,' Lily assured him just as Iris suddenly bustled in through the swing doors. She stopped, tilting her head to the side, her eyes glittering with warmth. 'Now don't you two make a picture?' She smiled at which point they both sprung apart.

'I've just been talking to one of the doctors, he's going to be fine,' she explained lowering herself onto a seat and wincing at the hard seat. 'As we suspected, blood pressure had dropped too low, but he'll be getting out shortly.'

Lily regarded Iris thoughtfully for a moment, her normally placid features etched with strain reminding Lily that no matter how strong and hearty she normally appeared, this morning's events must have given her a fright. The same thought seemed to run through Jack's head and he jumped to his feet. 'Can I get you something, Iris?'

'No thank you dear, not from here. She wrinkled her nose disparagingly in the direction of the vending machine. 'I'll wait until we get home. In fact, I'll take over now, you two can head off.'

Lily felt relief flood through her but she desperately wanted to see Angus, to see with her own eyes that he was okay. 'Actually I'd like to stay if that's all right.'

'Of course it is, sweetheart. Jack, what about you? You've done enough already and you must be needed at the centre?'

Jack checked his watch and then glanced at Lily, appearing almost reluctant to leave. 'You'll get back with Iris, then?'

'Sure.' She nodded. 'And thanks.'

They watched him leave, the waiting room suddenly feeling very empty without him.

'I'd say he's quite taken with you,' Iris stated.

Lily wasn't sure how to respond. It was true his gaze was capable of making her feel as if she was the only person in a hundred miles radius. Whether that meant he was *taken with her* as Iris so quaintly put, she wasn't sure.

She glanced sideways at Iris. 'He told me about the car crash and Adam's wife.'

Iris tutted. 'Such a terrible business. Sometimes I think that's why Jack never stops. Everyone has their own way of dealing with things, I suppose. He's a good man, you know.' She sighed, sounding wistful. 'And I saw the way he looked at you.'

Lily made an odd little sound. Perhaps she was feeling a certain chemistry between them but she'd made a massive mistake with James, misread the signals so badly and she wasn't about to let that happen again. Besides, Jack had made it clear he wasn't looking for anything. And that suited her because neither was she.

'He was pretty amazing today,' Lily conceded. But that was as far as she was prepared to go. Any more and she'd be in danger of giving Iris false hope of a burgeoning romance which simply wasn't going to happen. If she was lucky, one day she might find love. But if she didn't find it, then that was fine too. Look at Iris, she was happy and as far as she knew, single.

'What about you, Iris – do you miss not being married?'

'Goodness, no,' she laughed. 'Three times was enough for me but I'm not a cynic, I'm still a romantic at heart, still believe in love. And I'm on good terms with all my exes. But I have everything I need now. I'm always busy and I have my friends – good friends.'

Lily distracted herself for a moment watching a young child – totally oblivious to his environment and his mother's reprimands – race around and interweave his small body between the chairs. To him, it was all an adventure, a new territory to explore. To Lily, it was somewhere she didn't want to be. She turned to Iris who gave her a knowing look.

'Seems like yesterday, doesn't it?'

The days they had taken turns to sit with Patty were so deeply embedded in both their beings, they didn't need to say anything. Instead, Iris simply laid a hand on Lily's arm.

'My mum and Angus – did you know?' Lily asked quietly after a short while.

'I did.' Iris paused. 'But they were both very discreet about it. I think Patty quite liked the idea of it being a secret liaison even though there was no reason for it to be.'

Lily shook her head with a watery smile, it sounded so like Patty. Just then, a nurse came in to let them know Angus was ready to leave. Lily was unbelievably happy to see Angus back on his feet and looking so much better. They made their way slowly to the car park and all three of them bundled into Iris's small car.

As they approached the cottages where Iris and Angus both lived, Lily looked out in the direction of the old caravan park where she'd stayed for all those summers. Her mouth fell open in shock – was that actually the same place?

Iris let out a little laugh, seeing her expression. 'Oh yes, it's all changed now. It's got eco-cabins and chalets as well as five-star caravans. There's a café and a small grocery shop, and the play-park's all been fitted out – there's even crazy golf.'

Times really had changed in Carroch, Lily thought as Iris pulled up outside her cottage.

'I can go to my own home,' Angus said as Lily helped him to lever his large frame out of the car.

'You'll do no such thing,' Iris admonished, already leading the way up the garden path and through the front door which was framed with roses. Like Patty, she had green fingers. That was how the two women had first met. On their way back to the campsite one day, Lily's mother had stopped to admire the beautiful flowers in Iris's front garden. Iris had been happy to stop her pruning and dead-heading to chat and the lifelong friendship had been formed.

Like Aladdin's cave, Iris's cottage was pretty much as Lily

remembered, only busier if that was possible. Iris ushered them through to the back room which served as kitchen and living room. A low-ceilinged room, the walls were lined with shelves of cookery and gardening books and every conceivable space was taken up by trinkets, ornaments and photographs. An ancient range took up most of one wall and a large, worn, dark-red rug provided some warmth on the stone floor.

Although it wasn't cold, Iris lit the fire and sat Angus down on the armchair, propping cushions behind him and ignoring Angus's pleas to stop fretting over him.

'I'm going to heat some soup,' Iris told them, hanging her coat on the back of the door and swapping it for an apron.

The hospital had sucked any normality out of the day so that Lily wasn't sure what time of day it was, only that she was suddenly famished. 'Can I help?'

Iris waved her offer away. 'You stay with Angus. I'll just check on the chickens and then organise some food, so I'll leave you two for a short while.'

Iris disappeared and Lily joined Angus by the fire who was shaking his head at Iris's retreating figure. 'Feel like an old fool, causing all that fuss,' he muttered.

Lily gave him a small smile. 'Are you feeling all right now?'

'I'm fine now. You mustn't worry about me.'

They sat for a few peaceful moments, the fire crackling between them. Outside the sun was losing its battle against the grey clouds which stubbornly dominated the sky. Lily's thoughts drifted, her body finally beginning to unwind.

Angus seemed content just to sit. He had such a calmness about him and Lily wondered what might be going through his mind, if he was thinking about today and it occurred to her she didn't know if he had family he might want to tell.

'Do you have children Angus?'

'A son in Australia.'

'A long way.'

137

'He's married with three children and they've got a grand life there. Me and my wife, we used to visit them every year or else they'd come here. They manage the trip most years but of course, it's not always easy.'

Lily nodded in understanding as he carried on talking for a while about his son and his family, clearly very proud of them. As she listened, she could see why her mother had liked him. A big, handsome man. Solid and dependable. Was that what her mother had wanted?

'Do you mind if I ask you something, Angus?' she asked tentatively.

'Of course, absolutely.' If anything, he sounded eager to talk.

'Well, I know this might sound a strange question ...' She paused taking a little breath. 'But do you think my mother was happy?'

Angus stayed very still, his grey eyes soft and warm as they regarded her.

'I don't think it's a strange question at all. Whenever we lose someone close to us, we always seek reassurance that they were happy.' He seemed to consider his next words carefully. 'But I can understand why you might ask that about Patty in particular.'

'You can?'

He leant forward slightly, his large hands lying on his lap.

'I had never met anyone like Patty before. We grew close but it took me a long time to feel like I really knew her or at least at well as anyone could. She never wanted a traditional relationship. We didn't go on dates as such, she insisted on that. Just walks, the odd shared meal. But we would talk for hours and hour.' He stared into the fire, his eyes far away for a moment.

'I used to think of her as a butterfly, flitting from one thing to the next, never settling. If you were lucky you'd capture her attention for a while and then it was like the sun coming out after a long cold winter.'

Lily sat back with a sharp intake of breath hearing Angus express so succinctly and eloquently what she'd so often felt.

'She was one of those rare true free spirits,' he said. 'In one way she was complex but in another way she was wonderfully simple. She had this philosophy – you know, a sort of seize the day thing. She was good for me.' Unshed tears glistened in his eyes and Lily suspected that for a man like Angus, tears didn't come often or easily. 'I'm simply grateful that I knew her.'

Lily listened, soaking up every word. Since arriving in Carroch, she felt as if she'd been piecing together her mother's life. Although she'd been reassured she'd been surrounded by friends and had been making plans for the future, Lily still felt there were unanswered questions and something about Angus told Lily he perhaps knew Patty better than most. The last thing she wanted was to sound self-pitying but Angus's perception gave her the courage to say out loud the thoughts that until now had only ever circled uncomfortably in her own head.

'Sometimes everything feels so horribly unfinished with her. As if we were still to have all these conversations and everything would start to make sense,' she told him. 'I did all the things most parents would want. I behaved, I did my homework. I went to university. But there was always this feeling that somehow it wasn't quite right. Do you know she actually looked horrified the day I told her I was going to university?' She shook her head, blinking. 'I'm not sure I'll ever understand her.'

'Maybe you don't have to understand her. Your relationship with her might not have been like most peoples but that doesn't make it bad or wrong.'

Lily waited a few moments. 'Did she ever mention my father to you?'

'No.' Angus shook his head. 'She talked about you though.'

'She did?'

'Probably more than you would ever think. She told me about your career and how hard you worked.' Angus paused. 'She hoped one day you might take over the shop, thought you'd be a natural at it'

'The gift shop?' Lily was amazed.

'I think she wanted the shop to be something for you both, something for her to build for you in the future. It was her way of showing she cared about and loved you.' He took a breath. 'You know, I don't think Patty would mind me saying that there were certain things in life she regretted or wished she'd done differently.'

Lily had never associated her mother as someone who had regrets but of course she did. She was human. Her mother hadn't been perfect and neither was she. Lily understood now that her mother had probably rebelled against her ultra-conventional parents while Lily had gone the other way, seeking stability and security against her relaxed upbringing.

'You know Lily, she might not always have been able to show it, but the love between you was always there and always will be.'

Lily bit down on her lip, tears welling in her eyes.

Angus reached over and patted her hand. 'I want you to know I'll be here and you can always talk to me, Lily. Sometimes things don't seem quite so bad when you say them out loud.'

'You're right,' Lily sniffed. 'And thank you.'

Sitting there, Lily felt as though a warm comforting blanket had been put around her. She might not have not known her own father but she knew now it didn't matter. Family came in many guises and it was the people around you that mattered. Knowing Angus was there felt like being surrounded by a warming, comforting blanket.

Lily looked to him now, seeking guidance. 'Do you think it's time we scattered Mum's ashes?' It was important to her that he thought it was the right time to do it.

He nodded, a hint of sadness momentarily shading his features. 'As long as you feel ready, then yes. We can do it with Iris whenever you want, just say the word.'

Angus sat back, his expression lightening. 'Do you know I asked her to marry me several times?' The merriment dancing in his eyes suggested the proposals had been made in the spirit in which he'd known they'd be received. He chuckled, shaking his head. 'But she was having none of it.'

'Sounds like Mum,' Lily laughed with a small sob.

Lily laughed, tears of relief, grief and love merging into one as they trickled down her face. She wiped them away with the back of her hand just as Iris returned, the aroma of homemade vegetable soup wafting in behind her. She took one look at Lily and Angus and tutted. 'For goodness' sake, I leave you alone for a few minutes and look at you both!'

Lily and Angus exchanged glances and burst out laughing.

Chapter 14

When Lily told Iris and Angus she intended to open the shop they'd both insisted on being there. 'In the capacity of lending moral support,' Iris told her. Lily looked at them fondly now, Iris bustling around Angus and burrowing in her omnipresent yellow bag for goodness what and she felt a swell of gratitude and affection for both of them. Angus rolled his eyes in jest at Lily behind Iris's back.

'Can I make you tea?' she asked him, taking the chance to surreptitiously scrutinise his pallor. She'd missed him at the swimming but understood a few days off was probably wise. Apart from looking slightly pale, she was pleased to see him looking fit and well and despite his protestations for her and Iris to stop fussing, she suspected that secretly he didn't mind a bit.

'No need for tea,' Iris trilled appearing from the hobby room with three glasses set on a tray. 'I've made this especially for today so we could make a little toast,' she announced. 'Homemade ginger beer with a little something special added.'

It wasn't a day for celebration; they were all too painfully aware that this was a day Patty should have been there for. But it still felt significant in some way and so silently they brought their glasses together. Lily took a sip and spluttered, suspecting the something extra was highly alcoholic. Once she'd recovered and with a nod of encouragement from Iris, she turned the sign hanging on the door from closed to open.

Lily's stomach fluttered with nerves and excitement. 'Do you think Mum would have liked it?'

'She would have loved it. And she'd have been proud of you.' She squeezed Lily's shoulder, her voice wavering.

'You know I'd say you've got a real eye for this,' Angus added, swallowing a mouthful of Iris's concoction, his cheeks taking on a sudden ruddy glow.

'You think?' Lily smiled.

'Definitely – look at the place,' Iris exclaimed with an all-encompassing wave of her arms.

Lily took a moment to survey the results of her work over the last few days and had to admit the shop looked amazing. It was like a treasure trove, your eye unable to settle on one thing because there were so many lovely things to look at.

Outside the day was drizzly with grey clouds hanging over the loch but inside everything was lit up and looking wonderful. Lily felt a little lit up herself in some way, having made a special effort with her appearance. She'd chosen a cream blouse and black jeans with heeled boots and a pair of silver dangly earrings.

After years of poring over numbers and being marooned at her desk, Lily had loved getting the shop ready. She'd enjoyed creating the displays, the once empty cabinet and shelves now filled with pottery, scented candles and pewter hip flasks and the selection of silver and enamelled jewellery was now nestling prettily in the backlit glass shelves. Taking centre stage were Beth's oils, lotions and handmade soaps, and knowing it was important to let customers touch and smell them, Lily had laid out a few samplers and tester pots.

All the knowledge she'd absorbed in Bremners had come to the fore so she knew instinctively how she wanted to set out the shop. Immediately inside the front door was a welcoming space to encourage people to come in and let them see everything on offer. Her idea was to create a natural flow, leading customers round the shop and let them move to the things they liked.

Lily had priced all the stock at a reasonable level. It wasn't so much about making profit as getting it all sold. But she marked up the range of Highland Aromatics by a higher margin. Not just in recognition of their quality but she really wanted to be able to pay Beth a good price for them and hopefully show her what she could achieve.

Iris and Angus retreated to the hobby room where it was agreed they would be on standby if Lily needed any help. Angus, she had discovered, was a keen amateur artist and so had brought along his sketchbook and pencils and she watch him settle himself at the table by the window to make use of the natural light. Lily's imagination very unhelpfully shot into overdrive suddenly envisaging all the other uses for the room – art classes, kid's parties, ceramic workshops, the possibilities were endless. With a little shake, she stopped herself. She wouldn't be here so why even think like that.

All Lily could do now was wait and she paced around nervously. She had absolutely no idea what to expect, how busy it would be or if they'd even have any customers at all. Acutely aware the shop had no name above its door, the words *The Shop with No Name* kept swimming around her head.

She knew from Bremners, it was all about getting people through the door and that a window display was one of the most powerful ways of drawing people in. So in a bid to make the shop appear inviting, she'd strung some fairy lights in the windows and bought a couple of hanging flower baskets which Jack – always willing and able with his toolbox – had helped her to put up. Iris had provided some small wicker baskets which she'd filled with soaps and some empty boxes wrapped in sparkling paper had provided makeshift displays for the some of the other items.

As it happened, she didn't have long to wait. Within minutes the bell above the door jingled and the first customers stepped in. A middle-aged American couple, blissfully unaware their every move was being discreetly monitored by Lily trying to gauge their reaction, were curious as to what they might buy.

After several minutes and much to Lily's delight, they appeared at the counter with their selected goods which included a small glass paperweight and a hip flask engraved with a thistle design which they declared would make perfect gifts to take back to the States. Lily had been practising her gift-wrapping skills and felt a small glow of satisfaction as she handed over their prettily packaged purchases and waved them off.

After that, there was a steady trickle of customers. Mostly they were tourists but also a smattering of locals, some quite brazen about not wanting to buy anything and only wanting a good nose around. Lily didn't mind in the least, especially when they all seemed to have known her mother and were keen to introduce themselves.

Being at the counter was a totally new experience for Lily and initially she was hesitant. But after the first few customers she started to relax, finding herself enjoying each little transaction and exchanging pleasantries. She soon realised the need for local knowledge when it felt like every tourist had a question about bus times, the weather forecast or the best place to eat and Iris was called upon several times to impart her expertise. Knowing Iris and Angus were on hand had made all the difference and Lily had loved having them there as much as they seemed to enjoy being there.

Lily had spent time waitressing as a student and it had always surprised her how ready and willing people were to complain. But everyone had seemed relaxed and happy to spend time browsing and chatting, almost as if something about the shop seem to bring out the best in people. Either that or the incense sticks Iris had been burning all day really were having an effect.

Whereas Lily had begun the day considering the stock in terms of items to be sold, as the day drew to a close she began to appreciate them as gifts with meaning behind them. She was surprised how readily customers shared the reason behind their purchase; a scarf for a friend recovering from illness, a pair of silver earrings for a grand-daughter's birthday. A newlywed couple en-route to their honeymoon at a remote castle, looking deliri-ously happy and loved up, had chosen a few body oils. Lily had wrapped them extra specially and had waved them off wistfully, her mind suddenly alight with the idea of honeymoon gift sets. She'd been doing a bit of research herself on the oils in case of questions, discovering rosewood, jasmine and rosewood were known to have Aphrodisiac properties.

She mentioned the idea to Beth when much to her delight she came into the shop during the afternoon. Beth listened, her eyes sparkling and then revealed an idea of her own.

'I've been thinking a lot about what you said. I thought maybe it was time I gave things a real go with Highland Aromatics, look for more opportunities. So, I've arranged a meeting with the owners at the estate to see about supplying the holiday cottages with my range.'

She looked at Lily expectantly. There was a brightness in her eyes Lily hadn't seen before. Almost as if she was beginning to blossom in some way, find a new courage and confidence. Lily told her she thought it was a fantastic idea and had watched her go, amazed at the difference in the other woman.

By the end of the day, any doubts about opening had been banished. Patty had never been far from her mind and Lily felt sadness ripple through her that her mother wouldn't have the chance to live the life she was planning. Yesterday, she had gone with Iris and Angus and together they had finally scattered Patty's ashes. It had been a beautiful day with only a few wispy clouds high in the sky. They'd taken the urn close to the water's edge and gently released the ashes, letting them be blown away by the breeze and dispersed over the water. It had felt right and now her mother was at one with her beloved loch.

Now she could only hope she'd be pleased with today. Lily wasn't one for fanciful notions but as she locked the shop door, she felt comforted that she could feel her mother's presence more than ever.

***

'Fancy a drink?'

Jack held up a couple bottles of beers and Lily lifted her eyebrows at him with a smile. As if she was going to say no.

She started the ritual of emptying the till and tidying up, wondering where the time had gone. She could hardly believe the shop had been open for four weeks. This morning the air had been crisp and crystal clear and the water excruciatingly cold when she'd gone for her swim, reminding her that autumn was here and winter on its way. The days were shortening, the colours slowly turning to reds and golden-yellows, the sun blazing like a burnt orange low in the sky.

Earlier there'd been a small surge of customers when a busload of tourists had stopped in the village. Lily tidied and refolded the cashmere scarves, noticing there weren't many left. It wasn't just the scarves, all the stock was selling. Beth's products were almost finished, even with the new batch she'd brought in last week. She ran her hand over the cashmere, feeling its softness.

The thought that the stock was almost all sold made her feel uneasy in some way. What would she do when everything was sold? There would be no reason for her to stay. A proprietary feeling was growing within her, the thought of selling the shop and the little flat beginning to sit uncomfortably with her. She never thought she'd allow herself to be sentimental about the shop but suspected that's exactly what was she feeling. Once the shop was sold, every physical attachment to her mum would be gone forever and the thought of someone else moving in panicked her.

The days had slipped into a routine and most evenings after Lily closed the shop Jack appeared. A couple of times he'd brought some food from the café at the centre for them to share and they would sit and chat for a while, tentatively discovering more about one another. She had started to look forward to this time of day, becoming used to his company and feeling comfortable with him.

Sometimes he didn't stay long if he had something on at the activity centre but always long enough to make her grateful for his company and feel a pang of regret when he left. When she returned alone upstairs she would feel restless. It was becoming more and more difficult to say good night, their goodbyes becoming longer and more lingering.

'You should have one.' Jack's deep voice drifted over her shoulder now.

Lily jumped. 'What?'

'One of the scarves,' he said, appearing at her side. 'What's your favourite colour?'

Lily narrowed her eyes, thinking. She'd never given it much thought and no one had ever asked her before.

'Um, green I think. What about you?'

'Purple.'

She giggled. 'Purple?'

'What's wrong with purple?' he huffed, trying to sound offended. He lifted a scarf, holding it loosely against her cheek. 'You'd suit this one,' he said in a low voice, their eyes meeting. 'It would go with your eyes.'

Lily suddenly felt too aware of him, her pulse quickening. Their bodies seem to draw closer and the air between them suddenly felt heavy. Lily looked away quickly, flustered. 'Maybe I will,' she said lightly, turning from him. 'Is that beer open yet?'

He stood still for a moment then shot her a quick smile. 'Sure is.' He went through to the hobby room, dropping himself onto a chair and patting the seat beside him. 'Come and have a seat, I've got something for you.'

Grateful to get off her now slightly weak-feeling legs Lily sat next to him, taking the bottle he had opened for her. She swallowed a mouthful, her heart rate beginning to settle.

'Hope you're hungry,' Jack said, lifting the lid from a food container.

Lily held back her hair, leaning forward to see a rustic-looking pie made with golden flaky pastry. The most delicious savoury smell wafted its way to her nose, making her stomach rumble.

'What do you think?' he asked her eagerly.

'Looks great, where'd you get it?'

'Made it myself.' He grinned, looking pleased with himself.

'You made this?'

'Try not to sound so shocked.'

'Sorry, I just think – I mean, I wasn't …' She shook her head. 'I just wasn't expecting it.'

Lily felt her grip on the cold bottle tighten. The thing was, she wasn't used to any of this. She was used to living alone and now she felt suddenly as if she had been alone for a long time. Jack was in very real danger of making her feel special and that was something she didn't know quite how to handle.

She blinked, focusing back on Jack who was now handing her a wedge of the pie which had already been cut into slices. He'd even brought a few paper napkins.

'Susan at the activity centre café quite often gives me the leftovers – don't worry, they're not out of date or anything. She gave me some salmon so I rustled up this little pie for you.'

'Well, thank you, I can't wait to taste it.'

Lily was surprised at just how good it was. 'It's really tasty,' she said appreciatively. 'A man who can make pastry – impressive.'

'A man of many talents, that's me.' He winked, biting into his own slice.

'So who taught you to cook?' Lily asked.

'Myself. It was either that or risk having my mother come round with food all the time.'

'She worries you don't eat?' Lily really couldn't imagine a more healthy-looking male specimen and her eyes rolled appreciatively over Jack's body, her face reddening when she realised Jack had seen her eye-sweep.

'What can I say? She's overprotective.' Se shrugged breezily.

'Did your mum teach you to cook?' he asked.

'Not really, she didn't tend to cook much herself.' Lily brushed a little crumb from her lips, changing the subject. 'So how was your day?'

Jack lifted his bottle from the table, fixing her with a look before replying.

'Great. Well, apart from the two lads who thought it was a good idea to have a sword fight with the canoe paddles and one of them ended up with a busted lip.' He smiled with a shake of his head.

'Ouch!' Lily laughed. It was always the same, she thought. Whenever she asked about his day was, the response was always positive. She tilted her head asking, 'Don't you ever have a bad day?'

He took a slug of beer. 'Of course. But I try not to dwell on it. Suppose I've learnt not to stress the small stuff – at the end of the day most things aren't that important.'

Lily envied him his easygoing attitude. Although admittedly the last few days she had started to feel less restless and uptight than usual. As working days went, a day in the shop couldn't be more different from what she was used to. And at first, she had missed the routine of her old job, remembered how adrift she'd felt without it. But here, there were never any deadlines or rushing, as if all those months spent hunched over a desk she could begin to feel herself unfurling in some way.

'How was the shop today?' Jack asked in turn.

'Knitting club was this morning,' she replied, her voice warm.

It had become her favourite time of the week listening to their chat and laughter.

He gave her a look. 'Sounds like you're enjoying the shop.'

'I am,' she responded truthfully. 'I loved my job as an accountant but I'll admit I'm surprised just how much I've enjoyed the gift shop being open.'

'And not a spreadsheet in sight?'

'Not strictly true,' she countered finishing her last mouthful of pie. 'Couldn't help myself really, just to keep track of everything. Even managed to make a decent little profit,' she told him, not without a certain amount of pride. But the thing she'd delighted in the most was being able to pay Beth.

Lily stretched over to take a napkin at the exact moment Jack reached for his bottle, her fingers brushing against his forearm. 'Oops, sorry,' she murmured, every one of her nerve endings tingling at the touch of his skin. The air between them suddenly supercharged again and Jack's gaze locked with hers.

Lily could hardly believe it when just at that very moment her phone vibrated into life. They both turned to look at her phone which was on the table, Lily not knowing if she was relieved or not. She frowned at the number, mouthing to Jack she'd need to take it before hitting the accept button. Smoothing down her hair, she put the phone to her ear. 'Hello.'

Lily listened for a few moments, standing up to grab a pen and paper to scribble down a few details and then hung up, her heart thumping. Jack lifted a questioning eyebrow.

'It was one of the recruitment agencies I registered with. I've got an interview.'

There was a silence. Lily couldn't work out what she was feeling but it felt equivalent to having a bucket of cold water thrown over her. This was what she wanted, she told herself. But for some reason a small lump of dread seemed to have lodged itself in her chest.

The room had darkened suddenly and rain pattered against

the window. More for something to do, Lily went over and switched on the lamp, a soft light illuminating the room. She turned, avoiding Jack's eyes but could feel his gaze on her.

'What's the job?'

She cleared her throat. 'A financial company, just the usual accountancy stuff I should imagine.'

'So … that's good, right?'

Lily swallowed, feeling a stab of disappointment she couldn't understand. 'Yes. Yes, of course,' she said over-brightly. It was good, wasn't it?

She remembered how devastated she'd been after her redundancy and an inner voice was telling her it would be good to be back out there again. So why then did she feel confusion rain down on her?

The truth was that for the last few days she had found herself dipping in and out of a daydream about staying in Carroch but the call from the recruitment agency had just crash-landed into that little fantasy. A job would mean leaving here and she wasn't sure how that made her feel.

So much about the past few weeks had been unexpected and good and when she was with Jack, the attraction was undeniable. She felt as if her body was waking from a long sleep and the desire she was beginning to feel for him was difficult to ignore. A few minutes ago, she'd wanted to kiss Jack so badly, to feel him kiss her back. But if they had, then what would have happened? Hadn't he made it clear he was looking for a relationship? Warning bells were beginning to sound in her head. Maybe that call had come at just the right moment.

She turned to him now to find his eyes on her, his expression unreadable. Never had Lily been so glad to see Misty stroll into the room and she shuffled onto the edge of her seat, bending to stroke her.

'So when is it?'

'Day after tomorrow in Edinburgh.' An awkward sound came

from her, somewhere between a laugh and a sob. 'They sounded pretty keen.'

The mood had shifted and the silence between them thickened, Lily desperately wanting to say something but didn't know what.

'I'm pleased for you then,' Jack said eventually.

Bored, Misty sauntered off to investigate under the table. Lily moved too and was treated to a wave of light-headedness as stood up. Jack was by her side in an instant, his hand on her arm and the concern on his face only succeeding in making her feel worse. Suddenly all her confusion weighed too heavily on her mind. She needed to be on her own to try and untangle her messy thoughts. 'I'm fine,' she said abruptly. 'Just a bit tired, actually. I should probably think about an early night.'

Jack gave her a look, his voice flat. 'Of course.'

She locked the door behind him, turning to the emptiness and not understanding why she felt so low.

Chapter 15

Lily sat slouched on the stool behind the counter. She drummed her fingers on the counter and let out a sigh, possibly the hundredth of the day. Last night she'd hardly slept, her body tossing and turning almost as much as her mind resulting in a thumping headache which had stubbornly stayed all day.

She wasn't even sure why she'd opened the shop today. There was hardly any stock left now and it was all beginning to look a bit sad. Nor was she really feeling in any fit state to deal with customers. Not that it mattered – there hadn't been a single one anyway. Wisely, most people appeared to be staying indoors. Outside a storm seem to be brewing on the horizon, the sky and loch merging into one menacing mass of darkness.

Logically she knew there was no reason to open anymore but some invisible thread had pulled her down to the shop this morning. Perhaps it had been to keep her thoughts at bay or perhaps it was because usually being in the shop made her feel better in some way although that certainly wasn't the case today.

With something of an effort, she hauled herself to her feet and locked the door, turning the sign to 'closed'. She rested her head on the pane of glass for a few moments, staring out. The wind had picked up, whipping up small white peaks on the water and the rain was lashing against the window. For now all she wanted was to go upstairs, to the cosiness of the little flat, the feeling of being cossetted by it.

She turned away from the window, catching the delicate herbal aroma from the Highland Aromatics oils. Her eyes travelled to the shelf where there were only a couple of bottles remaining of Beth's oils. Perhaps a bath would be a good idea she thought. She picked up the geranium and rose bath oil – perfect for uplifting mood and spirits, the label promised. How could it possibly fail to work when it sounded so wonderful?

The roll-top bath seem to take an age to fill but after several long minutes, Lily finally sank gratefully into the hot water. She closed her eyes and leaned her head back, breathing in the aroma and allowing the oils to infuse her body. It felt utterly blissful.

The interview had been yesterday. It had been exhausting but she'd made it to Edinburgh and back in one day. Not wanting to leave Misty alone overnight, she'd left out enough food and then crept out to the waiting taxi, an early morning mist still blanketing the loch.

She'd dozed on and off most of the train journey and even though she'd arrived in Edinburgh after the morning rush hour everything had felt noisy and busy and she'd gone straight to her flat. After a quick chat with Mrs Robertson to collect her mail and make sure there'd been no problems while she'd been away, she'd headed up, opening the windows to let in some air and have a quick check around, something about it all feeling surreal. It all looked familiar yet she felt curiously detached from everything, almost like an imposter in someone else's home.

She'd dressed for the interview and examined her reflection in the mirror. Dark navy suit and cream tie-neck blouse. Heels and hair pulled into a neat chignon. It was like looking at her old self. This was the moment she'd anticipated but now that it was here, there was an inexplicable hollowness to it. Something had changed and she wasn't sure she saw the same person staring back at her anymore.

She'd smoothed down her skirt and brushed away an imaginary fleck from her shoulder and then with a measured breath and a final look in the mirror, she'd left. She'd quickly scanned the notes on her phone again. The offices of Abecon Financial Services were on the fourth floor of an office block a little distance from the city centre, she'd need to get a move on.

And then it was all over. Before she knew it, she was back on the train gazing out of the window as it trundled its way out of the station and making its way over the Forth Bridge to join the Highland line towards Inverness.

It had been a long tiring day, but Lily didn't realise how much it must have taken out of her until she felt herself falling asleep now in the bath. She peeled open her eyes, aware the water was rapidly cooling and she was in danger of emerging looking more like a wrinkled prune than the sleek mermaid-like creature she had envisaged.

Lifting herself out of the bath, she patted herself dry, her skin feeling sumptuously smooth. Her headache had subsided and she felt marginally better but she still felt a bit off.

In the kitchen she rummaged in the cupboard for something to eat, not sure she was really that hungry. Reaching for a tin of soup she spotted Iris's herbal remedy that she'd brought round the first day. Hadn't she said it was for an off-day? Deciding today definitely fell into that category, she knocked back a couple of mouthfuls. The taste left a bit to be desired but Lily knew any of Iris's remedies wouldn't do her any harm.

She finished her soup and washed up, wandering aimlessly around the flat as if she was looking for something. Even the flat didn't seem to be working its magic; something didn't feel quite right but she couldn't put her finger on it, a feeling that something was missing.

Pacing up and down Lily stopped suddenly, taking in a sharp

intake of breath. Misty – where was she? She felt a prickle of alarm. She hadn't seen her since the morning. She called out her name, running down to check the shop in case she'd somehow become stuck somewhere. But a search of all her favourite cubby holes proved fruitless.

It was only now Lily appreciated how much she'd become used Misty's presence, the way she silently padded around and – when she wasn't being too haughty – was quite often prepared to be stroked. If Misty wasn't inside, then it could only mean one thing and Lily really didn't like the idea of her being outside on a night like this. What was she going to do now? She certainly couldn't curl up and relax knowing Misty was out there. There was only one thing for it, she'd have to go and look for her.

After throwing on a jacket and trainers, Lily set out with a feeling of hopelessness and no idea how you went about finding a cat. It wasn't like a dog you could whistle for. Instead she attempted a few token *pssst* sounds between her teeth, hoping that somehow that would somehow summon Misty.

She started close to the house then ventured further, crossing the road. She couldn't see much, the visibility was so poor, but her eyes scanned up and down, hoping she might make the distinctive little patch of white fur on Misty's chest. Even then she knew there was a slim chance of finding her.

Scotland's bountiful rainfall might keep its lochs overflowing and flourishing but tonight it was the reason Lily was drenched within seconds. The rain had suddenly become heavier and she was woefully unprepared for her mission, her torch phone not making much impact on the darkness. The deluge was relentless, battering onto the ground and now the wind had strengthened too. The ground felt sodden beneath her once-white trainers which squelched with each step she took.

She kept on, heading down towards the loch. She remembered Jack telling her Misty very occasionally went to his place and her feet were already taking her in the direction of his house because realistically – and hopefully – she knew that's where Misty might be. And as much as she didn't fancy just turning up unannounced at Jack's, her concern for the cat outweighed her own qualms.

Wishing she'd put on more sensible footwear she trudged towards Jack's, her eyes squinting against the rain until she could make out the house that until now she'd only seen from a distance. Set amongst trees with its own small pebble beach leading down to the loch, it was as close as you could get to the water and despite the circumstances and the foul weather, some part of Lily's brain registered what an amazing spot to live, the views must be incredible.

Drawing closer though, she could see it was ramshackle, clearly still needing work done. But there was one light on, a warm glow coming from a downstairs window. Shivering, wet and miserable, her exasperation at the situation made her hammer on the door with perhaps more force than strictly necessary. Still, at least Jack had heard because a few seconds later the door was answered.

Jack opened the door, a look of puzzlement quickly replaced by one of a concern as he looped a hand under her arm, propelling her in. As she stepped into the warmth, her body suddenly started to tremble, her teeth chattering.

'God Lily, what are you doing out in that?'

He was wearing low-slung jogging bottoms and a snug fitting black T-shirt that showed off his physique, a towel round his neck which he had clearly just used to rub his damp and dishevelled hair. Lily felt her body tremble for a whole different reason now and didn't like to think what she must look like, pretty sure her plastered hair wasn't doing her any favours.

'It's Misty,' she stammered. 'I can't find her.'

'Ah, right – she's here. I only came home myself a few minutes ago and found her on my doorstep.'

'Oh, thank goodness.' For someone who thought she didn't care much for cats, Lily was inordinately relieved to know Misty was safe.

'She was soaked,' said Jack. 'She must have been out for a good while.'

Lily's face crumpled. 'Oh no. She never usually goes out and I didn't notice she was missing until a few minutes ago.'

'She's fine, she's sitting by the fire. Right now, I'm more concerned about you.'

Lily looked down to the floor where she'd managed to create a small puddle on the floor, her trainers now sporting more of a mud splattered look. 'Sorry, I've made a mess of your floor.'

'Seriously? Come on, let's get your jacket and shoes off for a start,' he said crouching down.

Her socks and trainers seem to be welded onto her feet. Jack had to wiggle them side to side to ease them off. By now Lily too miserable to feel self-conscious or embarrassed by the fact that he was holding her bare foot in his hand as he peeled off her socks.

A sudden gust of wind roared from outside, howling through the house and Lily gasped, her eyes widening in fright.

'Don't worry, the roof's only blown off once.'

She met his twinkling gaze, not sure if he was serious or not.

Jack disappeared for a moment, returning with a fresh, warm towel which Lily took and began to dry herself off, grateful that her jacket had managed to protect most of her body.

'Thanks,' she said.

'Come through,' Jack urged, taking her by the elbow. 'Still very much a work in progress,' he explained, guiding her through the hall which had clearly not been touched decoratively in years. Lily had never decorated a house from scratch herself but would love to one day and she wondered what Jack's taste would be like. Not that he appeared to have got round to doing much if the peeling wallpaper and bare lightbulb hanging from the hall ceiling was anything to go by.

But when she followed Jack into the front room, Lily was amazed to find one of the loveliest rooms she'd ever seen and not what she'd been expecting at all. The walls were painted the palest shade of grey with two large slouchy blue-grey sofas sitting either side of a cast-iron fireplace. One wall was taken up with a large bookshelf and the floorboards had been beautifully restored.

And there, sitting in prime position on a rug in front of the roaring fire, was Misty. Lily could hear her purring from here. She went over to greet her, rolling her eyes when she was totally ignored. 'And to think I was worried about you,' she huffed good-naturedly, stroking her ear.

'A law unto themselves, cats are,' Jack said following her into the room.

Lily straightened up, gesturing a hand round the room. 'It's really nice,' she said. 'Stunning, in fact.'

'Thanks, although I can't take all the credit. My sisters are responsible for all the colour and stylish bits – I wouldn't have had a clue where to start with any of that. I wanted to do the kitchen first but they assured me the living room was the place to start in case I ever brought a—' He stopped suddenly, looking down for a moment and raking a hand through his hair.

'A girlfriend?' Lily guessed with a smile although the thought caused a little stab of disappointment.

'I told them it wasn't going to happen but they insisted anyway.' He shrugged with a lopsided smile. 'And actually you're the first.' He stopped again, realising what he'd just said. 'Not girlfriend I mean. Person. Who happens to be a girl. That's been here.'

He shook his head with such a pained expression, Lily couldn't help laughing at his uncharacteristic bashfulness. 'I know what you mean. And your sisters clearly have good taste.'

'I'll tell them you like it, they'll be pleased. I'll, er, get something for us. Are you hungry?'

'Not really. I had something earlier.'

'I'll get us a drink, then. Make yourself comfortable.' He indicated with his hand around the room.

Left alone, Lily wandered over to the window trying to imagine Jack living here. It suited him, being so close to the loch. Almost as if it was part of who he was. Outside was dark, the rain still heavy and Lily could hear the wind buffeting against the trees. She turned with a little shiver, still feeling a little damp.

She went to one of the sofas, glancing at the half-finished cup of coffee and upturned book sitting on the low, dark wooden coffee table. She sat down just as Jack returned. He placed a bottle on the sideboard and then joined Lily on the sofa, handing her a glass. 'This'll heat you up,' he said.

'Thanks.' Lily looked at the small measure of amber liquid and took a precautionary sniff, the fumes hitting the back of her throat and her making her eyes water. 'What is it?' she blinked.

'Whisky of course, one of Dallochmore's best bottles. Cheers.' He clinked his glass against hers.

'Cheers,' Lily echoed, taking a small sip. Once she got over the initial shock, it went down quite smoothly.

'Welcome to my home, such as it is.'

Home, thought Lily, sinking back further into the comfy sofa. Such a safe solid word. 'You've lived her a few years, you said?'

'Yeah,' he said with a rueful smile. 'And long enough to have done more work.'

'You're doing it all by yourself?'

He nodded. 'Mostly. But I'm in no hurry, I'm not going anywhere. My brother comes and helps me when he has time.'

'That's nice.'

'Yeah, it is. Apart from when he mistook my arm for a piece of wood and almost amputated it and we had to take an unexpected detour to the hospital – that wasn't very helpful.'

Lily let out a small gasp as he lifted his arm to reveal a jagged silvery line running along his forearm. The thought he could have been seriously hurt disturbed her more than she'd have imagined. Without thinking she reached over, her fingers tracing

161

the scar tissue angrily snaking its way along his flesh. She lifted her eyes to find his gaze on her.

She snatched her hand away, feeling her face flare with heat. 'Looks quite nasty.'

'I'll live. Although sometimes I'm not sure if he and my sisters are more of a hindrance or a help.'

Despite his grumblings Lily heard the warmth and affection in his voice and had little doubt they were a strong, loving family who looked out for each other. She stared into her glass. She had no idea what it was like to have siblings, annoying or otherwise, but imagined it to be lovely. A small silence ensued and when she looked up, Jack's eyes were on her.

He hesitated for a second and then spoke. 'So how did your interview go?'

Lily put down her glass, her spine stiffening. She'd started to relax, feeling better than she had all day. Now she knew where Misty was and being here in this lovely room with Jack, she finally seemed to have shaken off that black cloud that had been following her around all day. Thinking about the interview made it loom large again.

Even now, twenty-four hours later she had trouble getting her head around the way it had unfolded. She'd got the shock of her life when she'd turned up at the interview to discover James there. It turned out Abecon Financial Services was a subsidiary of Dunn Equity, set up to focus specifically on small to medium size businesses.

Recruiting for its management team, James had seen Lily's name on the list of suitable candidates registered with the recruitment agency and had asked them to call her immediately. After being used and unceremoniously dumped, she didn't see why she should listen to anything he had to say and had almost walked out there and then. But even though she'd hated herself for doing it, some compulsion had made her stay to hear him out.

It hadn't been so much an interview as an informal chat. James had been at his persuasive best, assuring Lily he'd done everything to try and save her job at Bremners. 'You know the way these things work, my hands were tied. I always hoped we'd get a chance to work in the future again. As it turns out, I'd like to offer you something I think you'll be very interested in.'

She'd looked across the desk at James dispassionately. Now she could see him for what he was. Granted, he was a shrewd businessman but that's where it started and ended. All he'd ever been was a safe option for her. It had been easier to imagine there was something between them than risk the real thing.

Lily had almost gasped out loud when he'd offered her the role of an associate. It was the type of job she'd dreamed of, taking her career to a whole new level. But she knew she wasn't hungry for it the way she once was. A few weeks ago she'd have jumped at the job but things had changed, she had changed. Perhaps sensing her hesitation, James told her he'd be away on business and had insisted she take a few days to think about it.

She couldn't deny she was tempted. Too much of her old instinct had kicked in for her to be able to reject the job outright. All her years of studying at university, passing exams to become chartered and all the hours she's spent at work, it had been impossible for her to dismiss the offer outright.

Since she'd been offered the job she'd felt a bag of conflicting emotions fighting within her and she strongly suspected the main reason for it was the man sitting next to her now. But she had her future to think of and couldn't simply turn her back on her job and the security it provided. Her career mattered to her and she couldn't throw it away because she was attracted to Jack. She couldn't base any decisions on that, not at least without knowing how he felt.

Lily was jolted back to the present, aware Jack was looking at her expectantly. 'Um, it was all right. The job's for a new financial company.'

'Exciting.'

'I guess so.'

Jack watched her over the rim of his glass. 'You don't sound so sure.'

'Oh, you know.' She looked at him, then away again. 'There's a lot to think about. Misty, the shop ...' She took a sip of her dink and put the glass back down with a sigh. The real world had come knocking and she had a decision to make but all she wanted was to sit here in this little bubble with Jack for a bit longer.

'Anyway, I won't really know anything for a few days,' she said evasively, deliberately leaning forward to reach for the book lying on the table. 'What's this you're reading?' she asked holding it up. As a diversion tactic it was fairly blatant but she really didn't want to talk about the interview. She simply wanted to forget everything, at least for tonight. Funnily enough, the whisky seem to be helping with that.

Jack continued to look at her for a moment before turning his attention to the book in Lily's hand. 'It's all about whisky basically – everything from the process of distillation right the through to appreciating all the different styles and brands.'

Lily flicked through a few pages, stopping to read a description of a particular 10-year old single malt. 'It says it tastes like freshly chopped apples, rhubarb and gooseberries.'

Jack listened as Lily flicked another few pages. 'Ah, now I like the sound of this one,' she continued. 'Tastes like wet grass, butter, ginger and brittle toffee.'

'What about the whisky you're drinking – how would you describe it?' Jack challenged her with a half-smile.

She studied her glass for a moment. 'I'm not sure I'd know how to begin.'

'Here, I'll help you,' he said leaning forward holding his own glass. 'First swirl it around a bit. Just notice the colour and then gently breathe in the aroma.'

Lily copied Jack's actions as he went on. 'Most of the flavours you taste are related to smell. Keep your mouth slightly open and you'll realise you're actually tasting the aromas. This lets you get used to it, tells you if it's heavy or light.

'Take a small sip but let it stay in your mouth for a moment and then take a second sip. This time your palette has grown used to the complexity of the spirit and you should begin to notice the overall flavour. Now try to tell me what you can taste.'

Lily closed her eyes, her taste buds trying to evoke the flavour. 'Woody, I think. Or perhaps smoky?'

He nodded. 'I'd agree. You could also say peppery and there's a definite touch of citrus.'

She took another experimental sip. 'Yes, I think I can taste that. Oh, and vanilla?' She sampled another mouthful, beginning to quite enjoy this. Her glass was almost empty now so with a final swig, Lily tipped her head back to finish it off resulting in a rather inelegant coughing fit.

'You might want to slow down,' Jack said looking both alarmed and amused.

'So,' Lily squeaked, patting her chest. 'Are you something of a whisky expert?'

'Not at all.' He pulled a face. 'Thought it might be interesting to do some reading that's all – Adam is hoping to launch a new malt whisky at the distillery at some point.'

'Wow, that's quite ambitious.'

'Not for the faint-hearted, that's for sure,' Jack agreed.

Lily bit her lip deciding to put some of her knowledge to the test. 'A single malt is produced using only malted barley whereas a blended is a blend of two more malt and grain whiskies, is that right?'

Jack nodded, looking impressed. 'That's correct. Most connoisseurs would regard a single malt superior to a blended whisky. And they can certainly command a premium price which is why Adam is keen to give it a go.'

Lily smiled to herself, pleased she was able to talk with at least some understanding about a topic Jack was interested in. 'But it can take a long time before the whisky is actually bottled and ready for sale though?'

Jack's eyebrows lifted in surprise. 'It can take years,' he said. 'But Adam's got a long way to go before that. At the moment his priority is getting the distillery back on track. His father Jock is the nicest man you'll ever meet but well, he's let things slip over the last couple of years and maybe not made all the best business decisions. But it's not been easy for him, he was due to step down and Adam was all set to take over when the car crash happened.'

Jack took a second. 'When Maria died, Adam just couldn't face it and took himself off for a couple of years. After that, I think some of the heart went out of the place. Jock held on until Adam came back but the place has become a bit run down. To be honest we didn't even know if Adam would come back.'

Jack lifted himself from the sofa and went to the sideboard, rolling his shoulders and Lily could see how difficult and raw it still was for him to talk about what had happened. He picked up the bottle and brought it back over.

'But he's back now,' he said in a brighter voice, replenishing their glasses. 'He's got plans for the place and that's why he's so keen to be part of the festival this year. It'll be a chance to showcase the distillery and raise its profile.'

'I guess quite a few local people must depend on the distillery for work too?'

'Quite a few, yes.'

'So tell me more about the event,' Lily prompted.

'There's loads of things. Tours and tastings, masterclasses – even live music. Each distillery is hosting different events over a few days. You can go behind the scenes, see how the distillery works. Let me see, what else is there? I know, do you fancy a bit of speed-dating?'

'Speed-dating?' Lily spluttered.

166

'Yeah, apparently there'll be people from different distilleries and they each get ten minutes with at a table to present their whisky. After you taste it, you score it and choose your favourite.'

'Novel idea,' Lily commented. 'Although I don't think I would ever try speed-dating, for a partner I mean.'

She told Jack about her friend Erin who had tried it once. 'She said there was nothing like making you realise just how long five minutes can last.'

Jack laughed. 'Not my thing either, I have to say. What about a nighttime walk then, how does that sound?'

'Intriguing. What does that involve?'

'You're taken on a guided night time walk through the hills, retracing the steps of whisky smugglers in days gone by. Whisky under the stars, they call it.'

'Sounds romantic.' Lily tilted her head, visions of her and Jack under the stars floating pleasurably into her mind. Where on earth had that come from?

'What about Dallochmore?' she asked clearing her throat. 'What are they doing as part of the festival?'

'There'll be a few masterclasses running throughout the day, tastings and a tour of the distillery obviously. I'll be there to help Adam out with anything I can and my sister Isla, she's really into cooking and she's organised this food and whisky pairing thing so I'll have to go that or I'll be in trouble.'

'That sounds great fun, I'd love to go,' Lily enthused.

'Come with me, if you like,' he said easily. 'It's tomorrow.'

'Really, you're sure?'

'Of course,' he shrugged.

'All right then,' Lily said just as a sudden ferocious gust of wind rattled against the window. Even above the noise of the wind Lily could still hear the rain, making her feel blissfully warm and cosy.

'I'm glad I'm not out in that anymore,' Lily shuddered, sudden goose bumps sweeping over her skin.

Jack looked concerned. 'Are you all dry now? I can get you a blanket if you want?'

'I'm okay, honestly. It's my own fault anyway, I should have put on proper clothes.' She frowned, words from another time filtering into her consciousness. 'I remember my mum used to say there's no such thing as bad weather—'

'—only the wrong clothes,' Jack finished with a grin. 'Very true living here.'

Jack waited a couple of moments and then spoke again, his voice tentative. 'You must miss your mum?'

Lily nodded mutely, the unexpectedness of the question making her throat tighten.

'I'm sorry, I shouldn't have said anything.'

'No, its fine.' She gave her head a little shake, picking at a loose thread on her jumper. 'I miss her very much,' she said simply.

'You never came to see her here in Carroch though?' His voice was gently probing, not judgemental.

Lily glanced down, the usual cocktail of regret and grief swirling uncomfortably around inside her. She and Jack had talked a lot recently, their conversations covering a lot of ground. But Lily had always managed to neatly swerve the topic of her mother and why she hadn't been to Carroch before now. Coming from a family like Jack's, it probably appeared strange to him but she knew now that she wanted to try and explain to him.

Gazing into the fire, she gathered herself. 'You told me once your mum was overprotective? I guess you could say mine was the opposite. I loved her very much – everyone did and that was understandable, she didn't have a bad bone in her body. I'm not sure she had a maternal one either. At least that's what it felt like at times.'

Lily paused. 'We spoke on the phone and she came to see me occasionally in Edinburgh but we didn't live in each other's pockets. She wasn't the type of mum who wanted to know my every move or want me to know hers.'

Jack sat back and took a sip of whisky and with his eyes fixed on her, Lily started to talk. Suddenly it felt imperative to her that Jack understood, and she talked for what seemed a long time as she attempted to explain her relationship with her mother, her rush of words only occasionally punctuated by Jack's occasional comment.

'Then after she died, it all became too painful. My job was full-on which suited me, allowed me to keep putting it off. It was only after I was made redundant that I finally knew I had to come and deal with everything.'

When there was nothing more to say and with all her words spent, Lily curled her legs under herself and looked at Jack, his expression sombre. He laid his hand over hers for a moment. 'I'm so sorry Lily. And that you had to face it all alone.'

Lily gave him a grateful look.

'I used to see Patty and Iris around the village,' Jack remembered. 'Always looked as if they were up to something, always laughing and enjoying life, that's for sure.'

Lily smiled at the image, feeling lifted and lighter in some way. In fact, she was suddenly feeling extraordinarily relaxed. She glanced over at Misty who hadn't budged an inch and was still purring contently; Lily thought she might be beginning to feel the same way herself. The pain in her head from earlier had dulled. Everything had in fact, including her thinking and she thought perhaps the soup hadn't provided much of a lining for her stomach.

Her eye caught a selection of films on one of the shelves. 'That's quite a collection you have there,' she commented.

Jack followed her gaze. 'Yeah, I went through a stage of watching films a lot plus the nearest cinema is a hundred miles away.'

For some reason Lily found this amusing. She had the choice of two cinemas within walking distance of her flat and she giggled asking, 'So do you have a favourite film?'

'Easy. *The Godfather*.'

Lily rolled her eyes. 'What is it with that film? People rave about it and I've never even seen it.'

'You've never seen it?' Jack sounded rather offended. 'Do you want to watch it now?' He jumped up, pleased by the idea. 'There doesn't seem much point in you going back out in that yet.'

'All right then,' she agreed as Jack organised putting the film on and dimming the lights before re-joining Lily.

Lily wasn't sure of the exact moment but at some moment over the next two hours, as her rather woozy brain tried to keep up with the politics, the betrayals and the business-talks, she had fallen asleep, waking up in time for the finale soundtrack to find her head had made its way onto Jack's chest, his arm draped loosely around her shoulder.

With something of an effort she lifted her head, looking aghast. 'Gosh, sorry, I fell asleep. But I was enjoying the film, honestly.'

'Don't worry about it.' Jack was looking at her, a smile on his lips.

Admittedly he didn't seem too perturbed that she'd slept through most of his favourite film, his long legs stretched out in front of him. She flicked her gaze sideways at him, meeting his green eyes. They really were very dreamy. She almost wondered if she was somehow still asleep and in the middle of a dream herself. She gave her head a small shake which proved to be a bad idea, the room momentarily spinning.

Sitting up to the best of her ability, she stifled a yawn and stretched her arms out in front of her. 'I'm just so sleepy for some reason.'

Jack inclined his head towards the almost empty bottle sitting in front of them, raising an eyebrow to indicate that might have something to do with it. 'Perhaps that's why they call it a lullaby in a glass.'

Lily was delighted with this analogy. 'I really didn't expect to like whisky so much.'

'Well, I'm glad you enjoyed it.'

'I really did,' she sighed. 'And it was much nicer than the herbal medicine thing I took.'

'You took medicine?'

She waved away his startled expression. 'Not medicine, just a herbal thing Iris gave me.'

His eyebrows were still furrowed together as he spoke. 'Think perhaps it's time to get you home,' he said, pushing himself up from the sofa. He took Lily's hands and gently pulled her up, the slight roughness of his fingers against her skin feeling worryingly good. She took a moment to steady herself, pretty sure that if Jack let go she would fall backwards.

They were standing very close, so close Lily could feel the heat of his body. She tilted her face up to his, her hands on his chest. Lily wasn't sure exactly who moved first but somehow their lips met for the briefest moment and then Jack pulled back and looked at her.

His finger traced her jawline and his gaze dropped to her mouth, then back to her eyes. His body was solid against her and she could feel it respond as they fell into another kiss, this time deeper, more urgent. It had been so long since she'd been in a man's arms and Lily was lost in the moment as their mouths and bodies came together, the muscles on his back beneath her fingers, his hands tangled in her hair …

But just as quickly as they had come together, they broke apart at the sound of a deep throaty rumble coming between them – literally – in the form of Misty purring profusely between their feet. There was a moment of silence, both of them looking equally shocked and slightly breathless.

'Sorry I—'

'I should—'

Jack laughed awkwardly. 'Think we might have had a touch too much of Dallochmore's finest.'

'I should probably go,' Lily said, suddenly feeling a lot more sober than she did a few moments ago. She flushed, wondering if Misty had turned up just in time … Another minute more and she didn't think either of them would have been able to stop.

'Of course.' Jack took a step away, running a hand through his hair. 'Let's get you and Misty back.'

Chapter 16

Lily had woken the next morning with a dreadful hangover. She'd spent the day nursing a pounding headache and shuffling about the flat. But as the day wore on and painkillers and countless mugs of tea began to do their work, her head had started to clear and she'd been grateful of the time to be alone with her thoughts. She still had a decision to make about the job and time was running out.

Thoughts and ideas had swirled around her head like the fast spin cycle of a washing machine with the dizzying conclusion that in the space of a few weeks she'd managed to go from not wanting to come to Carroch to now not being sure if she wanted to leave at all. She felt as if a new life was being offered to her and part of her wanted to embrace it, grab it with both hands. Perhaps she wasn't so unlike her mother after all; perhaps she could find happiness here the way she had. But she was afraid too. She knew that's why she hadn't turned down the job because it was her safety net. It represented her old life the city, everything that was safe and familiar to her.

She thought back to the previous evening with Jack. Some of the finer points were slightly hazy but she remembered he'd walked her home, one arm guiding her and the other carrying

Misty. He had insisted on waiting in the living room while Lily got ready for bed which had basically consisted of scrambling into PJs and falling into bed. She'd fallen asleep within seconds.

She could be wrong but she was sure at one point Jack had come into the bedroom, tenderly brushing her hair from her face – and perhaps to check she was still breathing – but he had been so quiet and gentle, she thought it must have been a dream.

She'd almost forgotten about the whisky festival until she received a text from Jack. She had the mildly uncomfortable notion she might have invited herself to go with him and he'd only agreed to take her out of politeness but his text said he'd be here this afternoon in taxi to pick her up.

Now she was ready, pacing around nervously and checking the time every few seconds. It wasn't a formal occasion and obviously Lily didn't want to look as if she'd tried too hard but even so, she'd enjoyed some pampering. She'd spent ages blow-drying her hair so that it sat in shiny waves below her shoulders. She'd only brought a single dress with her, a green vintage-style tea dress and she'd slipped it on, completing the outfit with rose gold low wedge sandals.

She looked at her reflection in the mirror, and her skin and eyes shone back at her. Whether it was due to the make-up she'd carefully applied or because she was going to be seeing Jack, Lily couldn't be sure. Realising the taxi would be here soon, she decided to wait downstairs and so grabbing her bag, skipped down the stairs.

The shop was a different place when it was closed; quiet and still. Lily walked around, letting the silence wrap itself around her. She thought about arriving in Carroch all those weeks ago, feeling scared and unsure. She'd viewed the shop through the eyes of a grieving daughter and in some respects, even as an accountant. But since then, it had become so much more. She felt as if the shop had become part of who she was, almost part of her own identity.

She ran a hand along the counter thinking how much she'd enjoyed opening the shop for those few weeks. She loved that moment of turning the sign to 'open;, of unlocking the door and never knowing who would come in. Suddenly it was as though she could remember every single customer she had served, every item they had purchased.

And it hadn't just the customers that had made it so special, it had been all the times she'd enjoyed with Iris, Angus and the knitting club ladies.

Since that very first day she'd felt a connection to her mother through the gift shop. Lily had felt an attachment to it grow within her, a feeling that her mother had started something that she now somehow needed to finish. Patty might have bought the shop as a way of life more than anything else but Lily was certain the right person could run it as a profitable business and she found herself wondering if that person could be her.

The shop was capable of making a healthy turnover, she was sure of it and she'd done some loose projections, calculating that eventually she'd be able to draw enough of a salary to live on. In the meantime, she could use her redundancy money to use as capital until she was up and running. There'd be loads to think about – staffing, marketing, social media ... but none of it put Lily off. Instead she felt a bubble of excitement growing within her.

Her mind had gone into freefall, ideas coming thick and fast. She could expand the range of merchandise, sourcing good-quality local products, not just for tourists searching for souvenirs but for local people too. After all, giving gifts was something everyone did for so many different occasions, and being the only shop like it in the village should place her in a strong position. She could have themes, creating different displays and stock special gifts for Burns night, St Andrews day, Christmas and Hogmanay. And now she knew how well they had sold, Lily imagined the thrill of being able to place a large order with Beth at Highland Aromatics.

But of course, it wasn't only the shop that had been occupying her thoughts. It was Jack.

She'd replayed their kiss over and over. Even through a whisky haze it had been incredible, the intensity of it still burning within her. She tried not to read too much into it but surely she hadn't imagined its potency, Jack must have felt it too. A thrill of excitement shot through her at how it would feel to share something more with him, if that was effect a single kiss had.

The feelings Lily had for Jack had grown into something she'd never felt before and had caused her to dissect her previous relationships. It dawned on her now how much she had kept people at a distance, always managing to steer away from emotional attachments. She had protected herself from any possible hurt by pulling back if she felt they were moving too fast or becoming too serious. But with Jack, everything had changed.

Lily wandered over to the window, her gaze drawn outside. Soft velvety-looking clouds drifted across the sky and the sun sat low in the sky casting wintry rays of light over the water.

In some ways it felt as if she'd come full circle, all the way back to the boy she used to fantasise about all those years ago, almost as if her heart had always belonged to him. Initially the attraction had been purely physical – after all, the man was gorgeous. But it had become so much more than that. He'd been kind, made her laugh. He made her feel safe but at the same time he made her want to live more, experience new things, have adventures. When he looked at her, she felt as if anything was possible and she wondered if this was how it felt to fall in love.

If it was, then it wasn't something she wanted to slip away, at least not without finding out if he felt the same. This was entirely new to her, telling a man how she felt because she'd never felt like this before. Nowhere close to it. She was going to be brave, to find the courage within her and tell him how she felt and today was feeling like a now or never moment.

Lily startled. The taxi was here and Jack was already jumping out, waving to her through the window.

'Wow,' he said a moment later when he saw her. 'You look beautiful.'

He continued to stare at her for a moment and Lily smiled shyly at the effect her appearance seem to be having on him.

'Thanks,' she replied. 'You're looking pretty good yourself.'

Which was something of an understatement. Wearing dark navy trousers and a light blue shirt, jaw-droppingly handsome would be closer to the mark. And when he gave her that smile, the one he was giving her now as he helped her into the waiting taxi, she wasn't even going to pretend it didn't affect her. How could she possibly?

Lily was introduced to the taxi driver, a second cousin of Jack's who pretty much spent the entire journey putting the world to rights. Lily had to stifle a giggle at Jack's expression as he listened patiently, catching her eye with a wink.

They were finally dropped at the distillery, their taxi just one of many that the organisers had thoughtfully arranged to be available to ferry people to and from distilleries during the festival. The distillery looked like something out of a fairy-tale like with lights blazing from every window and the distinctive pagoda roof silhouetted against the sky. Lily could smell the smoky peaty aroma filling the air as they walked along a path from the carpark, Jack pointing out some of various buildings including the still house which contained the copper stills used for distilling and the warehouse full of maturing casks.

They passed under a wrought iron gateway displaying the name of the distillery in ornate gold lettering and through a cobbled courtyard. Just before they reached the visitor centre, Lily paused.

'Jack?' She glanced at him sideways from under her lashes. 'You sure you didn't mind me coming with you?' Not having had the chance on their journey to the distillery to clarify her little

177

niggle that she might have in some way forced herself on Jack to bring her, she needed to check.

Jack stopped to face her. 'Are you kidding? I wanted you to come. And besides, I really don't mind being seen with a beautiful woman. It should be me thanking you.'

Jack pulled open the heavy oak door, Lily unsure her legs were still working. They were met by a babble of chattering voices and a throng of people mingling in the entrance hallway. Jack seemed oblivious to everyone, his eyes fixed on Lily as he guided her through the door, the feel of his hand on her back sending a cascade of tingles down her spine.

The main room was a grand affair with panelled in dark wood and carpeted in tartan with a fire crackling in a massive open fireplace. Paintings depicting Highlands landscapes were dotted about and a huge glass showcase displayed dozens of bottles of whisky creating a wall of golden amber.

They weaved their way through the crowd, Lily very conscious of being seen beside Jack especially when it soon became apparent he knew a lot of people including various extended family members. Lily was having trouble keeping up. And if the number of handshakes, greetings and backslaps were anything to go by, then Jack Armstrong was highly thought of. The whole time he kept Lily close, introducing and including her in all the interactions.

There was a mixture of people, Lily picking up on the different accents and languages being spoken and spotting a few business-looking types. Various tours of the distillery were underway while in a smaller room named The Whisky Lounge a blending workshop was in progress.

As well as upturned oak barrels being used as tables, there was one single long table running the length of one wall which was laid out with different plates of food. Waiting staff dressed in tartan skirts or trousers and crisp white shirts were on hand, encouraging and advising people what to try.

'There she is,' Jack said, taking Lily's hand and leading her over to a pretty girl who was clearly in charge of the buffet table. She was a whirlwind, her honey-coloured hair swinging in a high ponytail, her cheeks flushed as she moved fluidly between guests and staff, ensuring everyone's needs were being met.

The girl's face lit up when she saw them approaching, her eyes swivelling to Jack and then Lily. Her distinctive green eyes were so similar to Jack's, Lily pretty much knew right away who she was before Jack looped an arm over her shoulder and made the introduction.

'Lily, this is my little sister the culinary genius, Isla.'

'It's lovely to meet you Lily, I'm so glad you're both here!' she enthused, turning to wave an arm around the room. 'What do you think?'

'Looks like you've done a good job, sis.'

'You need to try something, come on.'

She led them to the table, Lily's eyes widening at the selection of seafood, smoked and roasted meats and cheeses, all beautifully presented.

'I've made all the canapes to match the different whiskies,' Isla explained, giving Lily and Jack a small plate and napkin each. 'Basically it's all about balance, the whisky shouldn't overwhelm the food. See what you think of this.'

First, they tasted some delectable smoked salmon before Isla handed each of them a small crystal tasting glass containing an 8-year-old whisky. 'It's a light whisky, slightly sweet with a citrusy edge which should cut through the rich oily fish.'

They complemented each other perfectly and Jack and Lily both made appreciative noises before moving onto other Scottish-inspired tapas, all equally delicious.

'And I've saved the best till last,' Isla announced, producing decadent dark velvet truffles dusted with cocoa powder. 'Perfectly matched with this full-bodied, strong, smoky whisky.'

Isla watched, her eyes bright with expectation as Lily and Jack bit into their truffles and then followed with a sip of whisky. Lily hadn't tasted anything like it and rolled her eyes appreciatively. 'It's heavenly.'

Isla beamed with pleasure. 'I'd love to stay and speak to you more but duty calls.'

'Don't worry about us.' Jack grinned at her. 'And you're doing a brilliant job.'

'Praise from my brother.' Isla pulled a face at Lily. 'I knew today was going to be a good day.'

'That was lovely, Isla.' Lily smiled back at her. 'I really enjoyed it.'

'What would you like to do now?' Jack turned to Lily. 'We could try more whisky tasting if you like? You seem to be acquiring a taste for it.' Lily saw the tease at his lips, the sparkle in his eyes.

'Think I might have had more than my fair share of whisky recently,' she confessed with a rueful smile. Remembering her more private, intimate whisky tasting with Jack, she felt a flash of heat through her body. She took a small breath, letting a few seconds to pass before she spoke.

'I really enjoyed the other evening.'

'So did I.'

'And thank you for making sure I got home okay.'

'My pleasure,' he said solemnly.

Lily's heart suddenly felt like a runaway train, knowing this was her moment to find her courage. She licked her lips nervously. 'Um, actually, about that night?'

'Yes?'

'I was wondering …' She moved closer to Jack to be heard over the buzz of conversation. The room really was very busy. 'Do you think—'

Jack's two hands suddenly shot out to catch Lily as someone knocked into the back of her, almost sending her flying.

Jack frowned, taking her arm. 'You okay?'

'I'm fine,' Lily replied, although admittedly the jolt hadn't done much for her already slightly wobbly composure.

Jack scanned the crowd looking for a quieter spot, his face suddenly lighting up. 'There's Adam,' he said, his hand still on Lily's arm. 'Come on.'

Lily glanced over where she could see a striking-looking man mingling and chatting, his shoulders visibly relaxing when he spotted Jack. He made his way over to them immediately.

Lily watch them embrace each other, their easy familiarity speaking volumes. She didn't know what it was like to have a lifelong friend but she could see the closeness between them immediately, a look that said they had each other's back. Not only had they grown up together, they were bonded by a terrible tragedy too.

'Lily, this is Adam,' Jack said, turning to introduce them.

Adam gave Lily a warm smile, his dark brown eye regarding her earnestly. He bent down to kiss her cheek. 'It's good to meet you, Lily. Welcome to Dallochmore.'

'Thanks,' Lily smiled. 'Everything looks great, you've certainly got a good turnout.'

Adam nodded, looking like a man with a lot on his mind which was hardly surprising giving the circumstances. Taking over the running of a distillery was a huge undertaking and Lily detected a slight unease in his body language as his eyes scanned the room and felt an ache of sadness for him, imagining how different this would all be for him if his wife was by his side. They stood chatting for a few moments, Jack asking a few questions about how the day was going.

Both tall and equally broad, the two men standing side by side by made quite an impression. And judging by the number of furtive glances being aimed in their direction by the assembled female company, Lily wasn't the only to have noticed.

Adam turned to Lily, briefly touching her elbow. 'Would you mind if I borrowed Jack for a couple of minutes? Just need a bit of muscle to help shift some crates.'

'Of course.'

After reassuring Jack she'd be okay for a few minutes, Lily went to find the ladies' room, grateful to have the chance for a breather away from the throng of people. The ladies' was as opulent as the rest of the place with marbled floor and wood panelling. Lily stood in front of the large gilt mirrors and splashed cold water on her warm cheeks and ran a quick hand through her hair. Feeling particularly relaxed and mellow after all the amazing food and drink, she headed back out, anticipating finding Jack. It was unlikely they'd be able to find a quiet spot here to talk, perhaps she could suggest they go for a stroll by the loch later.

She walked out just in time to see Isla flying by with a tray of stacked dishes. Pushing her hip against a swing door to open it she disappeared into what was presumable the kitchen. A couple of seconds later Lily heard a crash followed by a muffled cry.

Lily rushed over, opening the door carefully, just enough to put her head round to see the cause of the noise. Lily glanced down where the contents of the tray lay smashed in several pieces on the floor. Looking distraught and standing in the middle of the debris was Isla. 'I knew it had been going too well.'

Lily stepped through the door. 'Are you all right? Did you cut yourself?'

Isla let out an exasperated sigh. 'I'm fine. I'm all fingers and thumbs.' Her face crumpled for a moment, dislodging her smile from earlier. She looked about to cry and Lily could suddenly see the exhaustion on her face. 'Sorry, its just today is so important to me.'

'Looks like you need to take a breather,' Lily suggested. 'Let me help – do you have a brush and shovel?'

'I can't ask you to do that. Please, you're a guest.'

'Don't be silly. Is it in here?' Lily opened the most likely looking cupboard by the back door.

Isla smiled. 'Thanks.'

As she helped tidy up, Lily took in the kitchen. Apart from a couple of modern appliances, the place looked like it was a need of an overhaul and Lily thought Isla must be a miracle maker to produce the array of dishes she had under these circumstances. She could see the amount of work that she'd done behind the scenes. No wonder she was overwrought.

'There, all done.' Lily scooped the last remnants into the bin and found glasses to pour them both some water.

'So, you did this on your own?' Lily's brow wrinkled looking around the deserted kitchen, surprised there wasn't a small army of staff beavering away.

'There isn't really anyone else,' Isla said matter-of-factly. 'When I started working here a couple of years ago Jock was still in charge and he was never really keen to expand the food side of things. I tried a few times to introduce some new ideas but he was never interested.'

She took a long sip of water. 'Cooking's always been my passion, the only thing I've ever really wanted to do. I'm hoping now that Adam's here, things will change. He's naturally cautious which I understand but at least I managed to persuade him to let me run the food pairing event for today.'

Lily was impressed. Between Isla and Beth, the entrepreneurial skills of women in the Highlands seemed in good shape and she felt a bubble of excitement at the possibility she might join their ranks if she opened the gift shop.

'It seems to have been a great success, you must be delighted.'

'It's gone really well. Well, up until ten minutes ago,' she said ruefully. 'I just want to prove that we could do so much more. My head is literally bursting with ideas, there's so many food and drink events we could run, cater for corporate and private hospitality—'

'This is where you're both hiding.'

They both turned as Adam appeared at the door. 'Everything okay?' he checked with Isla.

'Sure, everything's fine,' she replied quickly, Lily noticing the flush on her cheeks deepen.

'I'll leave you to it then.' He nodded then looked at Lily. 'Think Jack's looking for you.'

'Oh, right.'

Isla looked gratefully at Lily as Adam left. 'Thanks again for helping me. Wouldn't have wanted Adam to see all that mess.'

'It's no problem.'

'Right, back to it,' Isla said, heading to the door. 'You know, you're every bit as lovely as Jack said you were.'

'Oh.' Now it was Lily's turn to blush. Knowing Jack had said that to his sister made her feel a little giddy.

'Since the accident he's been so hell-bent on helping everyone else, making sure they're all okay. He feels so guilty about Adam losing his wife, sometimes it's as if he doesn't think he deserves to find happiness himself again.' Isla paused and turned. 'You did know about the accident? With Jack's ex and Adam's wife?'

Lily nodded. 'Jack told me.'

'He might be my big brother but I still worry about him. Me and my sisters, we tease him about him meeting someone but we know how difficult it is for him. It's nice seeing him today looking more like his old self.'

As Isla went back into the fray, Lily took herself off to find Jack, a definite spring in her step. Walking back through the hallway she stopped dead in her tracks. At first she was convinced she was seeing things. Her throat dried and her heart started to bang uncomfortably against her ribcage. She blinked, scanning a group of people in the far corner but there was no mistake. One of them was James.

Lily seemed unable to move, her brain frantically trying to make sense of his presence here. But before she had the chance to do anything other than stand gaping, his head had turned in her direction and he'd made eye contact with her.

For a split second he looked almost as shocked as she felt. But he recovered quickly, reminding Lily what a consummate professional he was in situations like these, his practised smile making an appearance as he strolled over to her.

'Lily? I didn't expect to see you again so soon but what a lovely surprise.'

'What are you doing here?' she stammered.

'Don't look so shocked,' he chortled. 'Remember I mentioned at the interview I'd be away on business for a few days? I'm here with some colleagues to enjoy the whisky festival and make some contacts. In fact, I've got a meeting here at Dallochmore.'

He quirked an eyebrow. 'What about you? I certainly wasn't expecting to see you here.'

Lily had never mentioned any connection to Loch Carroch or that her mother had lived here, the fact reinforcing to her how superficial all their conversations had been. She wasn't about to start going into detail now and skirted over the details, only saying she was here to deal with her late mother's property in Carroch.

'I didn't know you had links to this neck of the woods but what a happy coincidence. Do you know the owners here at Dallochmore?'

'What?'

'I'd heard there'd been a few changes recently, is that right?'

Lily shook her head, mystified. 'I think so,' she replied vaguely. 'But I really don't know anything. Why are—'

'Don't you see?' he pushed on, 'If you take the job, this could be your first project, liaising with the distillery.'

Lily's mouth fell open and then closed again. Jack was coming towards them, looking incredibly handsome and her heart started hammering. She felt the lightest of touches on her back as he came up behind her.

'There you are,' he murmured. 'Been looking for you.' His gaze flickered questioningly between her and James.

Lily's fist clenched at her side realising she had little choice but to introduce them. 'Jack, this is James Sinclair.' Her voice sounded strange. 'We, er, used to work together.'

185

The men shook hands, a look of confusion etched on Jack's face. Lily could almost see his mind making connections, like pieces of a jigsaw sliding together. With forced brightness in her voice she desperately tried to steer the conversation onto safer territory. 'Jack's sister did all the incredible food here today.'

'Really?' James's face lit up in interest and he homed in on Jack. 'Are you associated with the distillery Jack?'

'Family friends, that's all,' he replied in a measured voice. He glanced briefly at Lily and then regarded James, a look of distrust flashing across his face. 'Are you here for pleasure or business?' he asked him.

'Turns out a bit of both actually.' James slid his gaze pointedly at Lily. 'Our company is always looking to refresh and expand our product portfolio and the growth of Scotch whisky makes it ideal for investment opportunities. I've got a meeting here at Dallochmore, actually. I believe there's been a change at the helm recently, it could be just the type of place we're looking for.'

He held the glass of whisky he was holding up to light, considering its contents as he carried on. 'Of course it's not just whisky that's going from strength to strength – remember when we visited the gin distillery Lily?'

Lily had forgotten about that. James had been quick to seize on the gin trend, successfully securing a deal with a start-up business to supply Bremners with artisan gift sets.

'Couldn't have done it without you by my side Lily. Wasn't that the day we stopped at that nice little restaurant for lunch?'

Lily squirmed at how intimate it suddenly sounded. What made it worse was at the time that was exactly what she'd thought it had been. Intimate and personal. But in reality, it had only ever been about business, that's all it had ever been to James, the way it was now.

Lily stood helplessly and looked over at Jack, his expression unreadable. She swallowed, her stomach rolling with nausea at how this was beginning to look.

Thankfully a tap on his shoulder prevented James saying anything further. 'Looks like it's time for me to go and circulate,' he announced. He inclined his head briefly in Jack's direction then turned to face Lily. 'It'd be really good to work together again, Lily. Let me know soon about the job, I'll be waiting.'

Lily and Jack stood silently watching James's back disappear into the sea of bodies. She tried to move her lips but seemed incapable of forming any words, at least not the right ones.

Jack dug his hands deeply into his trouser pockets and turned, his eyes crowded with questions. 'He's the James you told me about, the one you worked with?'

Lily tucked a strand of hair behind her ear. 'Yes.'

'Did I miss something? He offered you a job?'

Lily let out a breath, not meeting Jack's eye. 'The interview I went to a few days ago in Edinburgh – it was with him. He offered me the job then.'

'I see.' Jack's voice was disconcertingly low.

'But I didn't know the interview was going to be with him,' Lily rushed on. 'When the recruitment agency called me all I knew was the job was for a financial services company – it was only when I got there I found out the company was a subsidiary of Dunn Equity.'

'And this is the man you worked closely with, the man you had feelings for?' he questioned, recounting fairly accurately what Lily had told him on the day they'd been on the boat.

'Yes,' Lily flustered. 'I mean we did work together but that was it. There was never anything between us.'

'You sure? You looked like you were on pretty good terms to me.'

Lily shook her head. 'I'm considering a job offer from him, that's all. There isn't – never was – anything between us. I know that now.'

Jack nodded thoughtfully. 'He made you redundant, right?'

'That's right.'

'Must be a hell of a job he offered you.'

Lily narrowed her eyes suddenly feeling defensive. She'd worked hard for her career and was good at what she did. She wasn't going to apologise for considering the job offer. 'Actually, it is.'

Jack regarded her, his expression darkening. 'Why didn't you tell me when I asked about the interview, why the secrecy?'

'It wasn't a secret. I was working things through in my own head, that's all. In fact,' she paused. 'I was going to speak to you today—'

'You knew he was interested in Dallochmore?' Jack interrupted.

Lily frowned. 'Not until a moment ago—'

'That's why you were asking all those questions, why you wanted to come today? You were doing your homework for him?'

'What? No!' How could he possibly think that? 'I had no idea James was going to be here until ten minutes ago.'

A small group of people suddenly surged in their direction chatting nosily and Jack stepped back to let them by, jabbing a hand through his hair distractedly.

'So is he serious about making a move on Dallochmore?' he asked, turning his attention back to Lily. 'Because from what you told me how they operate, somehow I don't think Dunn Equity would be good news.'

Lily blinked, wondering how to make him understand she didn't know anything. 'I should imagine there's a possibility but I have no idea,' she replied incredulously.

'So what would happen next if they want to invest?' Jack rolled his neck to one side, tension oozing from him. 'Do you think there'd be job losses?'

Lily shook her head in exasperation. 'I don't know – there're a lot of factors that would come in to play.'

Lily knew the way James operated. He'd want to maximise the returns but it would depend on the risks involved and he'd wait to see the state of the distillery's finances. She also knew there could well be redundancies and other consequences that might not go down too well. Even though she'd known nothing about any of it, the fact James had just asked to be involved made her feel horribly implicated in some way.

'Jack, I know nothing about it. We never discussed Dallochmore at the interview and I didn't know he would be here today. You do believe me?'

James nodded and there was a long agonising silence before he spoke again. 'So do you think you'll take the job?'

Lily was beginning to feel light-headed. This was not how today was supposed to go. She thought of all the things she'd wanted to say to Jack today and the conversation she hoped they'd be having. But that was before James turned up and now they were having a very different one.

Jack looked at her and Lily could feel the doubt she saw in his eyes begin to creep into her own thinking. She'd stepped out of herself these last few weeks and now she felt herself retreating again. 'I – I don't know.'

'Isn't this what you wanted, a job back in the city?' Jack's eyes softened for a moment. 'If it's something you really want to do, you should go for it.'

Only now did Lily wonder what she imagined might happen today. Had she really thought Jack was going to declare his feelings for her? Beg her to stay? Right now, she wasn't sure if he even trusted her.

Just then, Adam appeared nearby with a couple of people who he seemed to be showing around and called Jack over. 'I should go and see if he needs help.'

'Of course, you should go,' Lily told him.

Jack hesitated for a moment, looking at her uncertainly. 'I'll see you shortly,' he said.

Lily remembered Isla's words from earlier. Jack helped everyone. It was his way of dealing with what had happened. Helping her had simply been part of salving his guilt with what had happened. She'd thought it was her but it was everyone – Adam, Iris,

Angus … There was nothing special about her. Lily knew in her heart he was a good man but he had his own issues to deal with and perhaps he wasn't ready to move on.

The kiss they'd shared might have been passionate but it had been in the heat of a drunken moment. Hadn't he said he'd only had a few casual relationships since his split from Jessica and perhaps he'd only ever seen her as a possible casual dalliance while she'd been here. She'd misread the way he'd been with her as something much more than it obviously was. She'd been a fool, misread the situation with him just as she'd done with James. She could hardly believe what an idiot she'd been and humiliation swept through her. To think she'd almost spilled her heart out to him and revealed her feelings. Thank God she hadn't.

'Actually, I'm feeling pretty tired. I think I might go and see Iris,' Lily said, keeping her voice light. She inclined her head towards Adam who was waiting. 'You do what you have to.'

Jack hesitated for a moment, his gaze flicking to Adam and then back to her.

'I'll be fine,' she assured him.

Lily watched him walk away and swallowed hard. The last few weeks had meant so much to her. She'd dared to hope and dream of a future in Carroch with Jack but perhaps she'd got it wrong. Perhaps Carroch wasn't where she belonged, no matter how much she'd thought she wanted it to be. Opening the shop had been idealistic, a way of trying to connect to her mother but perhaps it had been a foolish idea. She'd been lured by the people, by the loch, the peace. By Jack.

She'd got carried away but this wasn't her life, it was her mother's. She should be living her own life. Carroch wasn't where she belonged, no matter how much she had thought she'd wanted it to be. She didn't want to walk away but that's exactly what she was going to do now.

Lily felt her guard come up. Knowing what she needed to do now, she turned and went to find James.

Chapter 17

'Mr Bell could see you at half past twelve tomorrow if that suited you?'

'That would be perfect, thank you,' Lily replied, figuring she'd be able to make it to Mr Bell's office and back in her lunch hour. She hung up the phone running her eye down her list, ticking another thing off with a satisfying stroke of her pen. You could achieve a lot in a week, she'd discovered, if you really put your mind to it. She sat back in her seat and finished her coffee. It was just about tolerable but given she was in a swimming pool café she supposed it could be a lot worse.

She'd been working for over a week now. Her new office was in a nondescript modern block just outside Edinburgh's city centre and coloured in a hundred shades of beige. It was nowhere near as charming as Bremners of course but when she'd discovered it was near a swimming pool, Lily had seen it as a sign and she'd been swimming every morning before work.

It wasn't the same as swimming in the loch by any stretch of the imagination. Warmer certainly but nowhere near as invigorating or life-affirming. With their moist walls and stray hairs the changing rooms were something to be endured but at least if she arrived early enough the pool was still relatively empty, just her and a few others determinedly clocking up lengths. She'd managed thirty this morning.

Lily bit down a sigh. How she missed the loch. She missed everything. It was still so difficult when she allowed herself to think about what she had left behind in Carroch and what could have been. For a little while her dream had held so much promise before it had turned into nothing more than a fantasy. Had she'd really believed she'd had a chance of finding happiness with Jack and making a successful business out of the gift shop?

But once she'd realised the dream was over and her life was back in Edinburgh she'd acted quickly and decisively, wasting no time after she'd left the whisky festival.

Galvanised by her disappointment, she'd returned to the flat above the shop, hastily packing her clothes and the few items of her mother's that she was keeping. What little furniture there was, she would just leave. Later and under the cover of darkness, she stole into the shop for a last look around, making sure everything was secure and given the place a final tidy up. After all, the next people there would be perspective buyers.

She'd gone to see Iris and Angus early the next day and explained her decision to head back to Edinburgh. It had broken her heart to see the small exchange of glances between them. Angus had agreed to take Misty on the proviso that Lily visited regularly which she'd happily agreed to. Of course she would – Iris and Angus were the closest thing she had to family and it meant the world to her to know they were there for her. She was determined to see them regularly and had decided a car would be a good use of some of her redundancy money. She wasn't exactly relishing the prospect of visiting car showrooms but it was next on her to-do list. That way she'd be able to drive straight up to the cottages to visit Iris and Angus whenever she wanted, avoiding the village and the risk of seeing Jack.

The knitting club would keep running until a buyer was found which admittedly might not take long, and Lily felt terrible about it. She tried to be optimistic that whoever bought the property would keep it as a gift shop and maybe – just maybe – keep the knitting club running. She'd have to go over it all with Mr Bell at her appointment tomorrow when she gave him the instruction to sell. No doubt Finlay wouldn't be too pleased when he found out she was selling though her own solicitor but she hoped this way she'd have more control over the sale.

And then it had been time to leave.

How she'd got through those first few days Lily didn't know – simply by putting one foot in front of the other and willing herself to get on with it. Nothing about it had been easy but with a grim determination she set about claiming back her old life, beginning with her new job.

Miles away, Lily was jolted back to the present by a group of elderly ladies shuffling their way passed her table heading to the early morning aquafit session. Realising it was time for her to leave Lily gathered her things together, ready to make the ten-minute walk to her office.

She'd settled in quickly. The work was all routine, she could practically do it with her eyes shut and in some ways it was as if she'd never been away. All her new colleagues were at their desk when Lily arrived at nine o'clock. She nodded, saying good morning and waving over to Gillian already in the middle of a call. A trainee accountant, she was full of energy and enthusiasm, something about her reminding Lily of herself – or at least how she used to be.

She kept finding herself staring at the screen in front of her, her thoughts drifting to Carroch. She thought of the view of the loch she'd woken to every morning and the sense of the tranquillity she'd felt. She imagined the blazes of colour, the oranges, pinks, purples and violets as the sun rose and set over the loch. And she thought of Iris, Angus and the knitting club ladies, wondering what they were doing.

But it was the thoughts of Jack that caused her heart to ache and made it impossible to focus on anything except how much she missed him. It took every ounce of her willpower to push them away.

She liked to think she was a still good accountant but the truth was, something within her had changed and she wasn't the same person anymore. If there was one thing the last few weeks had taught her, it was that she wasn't going to allow work to consume her whole life again.

From now on it was going to be all about finding the right life-work balance. No incessant checking of emails, no taking work home and definitely no more crazy-long days. Which was why exactly eight hours later at precisely five o'clock Lily left her desk. There was nothing so important it couldn't wait until the next day.

Her new office was too far to walk home from so she hopped on a bus and then stopped to grab some dinner at the Italian deli on the way back to her flat. With the weight of her shopping bag and her swimming bag slung over her shoulder, she was relieved when she finally turned into her cul-de-sac. She could see lights being switched on in downstairs rooms as people arrived home and settled in for the evening.

There'd been some rain earlier and the first leaves of autumn had fallen. The street lamps cast a glow on the wet pavements and Lily concentrated on stepping carefully over the leaves that lay slippery and golden. Lifting her head as she approached the stairs to her flat, she almost stumbled in shock.

Leaning against the black railings, huddled into a warm jacket with the collar turned up, was Jack.

He looked so out of place Lily thought she must be seeing things. She squeezed her eyes shut and opened them again but he was still there. They simply stared at each other, and for how long she had no idea. Time seem to stand still, her eyes drinking in every single detail of him as if they were thirsty for him.

He looked tired, his jaw shadowed by stubble and his dark

194

hair ruffled as if he'd just run a hand through it. Lily had never seen him looking so devastatingly handsome and every fibre of her being longed to touch him. But while her body might seem to thrill at the sight of him, her mind wasn't so easily convinced.

Her swimming bag slid from her shoulder and knocked the other bag out of her hand onto the ground. He was over in two steps, scooping up her bags and taking them from her. 'Here, let me help,' he said.

'Its fine, I've got it,' she muttered, the sudden closeness of him sending her reeling. God, she'd missed that deep drawl.

'What … why … how did …' She stopped, shaking her head in frustration. Forming some actual words might be helpful. 'What are you doing here?'

His eyes scanned her face. 'To speak to you.'

A terrible thought winged its way into her head. 'Is everyone all right – Iris, Angus?'

'They're both fine,' he reassured her quickly. 'I bumped into Angus yesterday, in fact.'

'Oh. How is he?' she asked in a small voice.

'He's doing great. Apparently Misty is missing you though.' He didn't smile but something sparkled in his eyes. 'Really badly, apparently. Can't eat or sleep.'

Lily shot him a look. 'Angus never mentioned anything when we spoke.'

'He probably didn't want to worry you.'

Lily narrowed her eyes. 'So why are you here then?'

'Like I said, to talk to you.'

Lily frowned, feeling whatever composure she'd achieved over the last few days begin to unravel. 'How did you know where to find me?'

'Iris gave me your address.'

Silently berating Iris, Lily's frown deepened. 'How long have you been here?'

'Not that long.' He shrugged, looking at his watch. 'Left Carroch about three hours ago.'

Lily flicked her eyes up and down the street and saw his Land Rover. She didn't dare to think how fast he must have driven. The Land Rover looked as much out of place as Jack did and was breaking at least parking four parking violations; Lily knew a particular traffic warden who would take great pleasure in slapping on the appropriate tickets.

'You know you shouldn't really be parked there,' Lily pointed out.

'What?' He squinted over at the land rover before switching his gaze back to her. 'Yeah, I'm really not too bothered about that right now.'

Mrs Robertson's curtain twitched and Jack gave her a coy wave. 'Nice neighbours you have, she invited me in for a coffee you know.'

Lily rolled her eyes inwardly, supposing they should get whatever this was over with. 'You'd better come in.'

She slotted the key into the communal entry door and headed up the stairs, leaving Jack to follow her. Her fingers fumbled slightly as she unlocked her own front door and headed straight through to the kitchen.

Jack came in behind her and Lily grabbed the bags back from him. Her kitchen, not exactly large at the best of times, suddenly appeared miniscule with him in it. She needed to keep busy. Dumping her swimming bag in the corner she opened the fridge, gratefully hiding her face in its coolness as she unpacked the Parma ham, roasted peppers and mozzarella, her appetite suddenly vanished.

'Can I get you a drink? Tea, coffee … think I've got orange juice …'

'I don't want anything. Not to drink anyway,' Jack replied patiently.

Lily clattered about finding a glass and pouring herself a drink, anything to keep from looking at him. She gripped her glass tightly, hoping he didn't see her fingers shaking. The clock on the wall suddenly seem to tick very loudly and Lily felt her heart banging in time with it. Eventually with no alternative she turned to face him.

'You all done?' he asked.

Lily nodded. 'Please take a seat,' she said politely, sounding ridiculously formal.

Keeping his eyes firmly on her, he lowered himself onto one of the two stools, his legs splayed in front of him. 'Adam told me you went to see him?'

'That's right,' she answered primly.

Lily thought back to the day of the festival. In some strange way it already felt a lifetime ago. After she'd left Jack, she'd gone to find James. She recalled the look of surprise on his face when she told him she was'nt taking the job, but he'd get over it, of course he would. After that, she'd managed to track down Adam and have a quiet word with him alone.

'He told me you're going to help with the financial side of things at the distillery?'

Lily nodded. 'I wanted to let him know about Dunn Equity and what it might mean if they invested.'

She could only base it on her experience at Bremners and she'd been honest with Adam – the investment may have secured the department store's future but it had also come at a cost to staff and the company's unique identity. Relishing the possibility of putting to use all the experience she'd gained in the last year working for Bremners to now help the distillery, Lily had offered to take a look over the distillery's accounts, fairly confident she'd be able to give Adam a few pointers in the right direction to steer the business back on track without outside investment.

'I knew the chances were that Jock had probably missed a few tricks, made a few errors of judgement. Hopefully we'll be able to help give the distillery a fighting chance to stand on its own two feet. I can do all my part remotely.'

Lily was delighted when Adam had accepted her offer and knew she'd be able to fit it in easily enough with the job she'd just started. A role with an export company, it had been one of the jobs she'd applied for when she'd been in Carroch and they'd been delighted when Lily offered to start immediately. She knew the role wasn't going to be too demanding and she'd have time to devote to the work for the distillery.

'I texted you later but you didn't respond. Then I came to the shop the next day but you'd gone.'

Lily shrugged. 'I decided it was time to head back to Edinburgh. Once I'd made up my mind, there didn't seem much point in hanging around.'

Jack studied her face for a long moment. 'I'm sorry,' he said. 'The day at the distillery … I don't think I handled it very well.'

Her heart thumping, Lily met his gaze evenly but didn't say anything.

'It was seeing you with James … knowing you were considering a job with him. Not only that, but that the distillery might be involved.'

Lily stared at him. 'You seemed so ready to believe I knew about Dunn Equity's possible involvement.'

'I know and I'm an idiot,' he said gruffly. He studied the floor briefly then lifted his gaze to Lily. 'Since the accident and Adam losing his wife, I've felt helpless.' Jack lifted his hands and let them drop again. 'There was nothing I could do for him. When he came home and decided to rebuild his life at the distillery, I finally felt I could do something. Be there for him, help him any way I could at the distillery.

'So imagine how I felt when I the woman I'd fallen in love with not only was considering a job offer with a man she'd had feelings for and was about to make a move on the distillery owned by Adam—'

Lily shook her head. 'Sorry. The woman you … me …?'

'The woman I fell in love with,' he repeated. 'Practically since the first moment I saw you.'

Lily flopped down on the stool opposite him, dazed.

'I knew you were the person who makes me happy and who I wanted to make happy but when I saw you with James and he started talking about offering you a job and investing in Dallochmore, I didn't know how to handle it, what to think—'

'I wanted to tell you about the job,' Lily broke in. 'I was planning on telling you the day of the whisky festival. There was so much I wanted to say to you that day but then James turned up.'

She paused, her breath shaky. 'There was never anything between me and James – I knew that as soon as I saw him again at the interview. But when he offered me the job I couldn't just turn it down. Growing up with Mum life was often uncertain, and I was determined to get a good job, provide for myself. And I did it. I was good at my job and I was happy with my life. Or so I thought.'

Outside rain was falling again, soft and steady against the window and Lily watched the raindrops trickle down the glass for a moment.

'Funny, all the years I went to Carroch with Mum, I almost resented it.' She smiled sadly. 'But I guess it must always have been part of who I was, more than I ever realised. When James offered me the job, I felt caught between two lives. Even though in my heart I knew I didn't want to take the job, I was scared to let go. I'm so used to being on my own, relying on myself.'

Jack reached over and took her hand. 'You don't have to be on your own anymore, Lily. Not if you don't want to be.' His eyes searched hers, his expression full of hope but Lily saw the edge of uncertainty as he waited for her response.

She stood up and took a step so she was in front of him, feeling a smile starting somewhere deep inside her. 'I don't want to be. I love you too, Jack. That's what I had wanted to tell you all along.'

Jack's face changed, his features suddenly relaxing and softening. He pulled Lily towards him and she sank into the strength and warmth of his arms and it was the best feeling she'd ever had.

'Nothing felt right after you left,' he murmured against her hair.

Lily lifted her face to him with a teasing look. 'So Misty isn't the only one who's been missing me?'

'Misty's doing fine.' He run a finger tenderly down her cheek. 'It's me who's been a mess since you left. When I found out you'd gone, I thought I'd blown it. It was Adam who told me to get my act together.'

'Adam?'

'He guessed I had feelings for you.' Jack gave a small laugh. 'Must have been more transparent that I thought. It was only then I realised how scared I'd been to find happiness again. Why should I deserve to be happy? Not when Adam was alone. Not when he had lost so much. But Adam told me to stop being an idiot and get myself down here.'

'I always thought he looked like he a wise man.' Lily smiled.

Jack gently cupped her face in her hands. 'I love you, Lily. Everything about you. I want to be with you, plan a future with you.'

He lowered his mouth to hers and kissed her, tenderly at first and then deeper, more urgently. Lily's hand slid over his broad shoulders and around his neck and she could feel him pulling her closer against her, their bodies moulding together.

When eventually Jack gently drew back his eyes roamed her face and Lily knew the love and desire glittering in his eyes were mirrored in her own. 'Will you come back with me now?' he asked.

'Now?'

'Well, maybe not this precise moment,' he said huskily pulling her towards him again. He peppered her neck with kisses, then along her jawline before finally finding her lips. After that, it was difficult to think of anything coherently.

Jack's green eyes glistened when they finally pulled apart. 'I'll take that as a yes,' he said.

Epilogue

'We're going to be late if you don't get a move on.'

Lily hurried down the stairs, fixing on her earrings. 'And whose fault is that?' She arched an eyebrow at Jack who was waiting for her at the bottom. He looked pretty much how she felt. Deliciously tousled and sleep-deprived for all the right reasons.

'Totally yours for being so gorgeous and irresistible,' he smiled happily.

Lily giggled as she reached the bottom step and Jack nuzzled into her neck. 'If you carry on like that we're definitely going to be late,' she murmured, reluctantly extracting herself from his arms.

Jack groaned and let her go but his gaze lingered on her. 'You look beautiful.'

Lily had never thought of herself as beautiful but today she felt it, her face lighting up as she smiled back at him.

'You ready for this?' he asked, shrugging on his own jacket before helping Lily on with hers.

'Absolutely.'

Jack closed the front door behind them and they stood for a few moments hand in hand at the water's edge. Lily breathed in the cold crisp air of a perfect winter's morning. The mountains in the distance were dusted with snow and the loch was illuminated by the sun in a cloudless blue sky. She felt like pinching herself, hardly daring to believe this was going to be on her doorstep every morning from now on.

Lily felt Jack's hand tighten around hers as they walked across the main road and approached the shop, both feeling the significance of today and they stopped again, this time to look up at the beautiful new façade of the shop.

There was only ever one possible name for the shop. It had come to Lily weeks ago but she'd kept it to herself, only daring to imagine that one day she might see the name above the door. And now that day had come.

Lily felt emotion well inside her as she gazed up at the sign bearing the name *The Rowan Tree Gift Shop*. The day Jack had stopped to show her the single tree on the moor had always stayed with her, reminding her just how precious life was. It was also the moment she had started to fall in love with Jack.

Angus had designed it to show the branches and dark red berries of a rowan tree woven cleverly into the dark green lettering and Lily had had it made especially. The exterior of the shop had been freshly painted white and all the woodwork restored. The morning light glinted off the latticed windows which were now brimming with festive displays of gifts.

'Isn't it perfect?' Lily said feeling her stomach fizz with nerves and excitement. Jack curled his arm around to bring her in for a hug and then together they went to open the shop for is first day of trading.

It had been a hectic few weeks since Lily had left behind her old life and returned to start her new one in Carroch with Jack. Although he'd d asked her to move in with him straightaway, Lily had waited a few weeks, wanting to concentrate on the shop first, determined to have it open in time for Christmas. It had been frantic at times but somehow she'd managed to source enough stock and the shelves were now filled with festive candles, scented pot pourri, hand-painted glass baubles and ceramic Christmas ornaments. Beth had created gift sets of handmade honey soap and wild raspberry body lotion contained in a floral embossed box and tied with tartan ribbon and these now took pride of place.

Lily had spent a day with Iris displaying all the stock, their creative thinking fuelled by mulled wine and Christmas songs. The windows had been decorated with snowflakes cut from white paper along with tree branches adorned with fairy lights and boxes painted with silver and gold had become props to show off products.

Lily knew it had all been worth it when a few hours later she stood back and looked at the crowd of people who had come to help them celebrate the first day of opening – it felt as if half the village had turn-up to wish her luck. The knitting ladies were there in force, already in the throes of planning a book club to be held every month, and of course Iris and Angus were there, offering glasses of prosecco or orange juice to everyone as they came in.

Misty was sitting behind the counter, mistress of all she surveyed. She appeared to have forgiven Lily for leaving her for a few days and was happily installed back where she wanted to be. Lily didn't think cats could smile but she could swear that's what Misty was doing right now.

As Lily looked around, she felt a bittersweet ache inside her that her mother wasn't here to see the gift shop finally open. The shop may belong to her now but Lily knew it would also always be her mother's. She was going to make sure The Rowan Tree gift shop flourished for Patty and that her spirit lived on it in it.

Theirs might not have always been the most conventional relationship but they had loved each other and that was enough, Lily knew that now. Finally, she felt at peace with her mum and her memory of her. She was confident she had found the place she was supposed to be in life. This was where her mother had been happy and although she hadn't expected it, Lily had also found happiness.

She had plans for the flat upstairs. One of the rooms was going to be used as a stockroom and the other would be an office for Lily where she'd be able to do her accountancy work for Dallochmore. She'd done the initial work pro-bono but when Adam had asked her to stay on as the accountant for the distillery which she had happily accepted, he'd insisted on paying her the going rate. It was still early days at Dallochmore but Lily was cautiously optimistic that no outside investment would be needed to turn its fortunes around.

She looked over at Jack, who was smiling and laughing with Iris. He caught her eye and she felt as if her heart could quite literally explode with love for him. The days before she met him seemed to stretch into a sea of grey, monochrome days. As if her life before had been in black and white and was now in full technicolour.

The future was bright and Lily couldn't wait for it to begin.

Aknowledgements

Thank you to my editor Charlotte Mursell for her invaluable guidance and all the wonderful team at HQ Digital.

And thank you to my lovely family and friends for their love and support which means the world to me.

If you loved *The Little Gift Shop at the Loch*
then turn the page for an exclusive extract from
Summer at West Sands Guest House …

Chapter 1

Molly Adams peered into the bottom of the laundry basket. The few items of clothing barely warranted a whole wash cycle but she reached down and bundled them into the machine anyway. She didn't want anything lying about tomorrow, least of all her dirty washing.

A surprising array of internet recipes and supermarket meals for one had taken care of her eating but laundry for one had taken her by surprise, an unexpected consequence of her husband leaving her.

Standing in the small utility room, she let out a sigh. With its integrated appliances and fitted shelves, she'd always quite liked the warmth and cocoon-like feel of the small space and she stood for a few moments almost reluctant to move. The silence of the house was driving her mad and even the gurgling and slurping of the washing machine was welcome.

Funny, it had been the laundry basket – or at least its contents – that had first alerted her. She could still recall the moment her insides had shifted uneasily as the unfamiliar scent wafting from her husband's shirt assaulted her senses. She had placed the shirt in the washing machine, setting the dial to the highest temperature – totally unsuitable for the luxury two-ply fabric Colin

209

favoured. Part of her had hoped the shirt might disintegrate in the wash. Perhaps if she destroyed the evidence, they could carry on as normal. Except deep down, she had known normal wasn't good. She had noticed a brightness in her husband's eyes, a spring in his step that she knew wasn't of her making.

She hadn't confronted him immediately, hadn't been in a particular hurry to have the conversation that might end their five-year marriage. Because although she had wondered about the state of their marriage for some time, she certainly hadn't expected her husband's infidelity to bring it to an ignominious end. She needed to live with the notion that her husband was having an affair, to bolster herself for what she knew was surely to come. She thought she should be rallying herself to put up a fight to save their marriage, except she wasn't sure exactly what she would be fighting for.

She had tried to pinpoint the moment their lives seemed to have veered in different directions. Molly had known Colin was driven but it wasn't until after they were married that she realised just how ambitious he really was. It seemed with every step he took up the corporate ladder he also took a step further away from her.

Molly supposed she'd always been more of a dreamer, not just in her career but in life generally. She liked to view the future as an unknown quantity, new things to discover, surprises still to come. Colin on the other hand was a planner and liked to look ahead – preferably with a spreadsheet involved. She began to feel caught in his tailwind, always trying to keep up with him.

A year ago, Molly had been made redundant at the same time Colin had gained a big promotion in the financial company where he worked. She was proud of his success and he was sympathetic for her loss but instead of pulling them closer, it had the opposite effect. While his career soared, Molly's had stalled and she'd taken a temporary position covering maternity leave. Colin clearly wasn't impressed with her temping status;

Molly suspected it annoyed him that she wasn't following a clear career path.

At school Molly had been undecided about her future, shuffling along to the careers teacher admitting she didn't have a clue what she wanted to do. Somehow between them, they'd conjured up marketing and so after school she started her degree.

In her first year at university, Molly had met Declan, an effortlessly cool and impossibly good-looking arts student from Galway who told Molly her wild red hair and emerald green eyes reminded him of home. Her hair was closer to brown than red and her eyes were hazel but who was she to argue with such romanticism? Until then, her only experience had been clumsy, fumbling encounters with boys she knew from school. She had never met anyone like him and she was soon spending every minute she could with him – all her good intentions of working hard flying out the window. When, after several months, the relationship ended as suddenly as it had started, the resultant fallout had been responsible not only for breaking Molly's heart but also for her failing all her exams.

Studying for her resits during a miserable summer Molly wondered if university was right for her. But she had buckled down, passed all her resits and started second year determined to do well. From that point on, when she wasn't attending lectures she squirrelled herself away in the library. It was there one day, when she was stretching for a book on the top shelf, that a safe pair of hands had reached out and prevented it from toppling on her.

She had turned to find Colin. Handsome and serious, Molly had immediately fallen for him, impressed by his focus and self-assuredness. She liked that he was organised and remembered important dates. What he may have lacked in spontaneity (Declan had once turned up with a picnic and whisked her away from classes to spend the day at Loch Lomond), he made up for in dependability (she recalled all the times Declan had never showed up).

Studying economics, Colin was two years ahead of Molly so that by the time she graduated, he was already on his career path. On the day of her graduation Molly had been surprised but delighted when Colin offered her a dazzling engagement ring which she had readily accepted. She knew they were young but she had seen that as a good thing, a sign they were meant to be together.

Using her parents' perfect marriage as her guiding light, Molly knew she had found the right man to follow in their footsteps. She had been full of hope on the day of her wedding; this was the start of her fairy tale and she had no reason to suppose it wouldn't last.

But then came the day of the laundry discovery. When several days had passed and Molly finally gathered her courage to talk to Colin, he'd admitted to the affair immediately and told her he was leaving. She couldn't believe that he hadn't wanted to discuss it, that he was so ready to throw it all away.

'Aren't we at least going to talk about it?' she'd asked him.

'It's too late, I'm sorry.' He'd shuffled on his feet awkwardly, unable to meet her eye. Beneath his contrite expression, Molly saw relief and she knew there was no way back for them. She looked at him, wondering what had happened to the man she had married.

Gone was the man she'd trusted and thought she'd grow old with. In his place there was a man she barely recognised. One who had become very particular about the clothes he wore and the car he drove, and preferred dinner parties to nights in the pub. One who spent more time at work than at home and took business calls before hers. One who had lied and cheated.

A woman at work was enough information for Molly. She resisted asking for the details – what good could come from knowing when it had started, if he'd bought her gifts, if they'd shared a hotel room at the conference he'd attended in Paris. No, she refused to acknowledge the cliché their marriage had become.

Colin moved out quickly, clearly in a hurry to get on with his new life. Strange, difficult days followed. At times Molly felt like running away – where to, she had no idea. But running wasn't an option; she had her job to go to and didn't want to let anyone down. And it had been the job that had acted as a life-raft of sorts, giving her a routine and a reason to get out of bed each day.

So Molly had remained in the house on her own, desperately trying to cling to normality. Functioning on automatic pilot, she went to work and avoided people. She'd told only those who needed to know, which turned out to be not many. Cossetted in what she thought was the security of her life with Colin, letting friendships fade had been all too easy. Colin told her to keep the house as if he were doing her a massive favour but the truth was, she'd never really liked the house.

It had been Colin who insisted they go and see a new-build estate on the outskirts of Glasgow. Molly's dream of starting married life in a spacious red sandstone in the West End, of weekends spent painting, varnishing floorboards and strolling around the bustling bars and vintage shops were slowly extinguished by the gushing sales advisor fawning over the flawless finishes of the contemporary kitchen and the dual-aspect bay-windowed lounge.

She'd turned to Colin, his eyes shining.

'There's not much character,' she'd whispered to him.

'Who cares about character? With the deal they're offering first time buyers we'll be quids in, we won't do any better than this.' With little or no knowledge on such things she had bowed to his financial acumen. She'd simply been happy there were four bedrooms and had felt a little inner glow as she imagined children filling the rooms.

She had tried to make the most of the house but no amount of coloured cushions, clever lighting or potted plants ever seemed to infuse any real warmth into it. It had always felt soulless to her. The first few times Molly had driven into the cul-de-sac of identikit houses, she struggled to recognise her own home and had resorted to placing a bright yellow plant pot outside their front door.

All their neighbours appeared happy enough with families coming and going. Some mornings Molly would see a group of women clad in tight black Lycra, meeting after the school drop to go for a power walk. Other days they morphed into sleek looking businesswomen, suited and booted, jangling keys and driving off in their Mercedes or BMWs. She thought maybe she'd join their ranks one day but anytime she raised the subject of children, Colin managed to sidestep the issue. Now she was certain he'd never had any intention of starting a family and the thought made her stomach knot in anger.

Wandering through to the front room, Molly wasn't sure how she had got through the last few months. She'd rattled about the house on her own, trying to find comfort in being able to leave clutter lying around, cry at romantic films and read until midnight with the light on, her once endearing habits that had clearly come to annoy Colin.

Colin hadn't wanted to take much and there was little evidence that he'd ever lived here. She almost marvelled at how efficiently he had extracted himself from her life. He handled the dissolution of their marriage the way he handled everything, and she was subjected to his ruthless efficiency for one last time. She certainly didn't want to prolong it or demean the situation further by haggling or stalling for time but all the same was shocked by just how quickly and clinically Colin was treating their divorce.

Apparently, if neither of them contested their 'irretrievable breakdown', it could all be over in weeks. With no children involved, all they had to do was agree over property and financial matters. He'd done all the paperwork and she just needed to sign on the dotted line. All so simple.

When Colin had brought round the papers for signing, Molly

had inadvertently seen The Other Woman pacing up and down at the side of Colin's car, taking a phone call. She had to admit, she didn't look a total lush. Ultra slim with a sleek bob and a dark business suit, Molly couldn't help thinking she'd been traded in for a more efficient model. Because although Molly hadn't grilled Colin for details, that hadn't stopped her imagining who the other woman was, how much more beautiful and talented she must be. In some ways, that she looked so normal made her feel worse; it was easier to think of her as some evil temptress intent on wrecking their marriage.

Molly also discovered that day why Colin wasn't overly concerned about the house and its contents. Not even trying to conceal his excitement, he told Molly he was relocating to the company's head office in New York – presumably with *her*. When he told Molly it was a dream come true, she had swallowed with difficulty. It was a dream he had never shared with her.

In the kitchen now, Molly glanced at the oversized retro clock hanging on the wall, willing time to speed up. Now that she was going, she wanted to get on with it. More for something to do than a desire for caffeine, she decided to make herself a coffee. She'd never got the hang of the fancy coffee maker Colin had insisted on buying despite its astronomical price. Still, it had outlived her marriage, she thought savagely as she watched the thick black liquid trickle into a cup.

Carrying it through to the hall Molly studied her reflection in the hall mirror.

On the surface, she looked more or less the same. Her auburn hair was longer than usual and the shadows beneath her large, dark brown eyes were certainly more pronounced. But inside, Molly knew she was different. Her self-esteem had as good as packed its bag and left with Colin.

Miserable introspection had been her constant companion these last few weeks and she knew her confidence had vanished. Anger, sadness, resentment all vied for each other as she tried to work out how she had got it so wrong. Each time she thought she had some sort of handle on her emotions, she veered another way until now there was just emptiness.

Taking a deep breath, she whispered her mantra to her reflection; *I'll be fine.*

She wasn't sure what would come next, it was almost impossible to contemplate. Her marriage may be over but so much of her identity was connected to Colin. It was odd to be considering a future without him. Occasional moments of optimism surfaced – hope for what the future might bring – but those moments were eclipsed just as quickly by fear.

At times anxiety and regret threatened to spill over but she forced them back down, determined not to give them a voice in her head. Her life with Colin had been dismantled and now she had to somehow reassemble her life on her own.

The walls had started to close in on her and she knew she had to make a decision. Selling the house was the only option – she certainly couldn't stay here, not now. The house was ready. Colin's penchant for minimalism had ensured Phil Spencer's top tip for selling – depersonalise and declutter – had been easy to achieve. No doubt a few eyebrows would be raised tomorrow when a For Sale sign was hammered into the small patch of clipped grass that constituted their front garden. There had been something liberating about handing over a set of keys to the estate agent's, entrusting them with the viewings. The young estate agent had all but rubbed his hands together when she'd given him the instruction, no doubt anticipating his commission thanks to the recently published league table which had put their house in the catchment area for one of the best performing schools in the country.

Molly checked, perhaps for the fiftieth time that day, her holdall sitting by the front door ready to go tomorrow. Hopefully she'd remembered everything she needed for the next few weeks. Now that her temping job had ended, she was free to embark on her summer escape, as she had taken to calling it.

A whole summer lay ahead of her and apart from selling the house she had made no other decisions. Something about it felt seismic, a sense she was on the cusp of change. This time tomorrow she'd be at West Sands Guest House and she couldn't wait.

Chapter Two

It may have been June and technically summer but that had never stopped the clouds sweeping in from the Atlantic and unleashing their load onto the west of Scotland and today was no different. Molly hated motorway driving, even more so in wet conditions, and her hands gripped the steering wheel tightly as she concentrated on the road ahead. Huddled in her faithful little red Ford, she stayed in the slow lane, silently cursing every time a lorry thundered by and sent spray lashing onto her window screen.

Earlier that morning she had slipped out of the house, locked the front door and driven out of the quiet cul-de-sac without looking back. In a few hours she'd be at West Sands Guest House in St Andrews and once again, she thanked her lucky stars the way things had worked out.

Molly had resisted running to her parents no matter how effusive she knew their welcome would be – that was assuming they even had room for her in their bijou apartment overlooking Palmira's golf course which was proving to be a very popular destination for friends and family to visit.

Molly's parents had waited for her to finish university before selling the family home in Glasgow where Molly had grown up and retiring to Portugal. Molly had in effect gone from living with her parents to living with Colin. This was her first time flying-solo as it were – albeit not by choice – and she needed to prove to herself as well as to them that she could stand on her own two feet.

She couldn't imagine anything sadder than having your divorced daughter barge in on your well-earned retirement. The thought of facing them, of seeing the disappointment in their faces was something she was quite willing to delay. Her fear was that she would somehow simply crumple and lose herself under their love and attention.

The truth was, Molly felt ashamed. Her happily married and loving parents would somehow reinforce her guilt and shame that she had failed to make her marriage work. She didn't want the fretting and the looks of concern – disrupting their lives would only make her feel worse.

Instead Molly had turned to her brother Stuart. After leaving the family home in Glasgow, he had completed his PhD at Oxford University and had then taken a job lecturing history at Manchester University.

Imparting the news of Colin's affair had produced a few choice expletives from her usually softly spoken brother before he shared his own news which had unexpectedly provided her with a welcome reprieve from agonising about her future – for the next few weeks anyway.

An old friend from his Oxford days had recently started work at St Andrews University, and had contacted Stuart regarding a job lecturing history and he had jumped at the chance. When they were younger, Molly and Stuart had spent a few holidays in St Andrews, mainly to accommodate their parents' love of golf and Molly knew Stuart had always coveted a move to Scotland's oldest university. He and his wife, Anna had decided to up sticks and move their family from Manchester to Scotland. Anna worked as a freelance software developer and after having a difficult year of her own, was happy to start afresh in the small Scottish town.

His friend from Oxford, Ben Matthews, had recently settled in the town himself and as luck would have it, Ben's wife ran a guest house which they could have until they found somewhere of their own to live.

'Come and stay with us,' he said simply.

Memories of those idyllic holidays flickered happily through Molly's mind. Carefree days before grown-up worries of relationships, careers and, in her case, divorces. Frankly, it sounded so perfect she could have wept but she sought reassurance she wouldn't be in the way.

'In the way? Are you kidding? We can always do with an extra pair of hands and the kids would love to see you. There's loads of room and Mum and Dad will be coming for some of the time too.'

Knowing her parents would be there had clinched it for Molly. Stuart and the family would provide a welcome distraction and ensure she wasn't the sole focus of their attention and hopefully by the time she saw them, she'd be feeling stronger.

Molly had hung up, relief filtering through her body. The next few weeks lay ahead enticingly empty, hopefully giving her the time and space she so badly needed to decide what came next. Or perhaps not to think at all. Simply to be herself again and not Colin's wife – she needed to try and remember what that felt like.

Now, as Molly continued to drive eastwards across the country, the rain eventually stopped and the clouds parted to make way for a pale blue sky. A good omen, she thought, feeling her shoulders loosen. She flicked on the radio, humming along to the music, feeling her spirits lift at the thought of the guest house by the sea filled with noise and family.

Soon she was passing through little fishing villages, navigating her way through narrow, windy roads and looking out onto sandy beaches and picturesque harbours. Approaching St Andrews, Molly slowed down, recognising the skyline of the grand, stately university buildings and other familiar landmarks of the town.

Molly had been delighted when Stuart had told her the guest house was at West Sands beach. Slowing down as she drew closer to the house, Molly let out a little gasp. A rather grand-looking Victorian house, it sat opposite a sweep of white sand with the sea stretching into the distance. Dark green ivy tumbled down the soft redbrick walls and the windows glittered in the afternoon sunshine. Terracotta pots brimming with small creamy flowers stood either side of the glossy blue front door.

The wheels crunched on the gravel driveway as Molly brought the car to a halt and she smiled, seeing the small welcoming party that had formed at the door to meet her. She felt her heart squeeze with love for them. Stuart lifted a hand and waved to her, his other arm around his wife's shoulders. Seeing Stuart and Anna standing there reminded Molly of her parents. Like them they looked so happy and made it look easy – they did marriage well in this family, all except her it seemed. If she didn't love them so much it would be easy to feel envious. She was barely out of the car before they swooped down on her with hugs and kisses.

'You're here!'

Wrapped in the warmth of Anna's embrace, Molly's suddenly shaky equilibrium was painfully tested but she swallowed down the tears that threatened, determined not to lose it now. Luckily the moment passed as her brother pulled her in for a gruff-like brotherly hug.

'Good to see you, little sis.' Molly grinned up at him, so happy to see her brother. At thirty-five, he was six years older than Molly. Growing up there had never been any rivalry between the siblings even though Stuart had given Molly enough reason for there to be one, at least academically. Instead she was proud of her brother's straight A record and subsequent offers from the country's top universities.

Tall, dark and totally oblivious to the effect his looks had on women, Molly had assumed the role of protector, vetting who was suitable. Operating on the premise that no one was good enough for her brother, Molly had been prepared not to like Anna, the first girl Stuart had ever brought home. But any fears Molly had were quashed within seconds of meeting her and she had pretty much charmed the whole family.

Not only had she been good for her brother – she had lovingly pulled him back from a life of crumpled corduroy and tweed jackets – she had become a good friend to Molly, too.

Molly turned to her eleven-year-old niece Lily. Wearing jeans and a sparkly T-shirt and sharing her father's reserved nature, she had held back slightly. She gave her aunt a shy look and Molly enveloped her in a hug. Luke, on the other hand, had no such reservations and stood beside Molly grinning up at her.

'Look at you! You've grown!' Molly exclaimed, ruffling his blond hair. Luke held himself tall, beaming a cheeky grin. 'I'm five now,' he announced proudly.

Stuart opened the boot and lifted her bag out. 'Brought your golf clubs, I see?' he chuckled.

'How could I not when I knew I was coming here. Thought I might see if you had time for a game.'

'What and be humiliated? Not likely.'

Molly laughed, shaking her head. 'I'll be totally useless now anyway, I haven't played for so long.'

It had always been a bit of a family joke that Molly was the son their father had always wanted. With his aversion to the great outdoors, Stuart preferred spending his time with his head in a book while Molly would be out tramping the golf course with their father.

Luke suddenly grabbed Molly by the hands, pulling her towards the house excitedly.

'Give Aunt Molly a chance,' Anna chastised him good-naturedly.

And in that moment, as Molly was swept into the house, she couldn't think of a single place she'd rather be.

****

'That was delicious,' Molly said gratefully, feeling nicely full from the paella Anna had made. The crisp Sauvignon Blanc had also gone down a treat. Sitting at the large oak table in the dining room, Molly felt herself start to relax as she caught up with Stuart and Anna.

It had turned into a beautiful evening and the adults smiled, hearing the shrieks of delight floating through the French doors from the garden where Lily and Luke were playing.

'You certainly know the right presents to bring your niece and nephew,' Anna commented sagely.

'Couldn't really go wrong with water guns, could I?' Molly grinned.

Stuart had been bringing Molly up to date about his new job at the university, which to all intents and purposes he'd already started. He and Anna had known for a while now that there was no such thing as long summer holidays for university lecturers and that the academic grindstone never truly stopped.

'I'm working on proposals for a funding initiative and supervising some students completing their final projects. I'm also preparing a workshop on the study of Medieval Scotland,' he explained with his usual enthusiasm as he topped up their glasses.

'Think I get the picture – no rest for the wicked,' Molly teased. 'So you've already met your colleagues?'

'Most of them, they all seem very nice,' he murmured vaguely. Molly smiled to herself. Often suspecting her brother's mind was somewhere in the fifteenth century half the time, she knew that even if his colleagues were awful, he probably wouldn't notice or comment.

With a sigh, Molly sat back in her seat and took a sip of her wine, her eyes sweeping the room. Buttermilk-coloured walls complemented the oak furniture and a large seagrass rug sat on the wooden floor. There was a small side table piled with brochures and local maps for visitors and a small indoor bay tree sat next to a comfy cream wicker armchair. The room oozed comfort and style.

Following her gaze, Anna smiled. 'Isn't this house just perfect?' she said.

Molly had felt it as soon as she stepped into the house earlier: an ambience which seemed to draw you into its warm embrace. And judging by the toy-strewn floor – she'd already had to avoid stepping on Luke's cars – the children had made themselves very much at home.

'So it's Ben's wife Eva that runs the guest house, is that right?' Molly asked.

Anna nodded. 'She used to run this house as a bed and breakfast but she lives next door now with Ben and her son Jamie. Obviously she knew our situation and she explained that as this was her first summer renting out the whole house, a longer let suited her perfectly. So, we've been so lucky to get it for as long as we need.'

'A case of good timing.'

'Definitely. Eva came round and had a coffee and stayed chatting for ages. She's just set up her own interior design business and her son Jamie is a year older than Lily so she'll be going to the same school as him.'

'Ben teaches physics, is that right?'

Stuart nodded. 'He's been showing me around the university and introducing me to a few people which has been really helpful.'

Molly nodded with a smile. 'Well, I'm glad to hear it's all working out so well.'

'And of course, as long as we are here, you can stay. There's no immediate rush for you to go back is there?' Stuart lifted an eyebrow.

Molly took a moment to gather her thoughts.

'Well, I'll have to deal with the house sale at some point but it's only just gone on the market. Then after that, I'll need to find somewhere to live – I was thinking I might rent for a while. And of course, I'll need to find another job.' Damn that little wobble in her voice. She cleared her throat, noticing the small exchange of glances between her brother and Anna.

224

Molly knew they had been concerned about her and she appreciated being able to speak them but she'd done enough sobbing down the phone. She'd told them she'd love to visit them in St Andrews but on the proviso there was to be no post-mortem of her marriage. She really didn't want to rake over the ashes of her marriage. She'd vowed she wouldn't let her newly divorced status intrude on their family holiday and so she drew in a deep breath, determined not to falter. *I'll be fine.*

'We just wish there was something more we could do.'

'Being here with you now is enough,' Molly said firmly. She gave Stuart a pointed look. 'And you don't need to tiptoe around me. You've never done it before and don't you dare start now,' she told him. Stuart held his hands up in mock surrender, lightening the mood.

'Okay, but remember I am still your big brother despite the fact you've bossed me about your whole life.'

'That's because you needed it for your own good,' Molly countered with a grin.

'Anyway, I'll have Mum for back up when she arrives.'

Molly rolled her eyes. 'You always were her blue-eyed boy,' she said affectionately. 'Do we know exactly when they're arriving?' she asked.

'Dad managed to get them tickets for the last day's play of the tournament at the old course in a couple of weeks.'

Molly took a gulp of wine, her mind calculating how long she had to shore up her defences before facing her mother's barrage of concern.

A sudden high-pitched scream from outside indicated delight had turned to disaster and five seconds later Lily marched in followed by a sheepish looking Luke. They were both drenched.

'Mum, he squirted the water at my face on purpose and hit my eye.' Lily was close to tears, her face puce with indignation. Anna sighed, automatically rising from her seat to mediate.

'Remember I said no faces, Luke? Say sorry to Lily, please.'

'Sorry, Lily,' he parroted. Then with all remorse instantly forgotten he turned to Molly. 'Is Uncle Colin not coming to see us anymore?'

'Shut up, Luke.' Lily scowled.

The simplicity and unexpectedness of the question took Molly by surprise, as did the tears that suddenly welled in her eyes.

'Right you two. Upstairs for showers now!' Stuart interjected. 'Tell you what,' he said, turning to his wife and Molly. 'Why don't you two take a stroll? Go and have a drink somewhere and I'll deal with these two little horrors.'

Molly wasn't sure she was in the mood to go out. All her recent interactions with people had been confined to work colleagues and even having a meal with Stuart and Anna had felt slightly alien. But Anna was clapping her hands together, rushing over to plant a kiss on Stuart's cheek.

'Come on, Molly, let's go before he changes his mind.'

After a quick freshen up – and in Molly's case a few private moments to compose herself – the two women were soon strolling along the cobbled streets, the setting sun casting the last of its golden rays over the town. Most of the shops had closed but there were plenty of people milling around, choosing where to have their evening meal.

Anna turned her head towards Molly. 'Sorry about Luke earlier. We didn't say anything to him but he must have overheard us talking.' She grimaced.

Molly waved her hand indicating it was nothing. 'Don't worry. Besides, he's only five. It's not his fault.'

'I understand you don't want to talk about things, but you are okay? Stuart has been worried about you.'

'I know,' Molly sighed, hating the thought of her family worrying about her.

She frowned, trying to remember the last time Colin had even seen her family, realising he had managed to extricate himself from any recent gatherings. She'd always hoped Colin and Stuart would have bonded but it had never happened.

'Colin and Stuart never did have much in common, did they?' she commented now.

'They were very different people,' Anna said diplomatically. 'As long as you know we're here for you.'

'Thanks. But honestly I'm fine,' Molly replied, forcing a bright smile.

Steering away from the main street and down a little lane, they found a rustic-looking pub and were soon ensconced at a table surrounded by the hum of conversation and the occasional peals of laughter erupting from a group sitting at one of the larger tables.

'Cheers.' They clinked glasses.

'You're going to love it here,' Molly enthused. 'What a great place for the children to grow up.'

Anna made a face, picking up her glass. 'I'm not sure Lily would agree with you, she's very unsure about the whole move.'

Molly had noticed Lily seemed a bit quiet, even for her. 'Is she really worried?'

'She's a bit sensitive just now – I think that's why she over-reacted with Luke earlier. It's fair to say she resents us for dragging her away from all her old friends to a new school. I've tried to tell her everything will be fine but she's so shy and you know how cruel children can be.'

'I don't suppose anyone wants to be the new kid at school, do they?'

Molly's heart went out to her niece. She knew all the reassur-ances in the world wouldn't stop Lily worrying about her first day at a new school not knowing anyone. 'Hopefully being in a small community will make it easier for her to make new friends.'

Anna agreed. 'That's why I'd like to try and get a new house sorted as soon as possible – I think being settled before the chil-dren start school will help. Plus if I stay in the guest house too

227

long I'll feel like I'm on a permanent holiday and that won't do at all.'

Molly looked affectionately at her sister-in-law. Her petite frame, elfin-cut blonde hair and large blue eyes belied the strength of the woman underneath. As well as being one of the smartest people Molly had ever met, she was one of the most driven with a work ethic that put lesser mortals to shame.

Anna had met Stuart when he had moved to work in Manchester. She worked for a high-tech company and did amazing things with computers that Molly didn't understand. After the children were born she set up as a freelance software developer and was so successful that now people came to her. She didn't do rest. For as long as Molly had known her, Anna had always been involved in some job, working long hours. And being your average everyday super woman, she appeared to balance it all.

Except looking at her now, Molly could see tiredness etched on her features, a lack of her customary sparkle. But then it was hardly surprising, she'd had a horrible eighteen months. She had lost both her parents and as an only child she'd taken the full brunt of the dealing with the illnesses that had claimed first her mother and then her father. Molly had met Anna's parents at the odd family occasion. They had been lovely and Molly could only imagine how painful it must be for Anna to lose them both.

'What about you, how have you been?' Molly asked her now.

'Oh, I'm fine,' she replied breezily.

'You don't have a job on at the moment, do you?'

'No, I'm taking a few weeks off for the move.'

'I'm glad to hear it. I know things have been difficult but hopefully this will be a fresh start for all of you,' Molly encouraged.

Anna attempted a smile but didn't quite make it.

Molly looked at her with concern. 'Are you sure you're all right?'

Anna sighed and looked down. 'I know moving here is the right thing. It's just the thought of starting over and meeting new people can seem a bit daunting I suppose. I've always lived in a city with Mum and Dad close by and I suppose I miss them more than I could have thought possible.' She lifted her hands then let them drop in her lap.

Molly reached over and squeezed her arm. 'It's going to take time.'

Anna stared into her glass before taking a deep breath. 'You're right.' She sat up straight, giving herself a shake. 'And as you say, coming here is a new start. Will we have one more before we go? This is your first night here and we better make the most of it. I'll make them large.'

Molly watched Anna make her way to the bar. She knew the alcohol had lowered her defences but it was still odd to see Anna, usually so strong and confident, sounding despondent.

She could only imagine how difficult it must be for Anna and wished she could find words to give her comfort. At least she knew she could be here for her and vowed there and then to do as much as possible to help in any way she could. It also showed her that her decision not to unload any of her own woes had been the right thing to do. Anna and Stuart had quite enough to deal with.

Anna appeared brighter as she brought their drinks over and proposed a toast.

'Here's to summer,' she said lifting her glass. 'I'm so glad you came.'

'As long as I'm not in the way.'

Anna shook her head. 'But I will admit, I do have an ulterior motive. I was hoping you'd help me look for houses – you know what Stuart's like. Ask him anything you want about medieval kings but he's not so hot on the merits of south-facing gardens.'

Molly giggled. 'Of course, I'd love to help you.'

'I've already seen an estate agent and got a viewing lined up.'

'That's exciting.'

'It'll be good to get the furniture out of storage and get settled.' Anna drained her glass, her gaze homing in on a group of men sitting across from them. 'Just think of all the nice men out there you could meet now.'

Molly shook her head. 'Not interested.'

'A few dates wouldn't do any harm though, would it?'

Even hearing the word 'date' made Molly feel slightly hysterical. Was that something she was going to have to do in the future? The idea was quite appalling.

'You need to get back out there,' Anna announced, nodding her head.

Molly wasn't sure about much recently – the foundations of her life had shifted – but one thing she did know unequivocally was that she was not interested in relationships, meeting someone, having a fling or anything else man-related.

She grimaced even thinking about it – she was so not ready at all for that. Far too soon and scary.

Another large glass later and, feeling quite pleased with themselves, Molly and Anna started to walk back to the house. Molly had consumed just the right amount of alcohol to put a positive spin on things. Her marriage wasn't a waste of precious years, she would find love again and somehow a career – or at least a job she loved – would miraculously appear. Yes, her life was looking much brighter through a soft-focus alcohol haze.

Anna hiccupped. 'I'm so happy you came.'

'I think you said that already.'

'Did I? Well, I am.'

'Stuart might not be so happy when he sees the state we're in. He'll think I'm a bad influence.' They giggled, linking arms as they stepped out onto the road.

Molly let out a yelp of surprise as car brakes sounded followed by an angry beep behind them. They jumped back on the pavement, Molly catching the striking blue eyes of the driver as he passed by with a shake of his head.

'Well, that was rude,' she said indignantly, managing to totally ignore the fact they had walked onto the road without looking. And laughing, they headed back to the house.

Chapter Three

Molly opened one eye and groaned. She lay still while her body processed the miseries of her hangover; nausea, pounding head and a dry mouth. Slowly she opened the other eye to see a room full of unfamiliar shapes and shadows and it took her mind a moment to piece together where she was and the reason for her current fragile state.

She had enjoyed last night and it had been good to relax and chat with Anna but getting drunk on her first night probably hadn't been the best idea. She remained motionless, listening for any sounds but thankfully the house was blissfully quiet. She wasn't sure she could cope with noise right now.

Very slowly she sat up and looked around. Her bedroom was one of five in the house and situated at the back of the guest house. When she'd arrived yesterday, Luke had insisted on giving her a tour of the house. Stuart and Anna's room was at the front of the house, a beautiful coastal themed room with duck-egg-blue walls and views of the sea. Another of the bedrooms was painted in pale green with a tartan armchair and a painting of the Cairngorms hanging over the fireplace.

Molly's room was unashamedly feminine with decorative floral wallpaper and cream embroidered bedding. A ceramic lamp and a pot filled with sprigs of purple heather sat on a traditional wooden dressing table in front of the window.

It certainly had to be the prettiest room to have a hangover in, she thought ruefully. Gently peeling back the covers she swung her legs over the side of the bed, eyeing her bag still full of her clothes sitting in the corner of the room. There hadn't really been time to unpack yesterday so that was a job for later. She narrowed her eyes against the daylight as she drew the curtains open. By the looks of the weather she had been right to treat herself to some new summer clothes.

When Molly had decided to sort through her summer wardrobe a few weeks ago, she had become painfully aware all the clothes had been chosen because she knew they would meet with Colin's approval.

For the last couple of years, Colin had been very specific about the holidays they had taken. He had taken to lording it up in five-star resorts, lounging at the pool all day and dining in the best restaurants. Molly hadn't always enjoyed that type of holiday – there were cities and places she dreamed of exploring – but she respected that Colin worked hard and needed his rest and relaxation. Priding himself on his skin being able to turn a particular shade of brown, the focus of the entire day had been rotating his sunbed to follow the sun and the only thing Colin wanted to explore after a hard day's tanning was the bar's cocktail list. Molly's summer clothes, therefore, were suitable for either lounging at the pool during the day or dining in restaurants where the dress code dictated she squeeze herself into formal evening wear.

Gathering up all those clothes, she had folded them neatly into bags and taken them to the charity shop and then taken herself to the shops.

With only herself to please now, she'd indulged in a spree of floaty, casual and feminine clothes – ditsy skirts and flowery dresses, brightly coloured vest tops and shorts, flat sandals – a world away from the restrictive clothes she had poured herself into. She'd also taken the precaution of packing a few jackets and jumpers; this was Scotland, after all.

Feeling mildly better after a hot shower in the en-suite bathroom, she dressed in skinny jeans, a stripy blue and white T-shirt and her comfortable trainers. As she made her way downstairs, a message pinged on her phone explaining why the house was deserted. Stuart's message said that he and Anna had taken the children off for the day to a nearby country park and that they'd bring home fish and chips for dinner. She baulked at the thought of food right now, but texted him back telling them to have a great day and that she'd see them later.

She wandered through the hall and into the front room. The cream walls were bathed in morning sunlight and two large sofas sat either side of a cast-iron fireplace. In one corner a shelved recess held a selection of board games and paperbacks for guests. Molly ran her finger along some of the titles reflecting on how much she liked being here in the guest house. Not just because it was so comfortable and stylish but because of its neutrality after the suffocating atmosphere she'd left behind in her own home. She liked that there were no reminders of Colin or their marriage. She felt free from the confines of her normal life and routines and that suited her. Spotting the title of a book she'd wanted to read for ages she made a mental note to come back for it later. A mug of tea and an early night suddenly sounded very appealing.

In the kitchen Molly saw the scattered remains of breakfast still in evidence and set about tidying up. She washed down the surfaces, wiping away splodges of jam and puddles of milk and put away a huge box of cereal. Once she had finished tidying, she found a glass and as she filled it with cold water, felt a pang of guilt, hoping Anna wasn't feeling as bad as she did. She drank thirstily, thinking how much energy it took to have children. Not that she would mind of course. She knew there was a flip side to all the worry and hard work. There was the love and laughter, both things she hoped to have one day. She sighed, rinsing her glass, not prepared to let her thinking go down that route.

In the meantime, she had the day to herself. The urge to collapse on that lovely squashy sofa was tempting but outside the sunshine beckoned and Molly reckoned a good dose of sea air was just what she needed.

Within minutes she was walking along the cobbled streets, mingling with families and tourists and enjoying the warmth of the sun on her skin. The last time she'd been here was as a girl with her parents and now she absorbed her surroundings with new eyes. The quaint, charming town with its eclectic mix of shops and cafés made the city feel a million miles away.

Out of nowhere Colin zipped into her mind and she wondered what he was doing, if he was happy with his new life. The only communication between them had been the odd email about the divorce proceedings. How formal and final it all sounded.

She took a deep breath of fresh air, determined not to let thoughts of her ex-husband infiltrate her mind. Instead, she tried to allow a sense of tranquillity wash over her. She was here to think about the future, not the past. For today though, she simply wanted to explore and get a sense of her surroundings.

Heading towards the water she took a few moments to admire the fine grandeur of the Royal and Ancient Golf Club before continuing through the leafy medieval streets where many of the university buildings were housed. She walked through St Mary's quadrangle, stopping to read the plaque by the decayed stump of a hawthorn tree which, according to legend, Mary Queen of Scots had planted on one of her many visits to the town. Molly smiled, knowing how much her brother was going to love this. The historical setting would be a dream for him.

She kept walking, following a path between the golf course and the beach which snaked along the coastline until it eventually started to turn inland. She crossed over a footbridge and then upwards through a wooded glen, pausing at a little burn trickling down the hill.

Molly enjoyed the peace and let her thoughts wander until she had to stop to catch her breath. Standing with her hands on her hips, she looked back the way she had come and although it afforded her a lovely view of the town, she realised she had walked much further than she had intended. She didn't suppose the hangover was helping but she couldn't blame that entirely for her current state which was now decidedly weak and wobbly. There was nothing like a good hike to show how unfit you were, she thought wryly, feeling the full impact of her recent car-reliant existence. With her slightly alarming heart rate and jelly legs, she promised herself there and then to try and improve her fitness.

Still, the pain was worth it because now she was surrounded by trees and lush greenery. It was so tranquil, almost like being in the middle of an enchanted forest. She was glad of the shade provided by the trees and wished she'd had the sense to bring water with her.

She noticed a path and, walking towards it, spotted a carved wooden sign announcing The Drumloch Inn lay ahead. Very fortuitously, the sign also indicated food and beverages being served all day. Molly, quite weak with fatigue and dehydration by now, felt herself sag with relief. The thought of a seat and drink sounded heavenly.

The inn, almost hidden by shrubs and trees, was a charmingly pretty two-storey stone building with wisteria growing up the walls. Baskets spilling over with purple fuchsias graced both sides of the double front door and, as she walked through them, Molly had the sense of being in a rather grand country house.

Inside, the floor was carpeted in tweed and the walls panelled in dark wood. A large vase of lilies sat on a mantelpiece above an open fireplace and a beautifully ornate chandelier hung from the ceiling.

Molly approached the small reception desk where a lady sat.

Molly placed her to be in her sixties although her stylish bob and immaculate make-up gave her an ageless glamour.

'Good morning, can I help you?' the lady asked. Her glasses were perched on top of her head, reminding Molly of her own mother and her smile was so warm and genuine Molly immediately felt at ease.

'Hello. I'm not a guest here but is it all right if I sit and have a drink. I saw the sign—'

'Of course!' the lady gushed. She stood up, knocking a sheaf of papers to the floor.

'Sorry, I'm all fingers and thumbs today. We've got a new computer system installed and I'm still working my way through this manual…' She gestured to the offending documents which she had now retrieved from the floor. Straightening up and looking slightly flustered, she smiled again. 'Now, where were we? Come with me and I'll show you where you can have a seat.'

Molly followed her through to a lounge area of seating in front of arched windows which looked out onto an expanse of rolling greenery. Molly took a seat on one of the sofas, grateful to be off her aching feet and was soon perusing the drinks menu that the lady had given her.

Molly ran her eye down the selection of drinks on offer, surprised and delighted by the choice; hand-pressed apple juice, traditional ginger beer, elderflower and cucumber or berry and mint refreshers. She eventually decided on a sparkling rhubarb and after a few minutes the lady returned with the drink in a tall glass, served on a little coaster with a serviette.

Molly took a drink and sat back with a sigh of appreciation. Feeling slightly conspicuous as the solitary customer, she glanced around. Tartan and gingham sofas, comfy chairs and dark wooden tables adorned with small vases of flowers created a relaxed, cosy ambience. There was another fireplace and a small brass-topped bar tucked discreetly in the corner.

After a while the lady came over to check if Molly needed anything else.

'I'm Judy, the owner here. Do you mind if I join you for a little while?'

'Not at all.' Molly smiled, indicating the seat beside her. 'I'm Molly Adams, it's nice to meet you.'

The lady eased herself down gracefully onto the seat and Molly instantly sat up straighter.

'How was your drink?' she asked.

'I really enjoyed it,' Molly answered truthfully. 'It was delicious and very refreshing.'

The lady tilted her head, looking pleased. 'Thank you. It was one of my creations.'

'You make the drinks yourself?'

'I do. I source all the ingredients locally and then I have great fun concocting all the different flavours up.'

Molly was impressed.

'I have an excellent local cook who comes in to do the evening meals and breakfast but drinks are my speciality,' Judy explained. 'I was a flight attendant and I think all those years serving up drinks to passengers must have rubbed off on me.'

'Well, it was delicious,' Molly reiterated.

'Are you here on holiday?'

Molly explained about her brother coming to live in St Andrews with his family.

'I'm sure they'll be very happy here.'

Molly nodded in agreement and then admitted how she had stumbled on the inn by accident. 'It's such a lovely location here although I hadn't realised I had walked so far.'

Judy pursed her lips. 'We are a bit off the beaten track here. Which can be a good and bad thing. Once people find us, they love it and we have a lot of repeat business. Other times, being so far from the town can put people off.'

'It's a very romantic setting.'

'It is, isn't it? We only have six rooms – four doubles, one single and one family room so it's mostly couples who book.'

'How long have you owned it for?'

'My husband and I bought this place six years ago. I was a flight attendant and he was a pilot and we fell very much in love and it was always our dream to own a place like this. We had ten very happy years together but unfortunately he passed away four years ago.'

'I'm so sorry. That must be difficult for you.'

'It can be.' She gave a small smile. 'But the business keeps me busy which is good. Especially now the golf school is open again.' She nodded her towards the window.

Molly gazed out of the window and only now did it dawn on her she had in fact been looking out at a golf course. In the far distance Molly could make out a flag marking one of the course's holes.

'That's a golf course over there?'

'Yes, that's Drumloch golf course and though you can't see through the trees, there's a golf school and range as well.'

Molly perked up with interest.

'It was run down for a while,' Judy continued. 'But it's recently been bought over by two golf professionals and I know they've got plans for the place.'

'I might take a walk over and have a look.'

'Do you play golf?' Judy asked.

'I used to play a bit with my father,' she replied. 'What about you, do you play?'

'Me? Goodness, no. Never understood the mystery of chasing a white ball about,' she laughed. 'Although George played and always wanted me to learn so we could play together.'

'Well, I should probably get going,' Molly said, conscious she had the return walk to undertake.

'Why don't you go and have a look at the golf course now?' Judy suggested.

Molly hesitated.

'It really is only a few minutes' walk. When you leave here, turn right and you'll see a tree-lined path. Just follow it and when you come to a little picnic area with a couple of wooden tables, you're practically there.'

'How much do I owe you?' Molly asked, getting to her feet.

'On the house,' Judy insisted. 'I've enjoyed meeting you and it's been lovely to have a little chat.'

'Thank you, I've enjoyed it too,' Molly replied, surprised by how easy she had found talking to the older lady. Outside in the sunshine again and feeling rejuvenated, Molly debated with herself whether to go and check out the golf school now or come back another day.

When she had known she was coming to St Andrews Molly had dug out her set of clubs languishing in the attic collecting dust. Now she hoped to have some practice at one of the ranges and maybe persuade her brother to have a game.

Both her parents had played but it had been her father in particular who had passed on his love of the game to Molly. When she'd been a little girl, Molly hadn't been interested in dance classes, swimming or any of the other activities on offer but had taken to hitting the ball. One day her dad had taken her to a range and she could still recall the look of surprise on his face when, with apparent ease, she smacked a ball a hundred yards down the middle of the fairway. After that, she was his caddy whenever possible and when she was older she played with him at their local club.

Her father was a quiet, thoughtful man and not one to talk much but it became their thing to do together and some of her happiest memories were of the two of them on the course together. She sighed thinking of those times. Sometimes the simplest things really were the best.

At this time of year Molly knew all the golf facilities in town would be busy which was why this location was so appealing. She could see the little path now. Overhung with trees and

240

surrounded by wildflowers, it almost seemed to beckon her. Molly made an instant decision – she was this close, she may as well check it out.

After a few minutes she passed the picnic area that Judy had mentioned and then the golf school came into view – a modern, timber frame building with dark wood cladding.

To one side Molly could see the practice range which consisted of a row of covered bays and to the other side was a small putting green. Further away and set amidst the rolling hills, she could see the golf course perched on the rocky shores of the bay with the North Sea as its backdrop. The sun beamed down and sparkled on the water below and Molly took a moment to appreciate the rugged beauty of her surroundings.

She pushed the door open into a reception area which was basically a large room with a few doors leading off it. There was a small counter and a couple of chairs beside a table with a few golf magazines scattered on top.

A tall, gangly boy aged about twenty wearing a tracksuit came bounding over, introduced himself as Kenny and asked how he could help.

'I'd like to come the range one day,' Molly told him. 'Do I need to book in advance?'

The boy shook his head. 'You can turn up any time – but it's empty right now if you'd like to play, I can get you set up?'

Molly hesitated for a heartbeat and then decided why not? A little surge of excitement shot through her, it had been so long since she'd played or practised.

The boy helped to get the bucket full of golf balls and, as she didn't have her own clubs with her, gave her a selection of practice clubs to choose from. After thanking him, Molly made her way to the furthest away bay.

It felt odd to be holding a golf club again. She rolled her neck and loosened her shoulders before she started, her father's voice in her head. *Straight back, knees flexed and head steady.*

She took a few tentative shots to warm up, some more successful than others. Molly knew that playing golf wasn't like riding a bike. If you didn't practice, you lost the feel for it. And that was why she wanted to try and use this time because she knew she could be a fairly decent player and with that came confidence – something she was sorely lacking at the moment.

It all came back to her why she loved it so much. The focus it required, the satisfaction of striking the ball. Soon she was enjoying herself, getting into her stride and finding that hitting the ball was quite therapeutic. Considering she had a hangover and it was a few years since she'd hit a ball, she was feeling quite pleased with herself.

After several minutes of hitting the ball Molly heard a door opening and glanced up to see a man coming through one of the doors. Disappointed her solitude had been broken and not relishing the prospect of an audience, she kept her head down hoping he would go away. She lined up her next ball and for some unfathomable reason gave her hips a little wiggle in an attempt to look casual.

Swinging the club perhaps a little too enthusiastically, she caught the edge of the ball with an almighty thwack and watched helplessly as it ricocheted off the roof and rebounded hitting her on the head.

'Ouch!'

Molly stood stunned for a moment, hoping it had sounded worse than it was. She brought her fingers to her head but apart from a small lump forming there didn't seem to be any other damage.

Out the corner of her eye, Molly could see her little commotion had caused the man to look up. Silently willing for him not to come over she kept her head down, but it was too late – he was already making his way towards her.

'Are you all right?'

Molly looked up upon hearing the deep voice.

'Mmm? Oh, yes I'm fine.' She managed a little laugh but couldn't stop a furious blush flooding her cheeks. They regarded one another for a moment and Molly's heart dipped as she recognised the driver who'd made the emergency stop for her and Anna last night. She cringed inwardly, dropping her gaze. She decided ignorance was the best plan and just hoped he wouldn't recognise her.

'Are you sure you're okay? Do you need someone to look at your head?' he asked looking at her with concern.

'No, honestly. I didn't feel a thing,' she lied, beginning to feel uncomfortable under his scrutiny.

'Have you been to a golf range before?'

Molly frowned. 'Lots of times actually,' she replied defensively, not liking the feeling he was assessing her in some way.

'Try to take care then, we don't want anyone hurting themselves.'

Molly bristled that his concern was now bordering on admonishment and wished he'd just go away. Perhaps sensing her irritation, he managed to impart a perfunctory smile. Something about his manner was distinctly reserved, almost as if he wasn't sure he wanted to be there. Or worse, didn't want her to be there. She hoped he wasn't one of the sexist ignoramuses who thought women shouldn't play golf because if he was she might just swing the club in his direction. Molly was just wondering exactly who he was when he introduced himself.

'I'm Tom Kennedy, one of the golf professionals here.'

So that explained his concern. He was probably making sure she wasn't going to make some sort of injury claim. And knowing he was a professional sportsman certainly explained his physique and healthy, outdoorsy look. He held out a hand for her to shake, her hand feeling tiny in his large, firm grip.

'I'm Molly Adams.'

'As long as you're all right, then,' he said gruffly.

Even in her slightly inebriated state last night, some part of

Molly's brain had registered the handsome driver as he passed. Sober and up close her assessment was the same. In fact, he was very handsome, she observed now, her eyes taking in his piercing blue eyes, short dark hair and square jaw. He was tall with powerful-looking shoulders and Molly felt a ripple of attraction run through her. Clearly the alcohol was still fizzing its way through her system.

Seemingly reassured she wasn't about to pass out he took a step back and leaned against the partition board, his large frame filling the small space. Molly's eyes drifted to his tanned forearms and swallowed hard.

'Are you here on holiday in St Andrews?'

She nodded. 'My brother and his family have taken a guest house for the summer so I'm staying with them for a few weeks.'

'Do you play much golf?' he asked.

Molly got the sense he was trying to appear friendly but it wasn't coming easily to him. If he was one of the new owners he might want to brush up on his people skills.

'I was captain for my local club's girls' team and I've played some great courses actually.'

She saw his eyebrow arch in surprise. Great, next she'd be saying she was best friends with Tiger Woods. 'I mean I've never played seriously or anything and I haven't played for ages so obviously I'm out of practice,' she back-tracked desperately, suddenly finding her feet fascinating to look at. Reluctantly she dragged her gaze up, detecting the tiniest flicker of amusement in his eyes.

'Are you planning on any more golf while you're here?'

'Hopefully. Just some practice at the range. See if I can drag my brother out for a game.' Molly wondered if he was really interested or just going through the motions.

'It's a good course here at Drumloch and it's only nine holes which is ideal if you haven't played for a while.'

'Um, sure, thanks. That's good to know.'

He shifted his weight from one leg to another and Molly detected an almost indiscernible discomfort as he did so. She sensed a suppressed energy from him, something she couldn't put her finger on and despite herself she felt her curiosity piqued by the man with the intense eyes standing in front of her. She gave herself a shake, deciding it was definitely time for her to go.

'I should be leaving,' she said, beginning to gather her things.

'You really are okay? You're not hurt?' he checked again.

'Definitely not hurt, thanks.'

He looked at her while running a hand across the back of his neck, appearing slightly awkward. 'Hope to see you again then.'

Molly smiled though doubted he meant that. She turned and walked away, noticing her hangover had totally disappeared.

Dear Reader,

Thank you so much for taking the time to read this book – we hope you enjoyed it! If you did, we'd be so appreciative if you left a review.

Here at HQ Digital we are dedicated to publishing fiction that will keep you turning the pages into the early hours. We publish a variety of genres, from heartwarming romance, to thrilling crime and sweeping historical fiction.

To find out more about our books, enter competitions and discover exclusive content, please join our community of readers by following us at:

@HQDigitalUK

facebook.com/HQDigitalUK

Are you a budding writer? We're also looking for authors to join the HQ Digital family! Please submit your manuscript to:

HQDigital@harpercollins.co.uk.

Hope to hear from you soon!

DIGITAL HQ

If you enjoyed *The Little Gift Shop on the Loch* then why not try another delightfully uplifting romance from HQ Digital?